By SUSAN LAINE

NOVELS
Falling for Rain
Genie's Wish
Sounds of Love

NOVELLAS
Love in Plain Sight
Twice by Chance
The Wolfing Way

Published by DREAMSPINNER PRESS
http://www.dreamspinnerpress.com

FALLING
FOR RAIN

Susan Laine

Dreamspinner Press

Published by
Dreamspinner Press
5032 Capital Circle SW
Ste 2, PMB# 279
Tallahassee, FL 32305-7886
USA
http://www.dreamspinnerpress.com/

Falling for Rain

Cover Art by Paul Richmond
http://www.paulrichmondstudio.com

ISBN: 978-1-61372-747-8

Printed in the United States of America
First Edition
October 2012

eBook edition available
eBook ISBN: 978-1-61372-748-5

This story is dedicated to all you Rains out there who battle against ignorance, prejudice, hate, and violence. Be brave. Stay strong. Be true to yourselves. You are not alone, and things will get better.

Acknowledgments

I would also like to give my thanks to Dreamspinner Press's Editorial Department for all their hard work on this story. It would not be the same without you. Thank you.

Chapter *One*

"*FUCKING faggot!*"

It's not like it was uncommon to hear such words, even coming from the alley beside the notorious gay nightclub V-Sin-ity at 11:00 p.m. It was, however, unsettling to hear the muffled sounds of a fight.

Matt Wetherton peered into the alley as he walked by to get to the nearby taxi stand, and what he found stilled his steps.

Two rough-looking men laughed mockingly while keeping a tall but lean third man trapped between them. They pushed and shoved him violently back and forth until one of them slapped him on the side of his face—hard. Down the man went.

At that point Matt's feet began to move on their own, rushing to get to the alley and the man getting bashed.

"Oh, look." One of the men turned to face Matt as he approached. The man laughed shakily, revealing just how drunk he really was. Funny how drink always brought out the very worst people had to offer in their bigoted minds, Matt thought in passing. "Another queer. Want some of this?" The man grabbed the front of his jeans-covered crotch in an obscene manner and squeezed. For a second Matt allowed himself the luxury of wondering what exactly about his work-suit-and-tie-wearing self screamed homosexual, or whether it was just his proximity to V-Sin-ity.

"Not even if you paid me," Matt replied, pulled the Taser from his coat pocket, and pointed it firmly at the man—who didn't stop pointing and laughing, like what he saw was nothing more than a joke.

Snorting, the other attacker moved closer to Matt, who didn't wait for the other shoe to drop. The man was almost in range, and judging by the way he fisted his hands and braced his back, he was going to make a move on Matt—and not in a good way, either.

Matt used the Taser. He'd never had to resort to it before, but he didn't hesitate. Two electrodes shot out of its tip at the guy's chest, like two darts, and pierced his T-shirt. The resulting jolt made him shudder in place like he was made of a mass of Jell-O instead of flesh and bone. Quivering and yelping, he wobbled until he collapsed on the ground, still moving in rapid judders while his eyes rolled back in his head.

The other guy froze in shock as his friend fell, then got his bearings and dashed toward Matt when the side door to the club opened and three laughing men exited. They stopped in their tracks to watch, stunned by the detestable scene in the alley.

"All you fags deserve to die!" the remaining thug shrieked. Just as the three guys at the door started for him, he ran away—though not before giving the man still lying on the ground one more kick with his military-style boot. A pained groan came out of the wounded man.

Dismissing the attacker, who was already halfway down the street, Matt rushed to the injured man and knelt beside him cautiously.

"Is he okay?" one of the men from the club asked worriedly, slowly approaching Matt and the guy who'd been attacked.

"I don't know," Matt said. The victim had curled into a fetal position after being kicked in the gut.

The man was tall, maybe six one or six two, very lean and slim to the point of being thin. But as Matt moved his hands over the exposed skin of his arms, he felt the muscles there, fit and firm. In the dark shadows of the alley mixed with the dirt and mud from the rain earlier that day, it was hard to tell the color of his hair, but Matt thought it could've been brown or red. His skin was fair but was now blotched with blood and bruises and grime. He had on a pair of skintight latex pants so shiny in their blackness that they resembled the fur of some fine jet-black big cat, while his torso was covered—well, barely covered—by a black sleeveless silk shirt so translucent he was in effect exposed and his chiseled chest highlighted to the point of shadowed nudity.

"Hey, can you hear me?" Matt asked quietly, hoping to calm the guy with the tone of his voice. Gently he reached for the guy's shoulder—but the guy shoved the hand away vehemently. "It's okay. I'm not going to hurt you. The men that attacked you are gone."

Matt heard the guy snort and sniffle in one single sound. "You must believe me to be *very* thick in the head, darling, if you think I didn't notice that," he said in a high vibrating voice.

A slender hand covered in colorful jewelry in the form of rings and bracelets brushed the dirty strands of hair aside in a gesture that seemed so utterly feminine that, for a moment, Matt thought he might've confused a man for a woman. But when those translucent green eyes arose to lock with Matt's blue eyes, he saw that there had been no initial error in judgment.

His face could only be described as full of character and personality—he was his own man, and well aware of it too. The guy's face was soft and pretty, like a woman's, with pearly-white skin that shone with facial glitter. Expertly executed thin black lines of kohl, along with long black lashes, gave his eyes a definite feminine look— which Matt suspected was the intention—even though the makeup was now raggedy and the fake lashes were drooping. Full, sensuous lips had had red lipstick on them but were now smeared with blood. His silk shirt was torn to shreds on the right side of the shoulder. He reached for the edge of the fabric, and when he found it in rags, he gave out a tired but unsurprised sigh.

"Always my favorite fabulous shirt when this happens," he muttered, his tone higher than a typical man's low voice—which again was, in Matt's opinion, purposeful. "Ruffians." The antiquated word that belonged more to *Sound of Music* than real life made Matt smile a little, as inappropriate as the gesture seemed in a situation like this. The guy, however, saw it and gave a ghost of a smile himself. "I know, honey. Poor choice of words."

"Can I help you up?" Matt asked worriedly, seeing the guy hold his arm around his chest, indicating without words that his ribs had taken a beating—literally. He offered his arm for support. The guy stared at his arm for a moment like it was a venomous snake about to strike, but took it eventually and allowed Matt to help him onto his wobbly feet. As the guy lurched, Matt quickly wrapped his arm around his waist to keep him up and hold his weight. The guy weighed practically nothing, or so it seemed to Matt.

"I do appreciate your kindhearted assistance, sweetheart," he murmured in Matt's ear as though he were amused. "But you can let go of me now."

Matt didn't have a chance to respond before he was violently pushed away against a cold, filthy dumpster. A colossal figure of a man—whose military attire was accentuated not only by his crew cut hair and huge musculature but also by his aggressive attitude—growled at him, "Get away from him, fucking asshole."

Chuckling, the injured man slapped the other man's massive arm—but the mannerism was familiar and friendly. "Hush, Tiny. Can't you see this valiant, dashing young knight in shining business suit rescued me from my heinous attackers? So let him be." The guy even winked at Matt through his broken fake lashes while attempting to stand up straight and hold his ribcage.

The bodybuilder type nodded quietly and glanced at Matt with a frown. "Sorry, man. Can't be too careful, you know?" Not waiting for an answer, Tiny touched the attacked guy's jaw with concern. "You okay, Rain? I didn't see them. I'm so fucking sorry." His low tone betrayed the anger, frustration, and shame he felt.

The injured man, Rain, smiled sweetly and brushed his bloodied fingertips over the other man's cheek. "Oh, don't be so melodramatic, darling. That's *my* job." He flashed a bright smile at the professional wrestler-looking jock, Tiny, and gave him a soft peck on the cheek, and Matt could easily discern even in the dark alley how the man blushed all over. Turning back to look at Matt, Rain gave him the once-over, which to Matt felt oddly out of place at a time like this. "Thank you, uh…?"

"Matt Wetherton," Matt replied, extending his hand in a reflex before even realizing it and quickly yanking it back when the reality of the situation hit him full force as the attacked man held his side, obviously in pain. "I, uh, I have a card here somewhere…," he managed to mumble, checking his work coat pocket for his business cards.

"Did you hear that, Tiny? He has a *card*," Rain repeated slowly with a Southern drawl Matt was only then able to detect.

For a second his fingers stilled, but as he had already found a card that wasn't too tattered, he offered the card to Rain anyway. Tiny beat him to it, however, snatching the card in a move that seemed way too fast for someone of his stature, like an ox suddenly engaged in a sprint. "Yeah, thanks, man," he said with barely disguised disdain. "Come on, Rain. Let's go back inside so I can patch you up. Can't have you looking like that on Saturday next."

Tiny had wound his wide arm around Rain's midsection and was already leading him toward the club's side entrance, more carrying than guiding him. But Rain was able to shout out over his shoulder, "See you around, Matt," and give Matt another wink and a flash of a flirtatious smile. Then the two of them disappeared behind the metal door, shutting out the loud thumping fast-paced music from the club.

Sighing, Matt couldn't help but be stunned at how rapidly the whole thing had gone down. It had felt like forever, but when he looked at his watch, he found it was closer to ten minutes. Shaking his head tiredly and raking a weary hand through his hair, he looked around. The three guys from the club had vanished into thin air just like Rain and Tiny.

After picking up his Taser from where he'd dropped it and yanking out the dart-like electrodes still attached to the passed-out attacker's chest, Matt sat heavily on a wooden box near the dumpster, dialed 911, and settled in for a long wait. He'd already had a shit of a day at the office—on a Saturday, no less—so why not have a shit of a night too?

INSIDE his dressing room, Rain was slowly beginning to unwind as the kinks in his strained joints started to settle and the tension drifted away—despite the aching bruises that would look like hell tomorrow and that were giving him tiny shocks of pain whenever he moved an inch. He felt the strange yet unfortunately familiar mix of sensations blurring into a single whole. This wasn't his first rodeo. There was numbness in his extremities, pain in his intestines, nausea pressing on his throat with a jolt of vomit, and a rattling in his brain, as though his head were a gourd with dried-up rice jingling loudly within.

There was also an annoying hustle and bustle around him. Typically he would've adored the attention, but right now he was in too much agony to enjoy it properly.

"Norma, please," he sighed for what felt like the thousandth time in the past fifteen minutes to no effect, "tell everyone to stop fussing and give me some privacy. I can't very well meet Mr. Right looking like this, can I, sweetie?"

In front of him, the tall black beauty with angular features, dressed in pink pearls, a pink curly wig, and pink sequined dress, nodded and, with a rapid wave of his hand and a whinnying noise, began to push people out—without ever touching them to do so, which was a particular talent of his. Crowd control. Finally the room was Rain's alone again, and he let out another sigh. Irritated, he shook his head, not wanting negativity to become a habit. His red-gold curls barely moved, as the dirt from the alley had hardened on them, and he longed for a long hot shower. His clothes were covered in muck and grime from the alley, and having dried, they cracked as he scrambled to his feet to find a soothing drink.

Norma returned quickly, lifting an enticing Long Island iced tea in a tall sweating glass with ice cubes. "Oh, darling, how well you know me," Rain managed to murmur appreciatively. He took a long hearty gulp and chuckled without feeling like his sides were about to be torn apart. Then he took another sip, relishing the sweet, fruity taste that hid the sneaky alcohol beneath the unassuming surface, and let the liquid work its magic on his bruised self.

Gay bashings were unfortunately nothing new to Rain, he reminisced ruefully as he allowed himself that single moment of quiet reflection, rubbing his aching flanks in a gentle massage.

From experience, Rain had known the futility of begging the men to stop their attack on him. Those violent, brutal, narrow-minded, hate-filled men had no mercy within them, no compassion, no caring, and no understanding of difference. The fortunate outcome was they'd been interrupted, because in the worst-case scenario, they could've gone on until Rain had either fallen unconscious or dropped dead.

But even then, in his most desperate hour, Rain had not let go of his values and had not fought back. He refused to fill his singsong soul with the kind of blind hatred and fear of the unknown as those men who had shown him the worst and ugliest face mankind had to offer.

And that was the last thought Rain gave to the whole sordid business. He put it completely out of his mind as if shaking rain from his curls like a dog, and refocused on his friend. Norma was Rain's dearest friend, a transvestite of the highest caliber, with an attitude to match. No one *ever* called him by his male name, not even off hours. Where Rain wore women's dresses during performances, and occasionally on dates, Norma wore whatever he liked whenever he liked, as befitting a true drag queen. Whether Norma felt more comfortable in his skin as a man or woman, Rain didn't exactly know, but Rain was certain Norma did not want to physically become a woman.

Norma pulled up a wooden chair and, smoothing his pretty pink dress with his jewelry-covered hand, smiled affectionately. "Oh, poor baby," he muttered with a low voice, now cracking with the intensity of his emotions.

"Now, now, darling." Rain comforted his best friend with a touch on his hand and a tender squeeze. "Can't have a queen make such a deplorable spectacle of herself, now can we? No, we can't. So dry your tears, dear, or your mascara will run."

Swishing his hand, Norma sniffled loudly into a silken white handkerchief. "Oh, it's waterproof, love. So, no worries." He took several deep breaths to steady himself, looking back at Rain through a veil of tears and blinking fast to try to get rid of them before they ruined his blush. "You could've been... oh, it doesn't even bear thinking about." He began to fan his hand in front of his eyes to dry the tears away faster.

"No, it doesn't, sweetie," Rain interjected with a calmness that surprised even him. "I'm fine. I know, it's not like what happened is an isolated incident, but seriously, sweetie, you know me. I say it's done, so we're just going to put it out of our minds. Tiny and his friends have sworn virtually by a blood oath to watch the street outside more. It's all we can do, really. Cops don't give a toss about what happens out here to a queer, let alone a queen."

Sighing, Norma nodded, decidedly displeased at the sad outcome that promised little safety for the future. "I wish that people would just leave us alone."

"I know, sweetie. I mean, if we don't care what the hets do in their private lives, why should they care about ours? Nosy busybodies and narrow-minded bigots, all of them." Rain gave his best friend a warm hug, patting him on the back softly, giving a small caress as well.

Suddenly, with a wicked grin, Norma moved back. "But you were rescued." He put his long-nailed hand against his heaving chest with a dreamy—and slightly envious—gaze. "And by a handsome stranger, no less. Oh, how romantic."

Rain smiled and even dared a little laugh despite the wrenching waves in his gut and the following pang of nausea. "It was just a coincidence that he even bothered to—"

"Oh no you don't," Norma scolded him rashly. "I won't let you dismiss the brave young man so casually. He did save you. You should thank him." After fishing down his low neckline, Norma took out a rumpled business card. "I snagged this from Tiny before he had a chance to throw it in the bin. Call him." With an amicable wink, he handed Rain the card. "Or better yet, go see him. Thank him in person. Face-to-face. It will show how much you appreciate him taking the risk to defend you against violent, bigoted gay bashers."

Knowing very well his best friend was right, Rain nodded slowly, taking the card and reading the embossed text carefully. *Matthew Wetherton. Griffin and Lyons Law Firm.* With a posh address uptown in the heart of the business district and a cell phone number written underneath it. For a mere white card with black ink on it in the form of letters, it was very efficient at describing the kind of vocation the man had. A lawyer, Rain repeated in his head a few times, in a high-profile law firm.

Well, Rain had never been to that part of town, so it would be a new experience, at the very least. And it would only be proper and polite to thank personally the man who had come to his rescue without a thought for his own safety. Rain had barely had a chance to form any kind of opinion about the guy, let alone pay accurate attention to his finer details through the throbbing pain and broken lashes.

Yes, Rain would have a good look at this man who'd saved his life.

Chapter Two

"MR. WETHERTON? He's over there."

Standing in the middle of the hallway, Matt looked up from the third—but unfortunately not the final—draft of the Wyndham tax files his colleague was showing him to find Rain leaning over the high wooden reception desk.

It had been three days since the incident at V-Sin-ity, about which there had been a small segment on TV three days ago. There had been video surveillance footage from the security cameras outside the club— but it was grainy and gray at best, and identifying the escaped perpetrator was iffy. The caught man had had a previous record for assault, and he'd been arrested. Political pressure from local gay and lesbian rights interest groups active in the area had ensured the incident remained an active file, and, according to the police, the investigation was ongoing. But in the media, it was yesterday's news now, and Matt had dropped the whole matter from his conscious memory, preferring not to dwell since he knew nothing of the injured man but his name.

Rain.

Right then the person in question followed the pointing finger of the receptionist and found Matt standing there. Matt felt his mouth hanging open quite a bit in surprise; he noted this with some reluctance and just a wee bit of embarrassment. But he had to come clean about it to himself since as soon as Rain saw Matt with that expression, his own wicked grin widened.

And then Rain was walking toward Matt.

There was absolutely nothing masculine about the way he moved. Swaying his hips in an exaggeratedly feminine manner and crossing his legs like a runway model with each step, he approached Matt, making a spectacle of himself. An old-fashioned show queen, Matt thought to himself while watching it all go down.

Rain was wearing what looked like dark-red leather pants. They hung so low on his hips Matt could just barely see the top of the patch of golden-red pubic hair, and the pants were so tight Matt wondered how in the world this approaching beauty could make his motions so casual and carefree and relaxed. He had on an equally skin-hugging sleeveless shirt of the same color but of a slightly lighter shade. It didn't descend low enough to hide a rather large sliver of the porcelain-white skin of his taut abdomen. Worse than that display was the glittery golden text on his shirt that spelled out *Twinks do it both ways. They suck and they bottom.* Well, at least the shining white leather jacket covered some of it with the swish of his walk. And lastly, there were the shoes—delicate, graceful, and feminine with long and tight leather tops and high heels that clickety-clicked with every step he took to get closer to Matt. They were white—so *very* white—and were encrusted with rhinestones in all the colors of the rainbow. Matt didn't know if they were brave or tacky or both.

Finally Rain reached Matt and stopped right in front of him, teetering on his heels and rocking his hips to the sides ever so slightly, like he was hearing trance club music others did not. There were no marks on his face. On his beautiful made-up face. He had glittery eye shadow, long black lash extensions, and thin dark-red eyeliner surrounding those amazingly and startlingly light-green eyes of his, like tropical seas, all serene and see-through. He had just a hint of blush, but mostly Matt noticed the glistening lip gloss that made his full lips seem red and swollen and luscious to the point of God-I-must-taste-them-now-or-I'll-die. The next thing Matt took note of was the perfume—the sweet fruity scent that surrounded him like a cloud of blooming orange blossoms, giving off pervasive whiffs at every motion he made.

"Hello, Matt."

That sweet melodious voice was packed full of feminine intonations. The Southern drawl emphasized the vowels, curling like his hair, which Matt noticed now had the hue of fine copper in sunlight—red and gold mixed together into a beautifully natural color tone. That tone not only matched the color scheme of his clothes and makeup but was one that Matt had no name for. He only knew that it equaled Rain in his associative mind.

"Hello, Rain." Matt even managed not to stammer.

"Rain Deveraux," Rain introduced himself formally. Matt was going to suggest they take this up in his office when Rain extended his hand in a greeting. Only he didn't offer his hand on its side, like one does for a handshake but instead lifted it upward palm down, like a woman did for a gentleman when she expected her hand to be kissed.

Matt took his hand and turned it to the side to shake it.

Wrong move.

Those green eyes the color of clear turquoise waters narrowed dangerously and flashed for just an instant—but it was enough, and Matt had never felt dumber and more ashamed in his life. Coughing his nervousness down, Matt turned Rain's hand back the way it had been and, without really giving it much conscious thought, rubbed his thumb over the soft skin between Rain's thumb and index finger. Matt hoped that that small gesture would give him a reprieve or earn him forgiveness. But when Rain's eyes flashed again, with contented heat this time, Matt knew that not only had he been forgiven but he was being flirted with—quite unexpectedly, if he did say so himself. Matt wasn't the type to be flirted with often, and certainly not in his office building at work with his gray work suit on.

Rain's smile melted into a playful pout, and once again Matt was reminded how Rain's effeminate nature extended far beyond his fashion sense. That gesture was what a woman sometimes did to make her lips seem bigger and fuller. Matt couldn't stop staring at her, uh, *him.*

Jesus fucking Christ, I'm such a blundering idiot.

Hiding the blush that was creeping up his neck toward his cheeks like a feverish rush with a wave of his hand, Matt requested Rain follow him to his narrow office. But as seemed to be his style, Rain brushed past him with his long legs and went into the room first. It was a typical office containing an extended desk with shelves above it and drawers beneath it. Apart from Matt's chair and a visitor's chair, there wasn't any furniture or pictures or anything of a personal nature.

Rain snorted with amused disgust as his gaze probed the room. "Good God. Who designed this putrid gray-beige-white color scheme here? Stevie Wonder?" Glancing at Matt over his shoulder, he winked with a grin. "What you need is *Queer Eye for the Straight Corporation*, darling. Because this is simply… ghastly." He uttered the last word like he was trying to physically push something out of his throat.

Matt laughed out loud. He couldn't help it. Rain made him laugh. He glanced at Matt again with a pleased expression on his beautiful feminine face. After closing the door, Matt made his way to his chair and sat down—and found Rain was still standing in front of the visitor's chair with an expectant and reproachful glare aimed at Matt.

"Oh." Matt blushed again and rose a little. "I'm sorry. Please, sit down."

Rain sat down—ladylike. There really was no other word to describe the manner with which he executed his move. Gracefully and slowly, he placed his bottom on the very edge of the chair, slid back almost lazily for a more comfortable position, and crossed his long legs like a woman. He looked at Matt under his fake long black lashes—did they have gold tips? Matt squinted to see better—with his crystal-green eyes, waiting for Matt to speak.

Clearing his apparently dry-as-a-desert throat again, Matt wondered what to expect from this surprise meeting. "You look better. I don't see any bruises on you."

Letting out a hint of a chuckle, Rain waved his hand dismissively—and theatrically. "The magic of concealer, darling. It's all in the wrist—and the proper shade, of course."

"Yes, of course," Matt agreed readily, not really an expert on any kind of makeup. "Are you… feeling any better?"

"Or is my flamboyantly stunning makeup the only thing holding me together?" Rain teased Matt with a little high-pitched laugh.

Again Matt laughed. "I certainly hope not."

Rain smiled at Matt, pursing his lips slightly, evidently pleased with him again. "Am I disrupting your busy work schedule, darling?" Matt felt he must've looked baffled because Rain chuckled. "You looked decidedly displeased with seeing me here."

Frowning for the first time in Rain's company, Matt fidgeted and readjusted his position, leaning toward him. "No, you're wrong. I'm not unhappy to see you. It's just that… when I left your friend my card I thought that maybe he'd call, or you'd call, to tell me everything's okay. I didn't expect a personal visit. But"—Matt emphasized his words with a smile he hoped was kind and inviting—"I'm most certainly not displeased to see you again."

Rain made Matt smile. It was a natural reaction, like birds singing in the spring, or flowers blooming in the summer, or the sound of gushing water during an autumnal rainstorm. Rain gave Matt a reason to smile without realizing it and without Matt being consciously aware of it. He only knew he wanted to keep smiling easily like this, with so little effort and absolutely no force.

Rain's luscious lips pursed again, and his shiny green eyes were hidden beneath the curtains of his lashes. "That's gracious of you, sweet pea." He looked around a bit, checking out Matt's laptop, rows of law books, and stacks of legal documents covering every available space on his desk and drawers and shelves. Matt could tell he saw only something vaguely amusing and not something interesting. "What is it that you *do*, Matt?"

"I'm a tax attorney for corporations and private citizens, but mostly the former." There was no change in the expectant glow of Rain's eyes, so Matt couldn't tell if he wanted him to stop or to continue. "I work in conjunction with the IRS, but my main concern is the US tax law, and I try to guide my clients through the legal jungle that is tax law to make sure they're not violating the law but aren't getting screwed over by the government, either."

Now there was a small sound like a muffled chuckle, so Matt guessed that, at least, had entertained him. "Sounds… dreadfully dull and utterly tedious, darling. How *do* you stand it?" Rain looked around again with obvious distaste, but all Matt heard was the way his slow drawl dripped the words out like honey and emphasized them all to an exquisite degree, pronouncing them clearly and distinctly, as though every word was a pearl of emotion. "Even jail cells have better décor and ambience than this dreary dungeon of a corporate cemetery. I've only spent a moment here, and already the stifling and stuffy lifelessness of this place is draining me of my colors." Rain pressed his left hand over his heart with a feigned and exaggerated pained expression.

Laughing, Matt shook his head. "The colors are designed for a purpose. The steely gray to indicate our resolute hardness, the beige to show that we have a creamy soft center after all, and the white to demonstrate our neutrality before the law." Suddenly, Matt winked. "Besides, you can't blame this place for doing that." Now Matt had Rain's full and undivided attention as one vivid mascara-accentuated eyebrow quirked in a query. "You have so much color, so naturally, this place, devoid of vibrant tones, wants to partake of them." Matt leaned forward like a conspirator and lowered his voice to a hush. "This office is envious of you."

Matt had his hand on the edge of his desk, close to Rain for reasons he wasn't too sure about, and now Rain's slender right hand landed over Matt's, gently pressing on it and caressing the skin with his soft palm. Yet there was strength there, underneath that silky smooth surface, that beckoned him with warmth. That simple touch made Matt's heart race while his belly filled with butterflies.

Rain was beaming, and he lifted his proud chin and batted his long black lashes at Matt. "Well, aren't you just sugary sweet, darling? You're giving me a toothache."

Matt honestly couldn't say why he was flirting with Rain like this. He wasn't Matt's usual type. Matt knew he was of relatively small stature—at least two to three inches shorter than Rain, anyway. He had muscles but they were compact and not protruding. He kept his health and physique up with daily trips to the local gym and by running the occasional marathon. He had no high hopes that one day he'd be a big beefy top with to-die-for muscles like tree trunks. Though his friends complimented him and said his hair was the color of cinnamon, he knew it was more akin to sand, with no discernible color. His eyes weren't striking or piercing or amazing or anything—they were just plain old blue. Matt was, for the lack of a more suitable word, average. He was average height, average weight, average appearance—and he was well aware of this fact. For all intents and purposes, sometimes Matt felt practically invisible.

But Rain… no one in the world, not even the blind, could miss him.

Matt liked Rain. He was so out of Matt's normal comfort zone and typical social circles that it wasn't just Matt's office that was envious of his flashy quality. Or was it jealousy, knowing that once this meeting with him was over, Rain would return to his colorful life and Matt would still be here, locked in this gray-beige-white office, buried in official papers and law books and office work for the rest of his foreseeable life?

"So…," Matt started up again after realizing he'd been staring, "is there something I can do for you? Do some accounting or settle your taxes, maybe?"

With a loud derisive snort, Rain rolled his crystal-green eyes and shook his head, lifting his hand away from Matt's—which made him feel rejected. "Oh, Matt. Are we really going to have an obvious, boring conversation?"

Matt contemplated replying with something, anything, but not a peep emerged.

Rain kept on expecting something but when he failed to get it, he sighed patiently. "Very well, then. I came here to thank you for your heroic intervention on my behalf."

Matt couldn't tell why, but he was disappointed—yet not surprised. "Anyone would've done the same, I'm sure," he said, dismissing the praise as casually as he could.

Now there was a distinct snarl in Rain's amused voice. "Wherever did you grow up, darling? The moon?"

Did Rain find Matt contemptible, too, aside from being boring? Apparently so, and Matt was beginning to feel uncomfortable and humiliated. "No, I'm not that delusional to think that everyone...." His voice trailed off, and, fidgeting in his seat, Matt braved on. "It's just something people say to—"

Rain chuckled but it was less than genuine. "Do you always quote what other people say, sweet pea? Do you have any originality left underneath that frightfully gray suit of yours?"

Blinking nervously, Matt licked his lips. "I hope so. About originality, I mean."

Suddenly the door to his room opened and a head popped in. Goodman. Matt's rival on the battlegrounds of office politics. The ambitious backstabbing prick was always itching for a promotion—and actively searching for ways to undermine and embarrass his colleagues up for the same career advancements. "Oh, sorry, Matt. I just came by to ask if you'd finished the Wyndham update yet. I guess not." His bleached-blond hair didn't stir at all with his head's movements, which to Matt was strange and unnatural.

Matt had to think fast, and it wasn't always his forte. "I'm with a client."

Looking at Rain intently with a dangerous gleam emerging from the black depths of his eyes, Goodman grinned—and Matt knew he was going to pay heavily for this surprise visit during the next department meeting as the office gossip started in full force. "Sorry again. I'll give the *two* of you some privacy." The bastard even winked suggestively at Matt before closing the door again, and Matt did his best not to fume his frustration in front of Rain, whose lips were pursed disapprovingly as he studied Matt and what he knew was his awkward expression.

"Obviously I was sorely mistaken, precious," Rain said at long last, with his typical drawl again. "Your ingenuity in lying is clearly excellent." And he got up from his seat, patting his leather pants to remove imaginary wrinkles.

"Wait," Matt said hurriedly, getting up too. "Goodman's a, uh, a kind of a rival. But I didn't mean to—"

"No, my dear," Rain interjected with a raised hand—and Matt saw he had bright-red nail polish which Matt, for some reason, hadn't noticed before. "I've overstayed my welcome. Please, don't let me keep you—"

"Rain, wait, please," Matt pleaded quickly, moving in between him and the door. "I, uh...." Searching for the right words—and knowing he was too rattled to find them within—Matt just blurted his tentative speech out in one breath. "Would you perhaps like to have dinner with me... sometime soon... maybe...?"

GOD, he looks so adorable. Rain found himself moved by the blushing, nervous man in front of him, asking him out. Still, he couldn't help but tease. "Like a date, darling? Or a business dinner with a client?"

Even more bashful, Matt smiled a bit. "The former. If that's okay with you."

Rain had to admit that this young man spoke to his wishful heart. Matt might not have been his usual taste of men—big and muscled and aggressive—but he was sweet and kind, if maybe a little bit in the closet at work. Yet he had saved Rain from a brutal beating. And he was cute in a nerdy kind of way. Shrugging, Rain glanced at the man from under his batting lashes. "Naturally a date is all right with me, sugar. Is it with you?"

Now Matt smiled more openly. It was by far the most sincere smile Rain had seen in a long time, which clinched the deal for him. "Yes, I'd love for it to be a date. How's, um, Friday? That's the day after tomorrow."

Rain lifted his eyebrows in amusement. Sometimes people thought because he had a bubble butt he was just a bubblehead, a male blonde bimbo. He snorted. "Surprisingly even queens nowadays know how to read a calendar, darling. Literacy isn't a new development. Even in gay studies."

Seemingly embarrassed, Matt brushed the back of his neck with his right hand. "That, uh, that wasn't meant for you. I meant it as a reminder to me. Here in the office, weekdays tend to blend in together in boredom until one's not sure what day it is anymore."

Oh, wrong assumption.

"I'm sorry, Matt," Rain apologized immediately. "I get a little defensive sometimes. I didn't mean to bite your head off. Forgive me." Great, a perfect start to a new relationship—with a stinker of a foot in his too-talkative mouth. Cursing at himself, Rain lowered his head in a regretful manner, hoping it would convey what he felt to the man in front of him.

Matt smiled softly and shook his head. "It's okay. I understand." Just when Rain was busy painting the man with light-filled halo in his imagination, Matt's smile turned to a grin. "If you want, you can make it up to me by taking me up on my offer of a date."

Because of that wicked playfulness, Rain knew it wasn't extortion in any sense, and he liked the new self-confidence and determination of this young man. "When you put it like that, how can I possibly refuse, my dear?" Adding a little wiggle room into his acceptance, Rain brushed his fingertips across the man's shoulder, as if cleaning an invisible piece of lint—any excuse to touch him at this point—and said, "But if you choose the time, darling, I get to choose the place."

Nodding, Matt grinned, glancing quickly at Rain's hand on him, and replied, "Sounds good to me. Is Friday okay?"

"Yes. Do you have a number where I can reach you to direct you to the right place?"

Rain found himself staring at Matt's lips. They weren't full but neither were they thin. In fact, they appeared extremely kissable, and Rain wondered what they'd taste like. Matt went to his desk with a knowing smile plastered on his lips as his eyes were set on Rain's gaze, ripped a piece of paper from a notebook, scribbled his private phone number on it, and gave it to Rain.

"Call anytime," Matt said, then hesitated for only a second. "During regular business and office hours, I might not be able to answer right away, but you can text me, and I'll get back to you as soon as I can."

Rain smiled amusedly. "Good God, what a dutiful slave to the clock you are. How do you manage such manacles?"

Matt chuckled. "Same as every other gay man in the world. Getting enough experience with handcuffs before allowing them to be put on."

At that quip Rain had to laugh out loud. If this was any indication of the hidden depths of Matt the busy worker bee, Rain might have a hard time keeping up with him. But boy, the chase would be fun. "Well, I'll have to test that theory," he taunted with a wink.

"No," Matt interjected, baiting him. "No theory. Practice."

"And has it made you perfect, then, darling?" Rain continued to ride.

Matt shrugged as if disinterested and looked away, but he was clearly still having a good time. "You'll have to wait until our date to find out."

Chapter Three

IT WAS true. Rain could hardly hold still and bide his time in anticipation of his date with Matt. Two days had felt like forever, but at long last the wait was over and Friday was finally here. And now Rain was frantic. It had been a while since his last official date that hadn't started out as an impromptu get-together or a casual meeting. But this was prearranged. This was a Date with a capital D—and with a man he liked too.

Rifling through his closet for the hundredth time, Rain searched for the perfect outfit—and failed. He was so frustrated he practically growled, and he never growled. It wasn't a familiar sound to his throat and ended up sounding more like a fake furious purr.

Norma chuckled at him from the deep cushions of the plump lounge chair, where he was nibbling on chocolates from a golden box. "Why are you driving yourself crazy over this? You know what you *should* wear." Rain's best friend's words echoed in the room, making him worry even more than before. Yes, he was well aware of what he should do since he wasn't one for hiding who he was. And yet the anxiety burned a hole in his throat and another one in his stomach. A firm believer that one should just dive into the deep end and paddle away even at the risk of drowning, Rain had trouble convincing himself of that particular principle tonight.

"I know, sweetie," he murmured finally, resigned, letting the light-green conservative shirt he had in his hands slip away. It was the most inconspicuous piece of clothing he owned, and he barely ever acknowledged its existence. It would be a cop-out and absolutely not him.

Taking a look at the dress he really longed to wear, to have hug his frame and kiss his skin, he made his decision, hoping against all hope he wouldn't end up choking on it.

MATT had followed Rain's text instructions to the letter. Yet when he stumbled onto the hole-in-the-wall's metal door on the side of a run-down building, he was certain he'd taken a wrong turn somewhere. Despite the fact that he wore his most comfortable faded blue jeans and a clean light-blue sweater with a light-brown jacket and dark-brown cowboy boots—his brother had bought them for him as a birthday present, and he really liked them—Matt still felt like he was improperly dressed for a place that looked as wild and threatening as this one did.

Still, he bravely stepped forward and knocked on the door.

Whatever he had expected, seeing Tiny's fierce countenance hadn't been one of them. "Oh, the hero," Tiny mumbled gruffly from behind the rectangular eye slit in the door, closed it with a clank, and opened the door to let him past. Matt had a distinct feeling the bouncer was checking his pockets and patting him down from a distance with just a gaze from his brown eyes. "Follow Tiffany," he added, nodding at the approaching overly made-up dark-haired usherette wearing a red corset, leather skirt, and fishnet stockings.

A few minutes later, Matt found himself sitting at an empty round table for two to four people in front of a low stage with dark-red velvet curtains. The lights were low in the room, and faint jazz tones drifted along with the distant hum of the air conditioner. There was a bar at the back of the room near the stairs that had led down here, and round tables all over. Not many tables had customers, though, and all of them seemed regulars. It wasn't easy to say why they gave off that vibe, but Matt was sure he was the only new face around here tonight. Scents of perfumes and colognes, cheap wines, and cigarette smoke floated near him from the manly men dressed in business suits and the effeminate men wearing evening dresses. Dust sprinkles danced in the candle flames and the soft yellowish spotlights of the stage.

Wiggling in his seat, nervous, Matt called another waitress over and ordered a G and T, wishing the lack of sweetness or bitterness of the cooling drink would discourage his nerves from wigging out. The scarcity of clients gave the waitress's feet wings, and soon Matt was sipping his drink.

Then a man's low, raspy voice spoke over the speakers. "Ladies and gentlemen, with great pleasure, The Sultry Sound is proud to present our very own lady of inclement weather and our dear dame of the daunting blues. I give you… Rain."

The remaining overhead lights now dimmed, and the only light emerged from the stage raw and naked as the red curtains pulled aside to reveal an unmanned piano. Then a tall, slim figure appeared from the side, stepped to the piano seat, sat down, and glanced at the audience from under his long fake black lashes.

Matt stared, dumbfounded, his mouth hanging open in surprise, at Rain at his most feminine yet. His red-golden hair had been slicked around his face in roaring-twenties style with curls plastered on his forehead and temples. His red-tinted smoky eye makeup was subdued, with dark tones, just like his long, body-cuddling black velvet dress— with some feminine padding underneath around the hips and bosom— which covered every inch of skin except for his face, hands, and a sliver of black silk stocking-covered leg visible through the thigh slit. On his feet he wore black high heels that made Matt admire his ability to walk in them.

His long slender fingers rose like butterfly wings and landed gently on the keys of the piano. A sorrowful melody haunted the silent room in an instant, caressing Matt like a touch and filling his ears and heart with the blues.

"This is 'Hiding My Heart' by the lovely Adele," Rain said low into the microphone.

Then Rain began to sing.

Not a lip sync, it was Rain's own voice with rich, deep undertones that hid his natural drawl beneath the languorously slow lyrics, definitely more languid than the original song.

"This is how the story went, I met someone by accident.

It blew me away, it blew me away."

Not even realizing that he'd stopped breathing, Matt listened to the most captivating and arresting voice he'd ever heard. Rain's soft and slightly hoarse sound rippled through his consciousness and slipped into his weeping heart, which was pounding away a mile a minute. Rain could *really* sing. He had a legitimate voice. The musical notes glided through the smoky veiled darkness of the club. Matt felt tears welling in his eyes for reasons he couldn't for the life of him fathom or define.

In his seat Rain swayed a little, his turquoise-green eyes closed, his full lips painted red as rubies.

Never had Matt been privy to the secrets of the universe, but at the moment, he was the favorite of the Fates. This essential truth he knew with crystal-clear certainty, as he was washed in sensations foreign and familiar. Rain's voice wrapped itself around Matt and tickled every nerve end and soothed his ears, just like Rain's usual Southern honey drawl—only this time through a woefully blue melody.

Matt didn't notice that Rain's hands had stilled and silence fallen over the club until he was surrounded by clapping—a bellowing noise that he joined in keenly just as the last echoes of Rain's tune died down. Rain turned on his seat toward the club's main room, with his ankles crossed, ladylike, and placed his right hand over his heart, dipping his head sweetly to his devout audience. As the sound of clapping hands increased, Matt glanced around and, to his surprise, found the tables filled. Apparently Rain was quite a success here in the dark underground club called The Sultry Sound, which was packed tight with the lovely low-sunken tones of the blues.

It was then that Matt saw Rain looking down at him with a hesitant hint of a smile on his lips and a question in his pale-green eyes. Matt returned an admiring grin and an encouraging wink. When Rain saw it, he seemed to release his tension and a light emerged all over his beautiful face, and to Matt, that was the look of an angel. Slightly debauched and lightly lascivious, yes, but still an angel.

After turning back to his instrument of choice, Rain laid his fingers on the keys again. The room quieted down and the music rolled from the piano in sweet tones, taking Matt's heart and lifting it up to soar in the skies along with the notes. He was soaking up the droplets of Rain's rhythm as his voice rose over the notes of the piano.

"This one is from the glorious Doris Day," he said with sincere respect and started.

"*You sigh, the song begins. You speak and I hear violins.*

It's magic."

As the sounds slowly dissipated from both the man and the piano, Matt was the first to clap until his palms tingled and ached from the force of his enthusiasm. Catching himself off guard, he found himself standing in ovation—and Rain looked at him like he hung the sun, the moon, and a few stars to boot. Matt felt a jolt in his heart and a punch in his gut, as though his insides knew what he wanted before he did.

"Ladies and gentlemen, our very own Rain will return in a bit. So just sit back, order a tall one, and enjoy your evening," came a man's voice through the speakers again.

Almost lazily, Rain stood up from his chair and curtsied gracefully. The lights on the stage diminished and the lights of the club rekindled as Rain took a few steps toward the little stairs on the side of the stage. Matt hurried to him before his conscious mind reacted, and held up a hand for Rain to take. With a delighted smile, Rain took the offered gesture and allowed himself to be guided to the table, where Matt pulled back a chair for Rain to sit.

His attentiveness made Rain chuckle. "Thank you, Matt," he murmured, pleased, following the man with his green eyes as Matt retook his former seat across from him.

For a still moment, silence hung between them as they sat staring at each other slightly warily, but the ambience was light. Matt was gleefully aware that he really liked the way Rain pronounced his name, like pouring syrup on pancakes.

"So...," Matt said, his word lingering like a thought bubble swimming before him.

Covering his gaze behind the curtains of his lashes, Rain shifted on his seat, as if uncomfortable. "Are you... all right...?"

Immediately Matt hated the timid, faltering tone of Rain's voice. "You were... just perfect," he gushed, meaning every word from the bottom of his heart. "Beautiful, and radiant, and lovely, and your voice took my breath away." Apprehension deserted Rain's posture, and Matt smiled appreciatively, letting his gaze rake and examine every feature on Rain's face and every inch of his body that he could discern, causing the man to blush further. "I'm glad you decided to show me this part of you."

Rain laughed a little shyly, biting his lower lip briefly. "I'm glad you didn't object."

"How could I possibly? You sang so beautifully. Like a veritable angel."

"Such high praise slips out of those sugar lips of yours, darling. You make me blush."

"Good," Matt teased with a grin. "I keep wondering if *your* lips are as sweet as your bedroom voice leads me to believe."

Murmuring something inaudible, Rain looked at Matt bashfully without actually being so. "I think I can arrange for you to find out, precious."

Wetting his lips in a rush of anticipation, Matt leaned over the table. "Don't keep me in suspense, Rain. I'm on pins and needles here. I'm sitting on the edge of my seat—literally."

Rain's smile faded, and Matt feared he'd gone too far and pushed his date against the wall with his overeagerness. He frowned and began to back away when Rain placed his hand over Matt's on the table, giving him goose bumps all over his body and making his heart flutter. Those ruby-red lips parted, trembling, as Rain licked his lips slowly and scooted closer. Over their small round date table, they shared a kiss.

For Matt, it was the perfect first kiss. Tentative and soft, yes, but promising the world. Both their lips were slightly parted, and there was a hint of tongue tips brushing each other. Rain's lips tasted like watermelons, sweet and moist and luscious. Matt would've given just about anything to have more of Rain's deliciousness and to extend their kiss into a deeper fulfillment and a more profound pleasure.

But he knew it was too soon.

Reluctantly he allowed Rain to break the kiss and move back first.

Trying to arouse a conversation instead of his dick, Matt began, "Your first song was almost like it was written with us in mind. Do you hide your heart too, like in the song?"

Rain shrugged a bit. "I try not to hide. It's not conducive to one's well-being. Pretense, I mean."

"It's not necessarily conducive to one's health, either," Matt replied slowly, frowning. "So, you don't hide even if—"

"Even if I get beaten up every day by drunken heteros trying to prove they're big men, certain of their standardized sexuality and physical prowess?" Rain's voice had lowered, but it was sadder more than menacing, and there was a definite undertone of disappointment. "Should I pretend to be someone I'm not out of fear? Should I cower from a mere look in my direction by every straight man several sizes bigger than me? Should I dial my flashy nature down to avoid any undue attention? I shouldn't have to. Or should I, Matt?"

Thinking about it for a moment, Matt had to admit the man was right. It was his right to be whoever he wanted to be and who he was in his heart. Still, he had to say, "I'm sorry if I hurt your feelings, Rain. I didn't mean to sound stupid or condescending or oppressive. After what happened to you, you can't blame me for being concerned about your safety. I'm not saying that I'm right here, or even that I have the right to worry. I just... I can't help thinking that if you didn't draw attention to yourself—"

Matt stopped in midsentence. Rain didn't have to say anything because Matt knew he'd crossed the line and said too much. Unsure but needing to voice his emotions anyway, he said quietly, "I'm sorry, Rain. I, uh, I just like you, and I—I... I don't want anything bad to happen to you ever again. I didn't want to lie to you or hide how I felt."

IT WAS strange how this young man could make Rain feel annoyed and giddy at the same time. There were several feisty opinions bubbling inside Rain, trying to gain enough momentum to rear their ugly heads and ruin his first date in what felt like forever.

"I understand how torn you must feel, Matt," he said finally in concession. "I feel the same way. Sometimes I feel brave and indestructible and strong enough to be comfortable in my own skin—and flamboyant clothes too. But other times I know the reality and the potential outcome of being the way I am. I'm not ashamed and rarely scared, but I do get it." Matt smiled in obvious relief, and Rain felt blessed that Matt comprehended the point he was trying to make. "Oh"—he waved his hand in front of him in light frustration—"this is a depressing topic. Shall we change it?"

"Yes, please," Matt laughed. "So, when did you start singing?"

"Like this, as a bluesy wishful show-tune queen, or in general?"

"Either. Both."

"I've been singing since I was a toddler, practically," Rain joked. "I've loved singing all my life. And being a flaming gay man who likes to wear women's clothing, this sort of place seemed a far better alternative than, say, *American Idol*. Besides, my cadence is a bit on the subdued side, fitting for the blues, and just a little raspy, fitting for jazz. Here I can do both. No, there isn't much money in it, but I make a fairly decent living at it."

Nodding, Matt asked, "Your accent is Southern, isn't it?"

Pursing his smiling lips, Rain winked. "It's not that hard to miss, is it, darling?" Rain laughed wholeheartedly. "I'm from Mobile, Alabama, but I didn't stay there for very long. I left home when I was sixteen, and I've been on my own since then."

"You still have folks there?"

"My Gram, Daisy," Rain answered with softness creeping into his voice and a longing sadness rising in his green eyes. "She's still around and will probably outlive us all. She's a witch, you know. That old black magic, Cajun secrets, and all that jazz."

There was a definite sparkle in Rain's eyes as he tried to coax Matt into stunned silence, and succeeded. Matt's face turned perplexed and unsure whether Rain was serious.

"Really...?" Matt asked, wavering between disbelief and amusement. "You're having me on, aren't you?"

Snickering, Rain waggled his delicate hand in front of him. "Maybe, maybe not."

The truth was he was serious. Daisy had knowledge that extended beyond this world, of that Rain was certain. He remembered fondly one rainy night in her house by the bayou where old trees swayed in the wind and the smell of swamp water was horrid in the evening after hot days, while the scent of jasmine lingered in the morning after cool nights. All through that day it had rained by the bucketloads, and Daisy had made Rain lemonade from scratch and sat with him on the verandah, swapping stories. Rain had been thirteen, and it was the first time he'd dared reveal to anyone that he liked men. Daisy had smiled knowingly, as if she'd heard it all before, winked, and said, "The cards told me that long ago, sweetheart, just like that your mother's dresses fit you far better than her." And just like that, Rain had become a believer.

"She taught me to be true to myself," Rain explained with a sigh. "Even if that someone is a flaming queer transvestite slash lounge singer."

"It's always good to have an affirming adult presence in your life when you're going through stuff like that," Matt agreed. "I had my brother, Mitchell, who was a jock and homecoming king, the most popular guy in high school. I feared telling him the most. But he just stared at me like I'd grown two heads and said, 'Yeah, so what else is new?' And that was that."

Rain sniggered for a bit. "Good for you. Family is the hardest to convince that you know who you are and that you know what you're doing—even if you're scared out of your wits."

"So how come you like women's clothes?"

Rain stared at Matt intently, but all he saw was curiosity, nothing judgmental. "I don't always know exactly," he replied with a drawl, the admission feeling strange but honest on his lips. "They make me feel beautiful and sexy. I like the way they feel on me, soft against my skin, light and pretty. The fabrics and textures are smooth and silky, the colors warm and inviting, and the shapes accentuate lines and curves equally. They are a bit of luxury in an otherwise harder reality, like a pair of Louboutin shoes or Egyptian cotton sheets, you know?"

Matt chuckled, shaking his head, baffled. "A little out of my price range, I'm afraid."

"Everyone needs a little luxury in their lives," Rain scolded gently. "What is luxury for you, darling?"

Apparently Matt had rarely given it that much thought, because the look on his face was positively pensive, and Rain wondered if anyone had ever asked him that question before. "To me, luxury is a couple of days off work, I guess. Held consecutively. And that's a rarity, I can tell you," Matt added with a wink.

"Goodness, sweetie, are you a workaholic or a slave?" Rain smirked dryly. "What do you usually do on these precious few days off, then?"

"Um, I run in the park sometimes, read, cook, go to the gym, nothing special."

"Date?"

Matt shook his head, and to Rain, he looked sad. "Nope. Rarely."

"Why not? You're not wholly unattractive, darling." Rain added a suggestive grin to his statement, making Matt chuckle.

"Well, you know how it is with gays. The measuring gaze and the sizing up—and then the inevitable follows. They come in, look me over, and they see me, and… first their look is expectant, but then I see the disappointment that I'm not a six-three Norse god with muscles up the wazoo and a nine-inch cock. One can only take so many rejections before hello."

Rain nodded in complete agreement. "I understand, lovey. For me, it's anticipation first, shock and dismay right after. I know I can be a little, um, extravagant at times. I just happen to favor the principle that one should show his or her true self as soon as possible to dispel any accusations later on about dishonesty or some such."

"I agree." Matt nodded, checking Rain out from head to toe. "You're unlike anyone I've ever met before. I like you this bold. In fact, you're the most audacious person I've ever met. I mean that as a compliment."

Rain laughed because he was happy. "There you go again, darling. You and those sugar lips of yours. Sweet as honey, they are," he added, batting his long lashes.

"I hope I'm sweet all over," Matt said slowly, blushing bashfully.

"Tell me… Matt," Rain quipped with his usual drawl, "what do you hope will be the outcome of this evening?"

Rain watched Matt lean back in his chair, rubbing his stubbly chin, lost in thought as he carefully chose his words. "Well, first and foremost, I'm going for enough charm that there'll be another date in store for us." Rain let his eyebrows rise in a silent *and then?*, which made Matt chuckle again. "Second—and bear in mind that just because I crunch numbers for a living I don't always count everything I say—I was kind of hoping for a, uh, a heartfelt kiss goodnight."

Inside, Rain's heart was doing summersaults. The way Matt's blue eyes held his, showing the growing hunger there but holding it at bay, made Rain's stomach flip, knees buckle, and toes curl. "But… nothing more?"

Matt lowered his gaze for a moment, but when it came back up, his eyes were lit with flames. "You, Rain, are a lady, and I want to romance you. I'd love to take you back to my place and see what your face looks like enraptured with pleasure—but I will wait as long as you want. I don't want to mess this up."

Hearing the words was one thing, but seeing the sincerity in Matt's eyes, Rain felt out of breath, his heart hammering in his chest like a drum. His mouth went dry but his palms sweated. However, he didn't get the chance to reply before one of the waitresses came over and whispered in his ear that his second set was about to begin. Nodding in agreement—even though all he wanted was to stay near

Matt and have him sweet-talk to him some more—Rain smiled apologetically at his date.

"I have to go sing again—"

"Go. I'll still be here when you're done. I promise." The smile Matt gave Rain nearly melted his brain to mush, and he had to brace himself gently against the table to avoid falling to his knees. As he scrambled to his feet and skittered up to the stage, Rain could barely hold back the grin threatening to split his face in two. Oh, this had to be the best date he'd had in years.

Chapter
Four

MATT'S eco-friendly Toyota Prius accommodated them both, though the spacious hybrid car was rather compact. After his second set, Rain had retreated to his dressing room to remove his stage persona makeup and change his clothes. Matt glanced at the passenger seat over and over again, looking longingly at the long legs encased in pink latex pants, hugging Rain's sleek figure like a second skin, just like the pink sleeveless shirt he wore over his torso. He'd removed the oil from his red-gold hair, giving him a just-crawled-out-of-bed look, which Matt found fascinating and arousing. Rain had discarded the strong makeup in favor of a light coating of pink facial glitter and an equally thin covering of black mascara on his own lashes. Without lipstick or lip gloss, his lips appeared even more plump and scrumptious than before, causing Matt's cock to stir.

As Matt was busy readjusting his swelling dick inside his jeans, Rain looked over at him briefly, covering an amused tug of upturned lips behind his hand. Noticing the gesture from the corner of his eye, Matt smiled too. "You do such sweet things to me, Rain, without even touching me."

Seemingly pleased, Rain caressed Matt's hand over the gearshift, his thumb moving gently across the back. "So, is this better or worse?" he teased huskily.

Matt tried to reply, but his tongue was glued to his palate as his heart rate began to rise, and he had to take a breath to calm himself down. Readjusting in his seat again, he warned, "Careful, Rain. I might blow up in my pants, or I might regress to a teenager and take you to the backseat for an intense make-out session."

With a giggle, Rain glanced over his shoulder at the empty backseat, as if sizing it up for just such a suggestion. Looking back at Matt, he grinned. "Now, as much as I like that idea, darling, I prefer my own king-size bed with its Egyptian cotton sheets. They're pale green."

Matt smiled at the challenging comment. "You gonna show me?"

Falling silent, Rain settled more comfortably in his seat, still holding Matt's hand.

"COME on in," Rain welcomed, leaning on the door and stepping aside to allow Matt entry. "Let me give you the tour. This is the luxurious foyer." He gestured at the tiny space they were standing in. "At the back over there is the spacious sitting room." Rain waved at the open medium-sized room with a couch. "Next to it is the dreamy kitchen and adjoining dining room." He pointed at the kitchenette with an attached bar table with stools. "Here is the main bathroom"—he showed the narrow rectangular room opening from the foyer—"and over there is my *very* accommodating bedroom," Rain finished with a hint of a smile by moving aside to show the last room with its king-size bed, culminating in a huge metallic headboard, dominating the room. The bedroom was just like all the other rooms in the apartment, situated along a single hallway.

Rain's apartment was an amalgam of styles, colors, and shapes, drowning Matt in vivid visual sensations. The tiny third-floor apartment had little floor space—even less with Rain's stuff occupying nearly every available inch—creating narrow passages where one could barely navigate. Never mind the green couch with leaf patterns, or the bright-red recliner, or the bookcases filled with CDs, or the old wooden chests covered by linens or open with accessories of all shades flooding out. Never mind the dust falling from the ceiling as a result of someone playing the cello loudly in the apartment above, or the low pulsing screech emanating from the radiator, or the abiding smell of days-old salad dressing. Never mind the long silken curtains of various colors hanging over the windows and doorways, or the absence of noticeable light fixtures in the overall shade of the place, or the haphazard mash of everything Rain liked.

All that was relevant to Matt was the sight of Rain's apparent pride and happiness over the state and appearance of his own apartment. "It's nice," he said finally, looking cautiously where he stepped so as not to trample anything important. "It's certainly lived in."

Rain watched Matt approach but didn't say anything until Matt reached him. And then there was no need for words when Matt slid his right hand tenderly to the back of Rain's neck and pulled his head down for a kiss. With a soft whimper, Rain parted his lips and allowed Matt's tentative tongue entry into the smooth wet heat as he seemed to melt against Matt's body, bending his knees to accommodate Matt's two-inches-shorter height.

When they parted, both men were panting through their kiss-swollen red lips. Smiling, Rain pushed Matt's jacket over his shoulders and let it drop to the floor. "Am I moving too fast for you, darling?"

Liking the way Rain pronounced the word *darling* with the final G missing, Matt lifted his eyebrows amusedly and chuckled. "As long as *you* aren't moving too fast for you, I'm good." Winding his arms around Rain's slender waist, Matt straightened his back to gain an inch and recaptured Rain's heart-shaped lips that tasted like watermelons.

Laughing a little into the kiss, Matt licked the delectable taste off his lips. "You have a fondness for watermelons?"

The look of surprise lasted only an instant before Rain laughed. "You could taste that? Yes, I had a few slices before I went on stage. Yes, I love all fruits—and yes, I know *exactly* how that sounds, precious. But yes, I have taken a special liking to watermelons, honeydew melons, and squashes." Batting his eyelashes, Rain pursed his lips. "You disapprove?"

"Quite the contrary, I assure you." To emphasize the honesty of his words, Matt kissed Rain again, teasing the tip of his tongue over the seams of Rain's full lips and gliding in softly. For a moment their mouths fused as Rain's hands traveled over Matt's shoulders to run through his hair, and Matt pulled Rain's slender stem flush against his own slightly sturdier frame. They hung on to each other as Matt began to walk Rain backward from the foyer toward the bedroom.

As Rain's thighs hit the edge of the bed, Matt grabbed the hem of Rain's pink shirt and pushed it up over his lifted hands and head, then tossed it on the floor. Feeling the heat of Rain's body even through his own sweater, Matt slid his hands from Rain's back across his flanks to his chest. He fondled and pinched the tight rose-red nubs of his nipples, causing Rain's body to shudder while a high moan escaped the confines of his throat into Matt's mouth.

"Oh, sweet pea, your fingers can certainly do the math," Rain cooed against Matt's lips with a low laugh that mesmerized Matt as he breathed heavily into his lover's mouth.

"Well, I was an accountant before I became a tax attorney."

"How *utterly* exciting, darling."

Matt could hear the playful baiting in Rain's voice and couldn't help but smile. Stepping back to study the lax, pleased expression on his lover's face, Matt twisted the rigid nipples he had his fingers around, and Rain practically jumped, his laugh shifting to moaning in a heartbeat.

"See? You harass me, I punish you," Matt warned Rain with a husky tone.

But impudent as he was, Rain merely laughed again. "With a hand or a paddle? I assume you mean to spank the living daylights out of me, darling."

"I'll make you eat those words, babe," Matt cautioned with a sly grin. "Or make you eat something, at the very least."

Rain's eyes sparkled as he chuckled so hard his whole body vibrated. "Well, aren't you positively cocky tonight, my dear."

Mashing his erection against Rain's thigh, Matt nodded. "You tell me if I have a reason to be." Grinding slowly, he made his point, moving his hands down to cup the soft firm globes of Rain's behind and bumping their groins together, rubbing just enough to create delicious pressure on their rock-hard cocks even through their clothes.

"Oh, Matt…," Rain mumbled almost incoherently as he closed his eyes and wound his arms even tighter around Matt's neck until their foreheads touched. This was how Matt wanted Rain to feel in his arms, unable to restrain himself or resist giving in to the pleasure. Rain might have been taller than he was, and skinnier, but there was precise muscle definition all over his lankier body. His chest was sculpted like Michelangelo's David, giving an impression of a healthy physique and youthful exuberance. Rain might have tasted like watermelons, but his smooth, hairless skin felt like silk and velvet to Matt's perusing fingertips and palms, which longed for nothing more than to search and reach for every inch of his lover's beauty. Rain might have looked divine in makeup and drag, but naked he was all man, and his gorgeous figure portrayed a perfect athletic male form.

Emboldened by Rain's passion, Matt kissed his lover again, not wanting to presume he had any liberties but still taking over the kiss with all the need that coursed through his veins and pumped in his heart and cock. Their tongues tangled and curled to probe and suckle, and they took their time to get to know each other's tastes, styles, and kissing preferences. Matt learned that Rain had no qualms about his mouth being taken over by another man, so he took what Rain gave without hesitation, tilting his head and slanting his mouth to deepen their kiss further until he was almost eating the man up.

Unconsciously he moved his fingers from Rain's perfect bubble-butt to his pants and belt buckle and yanked it open as fast as he could. When Matt realized, through the heady haze encapsulating his lust-filled brain, what he was doing, he stilled his hands and broke the kiss.

"Uh, is this all right?" Matt inquired, hearing how hoarse his own voice was. "Do you want to stop?"

Now Rain's pouting look was absolutely derisive. "I do believe, darling, I can find the words by myself if I wanted you to stop."

Cheeky. "I don't doubt your abilities, eloquence, or vocabulary, Rain. But if you're even half as into this as I am, reason will soon fly out the window—not to mention self-control or being able to quit in the middle of things." Matt needed Rain to understand that he didn't want to move too far ahead and blow his chances of making a good impression and making sure they'd both enjoy this equally. He liked Rain, and since it was only their first date, there was no real pressure to do this now. They could wait until date number two.

CEASING their amorous encounter had never even crossed Rain's mind until Matt stopped his hands from working their way to exactly where Rain wanted them. He did understand why the man hesitated, as this was their first date, and good girls and boys didn't always put out on the first date.

"I do appreciate you asking me, Matt," Rain finally admitted with his habitual drawl. "I am glad you felt you should ask before plunging for the prize, so to speak. I want you. If you think this is too soon—"

Shaking his head, Matt said, "I'm game if you are. I just want you to be sure. I don't know how I'd take it if you regretted this in the morning."

Being asked to verbally confirm the passion they felt for each other was a nice gesture, Rain thought. The idea that he might regret this the next day was insane and impossible. "You have my permission to continue, precious," he teased, chuckling.

Matt smiled, relieved and amused. "Orders received and understood."

"Sir, yes, sir," Rain murmured and stuck his tongue out between his teeth. He really liked Matt's playful side, which was so different from his formal work persona. Like he was a gay superhero, all mild-mannered and unassuming during the day, but at night transforming into a sexual, funny, smart, and charming lover who seduced with his attentiveness and kindness, not to mention his special brand of kissing. It was becoming apparent that there wasn't much about Matt that Rain hadn't already taken a shine to.

As Matt's fingers unbuckled his belt, Rain doubted he could withstand this sensual onslaught for much longer—not standing up, anyway. He longed to feel Matt's body against his own, above him and on him. Tangling his fingers through the silky bundle of hair, Rain fell into Matt's kiss again, feeling the touch on his tongue all the way down to the tip of his cock and his tippy-toes, as if there was a direct connection between them.

After pulling Rain's belt from around his waist, Matt moved on to the button and zipper, popping them both open so fast Rain felt his head swimming in anticipation of the touch that awaited him. And he was already so good at jumping right into the deep end.

Matt's probing fingers found their way inside Rain's fly, brushing softly against the tiny pink boxer briefs he'd had to dye himself to get the color tone right. Then those marvelous fingers caressed the hard upright length of his cock through the thin layer of fabric, and Rain's head spun and hummed as he let out a lingering moan.

"What do you want, Rain?" Matt whispered against Rain's kiss-swollen red lips without breaking the kiss for long, and Rain felt the small singe of Matt's slight stubble whenever their faces rubbed close enough. "Or should I learn on my own? Search for all those special places you hide from all others but lovers, and those fanciful ways you like to be touched and pleasured?"

Unable to find enough strength in his throat or air in his chest to reply to Matt's taunting tone with a verbal quip, Rain puffed into Matt's mouth, "I want you inside me, lovey. How you get there will be half the fun."

"Only half?" Matt chuckled into the kiss. "Your wish, my command."

Drawing a hot wet line from Rain's smooth jawline—not a hint of stubble—down to his neck, suckling on the sensitive spot beneath his ear, Matt slowly and gently pushed Rain's pants down past his hips until they slipped down to his knees and further down to his ankles when Rain did a little shimmy. Matt repeated the smooth move with Rain's underwear, eliciting an appreciative sigh from Rain.

"You taste heavenly," Matt murmured, moving his lips from his lover's neck down to the collarbone and then licking the little dip at the base of Rain's throat. Rain shuddered at the sensation—and music began to echo in his soul, synchronized with his heartbeat.

"We lived our little drama, we kissed in a field of white

And stars fell on Alabama last night."

Yes, shooting stars of love were definitely falling on one pretty boy from Alabama tonight, Rain mused as his mind drifted along into a heady haze of jazz and sex intermixed. He rarely heard music while a lover was taking him to bed—even if it was the divine low, raspy sound of Ella Fitzgerald. But Matt was different—vibrant with pulses of passion-red music floating out of him, filled with a kind of tempered masculinity and hushed vitality that drove Rain off his rocker.

Unaccustomed to his inner music coming out so clearly as he was wrapped in the embrace of a lover, Rain swallowed—and Matt caught the move with the tip of his tongue, surrounding the bobbing Adam's apple with his lips. By then Rain was already a goner and could no longer keep his upright stance. His knees buckling, he slipped out of Matt's hold on him and fell on his bare butt on the bed.

Chuckling, Matt caressed his cheek. "You all right, baby?"

Could he have sounded more pleased with himself? Rain pushed back on the bed, sliding up to the middle. "Smug bastard...." At this slight Matt only laughed louder, grabbed Rain's bundled pants and underwear, still trapped around his ankles, and worked them off him along with his socks. Though he expected to find it unnerving that he was stark naked when Matt still had all his clothes on, Rain felt cozy enough to slither his right hand down his hairless chest and past his white stomach to his angry-red erection and stroke himself slowly, his green gaze fixed on his lover, who stood at the foot of the bed, watching intently.

Apparently Rain wasn't doing a half-assed job at it, since Matt chucked his clothes off so fast they ended up tossed all over the room. *Not so smug anymore.* Rain chuckled contentedly as Matt splayed himself over Rain's body and began to kiss the breath out of him. Shivering, Rain wrapped his legs and arms around his lover, surrounding Matt with his tall frame and lithe limbs, giving back as good as he got. His hard cock was jutting out against Matt's lower abdomen, stuck between their writhing, heated bodies, and his lover's equally distressed organ pressed against him.

"Where?" Matt mumbled against Rain's lips.

"Huh?" All the blood in his brain rushing south too fast made Rain's head spin, and for the life of him, he had no idea what the man was talking about. It took an arrogant chuckle from Matt for Rain to get it. "Nightstand. Drawer. Condoms. Lube. Both flavored." Yes, the tastes of lube and latex were horrible and sometimes mood-deflating or even nauseating. As Matt expertly rummaged through the drawer and fished out the necessary items, Rain didn't need to check what flavor they were. He'd found that strawberry, lime, and vanilla worked best. Other tastes were less like the real deal, or too strong, or too weak, so he'd discarded them quickly enough.

After dropping the items on the bed, Matt resumed his former position and kissed Rain—apparently to his heart's content. "Oh, you feel so good, sweet-cheeks," Rain whispered into the kiss, encircling his lover like a climbing vine around a protruding tree.

Matt laughed heartily upon hearing Rain's use of the term of endearment, obviously finding it quaintly amusing. This annoyed Rain a bit, and he bit his lover's lower lip, and Matt let out a little cry that turned into a moan as his body jolted. "Oh, Rain, I want you so bad."

But Rain had other plans than to simply let his lover off that easily.

"I want to suck you, cowboy." To emphasize his anxious words, Rain sucked Matt's tongue into his own mouth, curling his tongue and resorting to a deep suction that made his lover groan in appreciation and need. That desire they both shared. But Rain had an appetite for Matt's unique taste—though he typically used condoms for oral sex—and he didn't feel like waiting for it, so using his natural agility, he swiftly flipped Matt onto his back and straddled his hips. "Oh, you're such a sweet dish, darling. I can't wait to taste every inch of you and suckle your cock all night long."

Gasping, Matt nodded. "All yours, babe. Have at me."

A strangled whisper was all the invitation Matt managed to add. Rain bowed his head to rub his cheeks and lips, his face, all over his lover's skin but without kissing or touching. Matt pushed up from the bed in an attempt to get some contact, but Rain wouldn't have it. "You're not the only one who can tease, sweetheart," he said, moving lower until he was kneeling between Matt's legs and his open mouth hovered above his lover's groin. There he had ample opportunity to admire Matt's dark, thick erection, which bounced against his taut abdomen and was surprisingly bigger and longer than Rain had expected from the compact man. All those men who had taken a look at Matt's inconspicuous conventional face and decided he wasn't worth the effort would've kicked themselves had they found out about this splendid, scrumptious prize.

That's when Rain observed the inked artwork. "What's this?" His fingers grazed gently over the black-and-white tattoo on Matt's right hip. It was a troll of some sort, unlike anything Rain had ever seen before. The hideous face was not, despite its ugliness, unfriendly but strangely shy and warm. The art had an otherworldly beauty that Rain kind of liked from the get-go.

Matt looked down where Rain was pointing and grinned sheepishly. "Indiscretions of youth."

"It's beautiful. Wherever did you get it?" He let the admiration ooze into his voice for Matt to hear.

"The art is by John Bauer," Matt explained matter-of-factly. "His art was used in fairytales and folklore books, and my mom used to read them to me when I was young. I guess she believed that when you read to your child, it would influence how educated he or she would eventually become. Considering I'm the first in my family to attend a university and graduate, I guess she had a point."

"What about your brother?" Rain hushed his tone, dipping the tip of his tongue to swirl around Matt's navel and then licking the gray-shaded picture like an eager puppy lapping a flavored drink. He was fast growing accustomed to everything that was Matt.

"Mitch?" Matt sounded breathless when he spoke, which pleased Rain to no end. "No. He was always more of an athlete than a bookish nerd—not like me. He plays for the Denver Broncos as a reserve wide receiver, has for about two years now. The whole family is real proud of him." Glancing up at Rain, who blew warm gusts of air at his dick, Matt sounded impatient, almost akin to a petulant child, when he said, "Are we going to keep yapping? Or are you going to suck me?"

Oh, the man was definitely going to get punished for his lack of greater forbearance, Rain decided then and there, and so he changed his method from arousing to tormenting in a single breath. Ah, the exquisite pain of pleasure.

THE heated breath on his dick turned to a cold breeze when Rain changed tactics in midmotion, leaving Matt goose-bumpy all over. "Good things come to those who wait." Rain kept on hounding him with his humorous giggle and teasing his tense-skinned cock, and Matt swore that he'd give Rain the ride of his life the first chance he got.

But at long last, Rain's tongue made its foray against the small slit of Matt's penis. He stuck the darted tip of his tongue against it over and over again, leaving Matt wiggling and bucking for his life. "Oh, for God's sake, Rain...." Yes, Matt had been on the receiving end of getting head before. Yet with Rain, it felt like the first time. He'd been fifteen when he finally figured out what all the various erogenous zones and nether-regions of his were for and could accomplish on their own—and especially with an ardent partner. What Rain was doing with his slit bordered on painful overstimulation.

"I see it's not just your lips that are sugary sweet, babycakes," Rain murmured against Matt's sensitized skin, the huff of hot air almost as distinct as a touch. But Matt didn't get a chance to respond in any meaningful way because Rain fastened his lips around the crown of his cock, suckling gently.

But that wasn't all Rain was doing. Matt felt Rain's saliva-dripping index finger sliding along the silkiness of his crease to caress his perineum. Applying just a little bit of pressure against the initial resistance of the anus, Rain caressed Matt's hole with shallow brushes and little jabs. Unable to contain himself, Matt opened his legs further, spreading all of the glory of his sex for Rain to do with what he willed.

Apparently what Rain desired at that moment was the natural zest of Matt, since those perfectly full lips moved from the head of his cock lower to lick and nibble Matt's inner thighs. So soft and tantalizing was the touch of his mouth, tongue, and teeth that Matt felt like he might cream himself before any penetration even occurred.

And still present was the teasing moist finger encircling his hole, leisurely advancing on the tight ring of muscle but never breaking through. There was a cry of pleasure trying to come out of Matt's throat, deep and profound.

Rain moved on to enrapture Matt with his mouth by latching on to his balls, the dark sacs covered with light fuzz, and, taking them in, sucking steadily with a rhythm so basic and irreproachable that Matt felt it from the tip of his feverish head to the curling tips of his toes. "Oh, oh, Rain, yes, yes...." His vanishing voice cracked, and all he could do was moan.

Rain chuckled low, the hot breath tickling the wet skin of Matt's thighs. "Oh, darling, I can't wait for you to open me up, stretch me wide with your fingers and your cock, and fuck me senseless till I scream or sing or both."

Matt had never heard Rain speak so coarsely, as if talking about fingers and dicks in asses was perfectly commonplace—even though their bedroom setting was designed for just such trashy pillow talk.

"Why?"

Lifting his head from his lover's exposed genital area to look into Matt's eyes, baffled, Rain could barely spit out the question, "Why what?"

"Why do you assume that it will be *my* cock stuck up *your* ass?" He knew he was being just as crude as Rain had been, but concluded that it was fitting considering the circumstances and the venue. Besides, he did have a point to make.

Suddenly Rain lifted up to sit on his heels with his hands resting on the top of Matt's haunches, remaining immobile in every respect except for his mobile mouth, which pursed into a rosy query of puffy red lips. "Do I look like a guy who gets to top, darling?"

Matt chuckled just as indignantly. "Do *I* look like a guy who always tops?" Interpreting Rain's dumbfounded expression wasn't difficult, and Matt shook his head patiently. "That's not even the question."

"No?" Rain's amazed tone had risen to a near shrill.

"No," Matt confirmed slowly, imitating Rain's typical drawl rather well if he thought so himself. "The question is do you *want* to top?" No, Matt didn't routinely bottom, but neither did he top every time. To him, sex had always been about pleasure—both giving and receiving. With a tendency to dive into the thick of things, Matt had found that versatility helped him through awkward situations, like if the other guy had either wanted to be taken or to take him, but had not phrased his wish well. Misunderstandings could ruin the mood fast. So to be on the safe side, Matt had set out to explore every facet of gay sex. Categorizing roles and labeling things might've made things easier on dates sometimes, but in bed, articulating the sexually diverse methods he was capable of was clearer. And it worked even better when shown instead of told.

This time, however, Matt wanted things to be laid out before them clear as day. Everyone—gay and straight alike—assumed that an effeminate man like Rain would prefer to bottom. Always and without exception. But things were never that simple and clear-cut. Matt knew that not all male transvestites were, without fail, gay, just like not all feminine men were necessarily bottom-only. People just felt comfortable with clarifying labels and visible signs, especially when it came to sexual minorities and gender appearances.

Matt wasn't like that—and absolutely was not going to be so with Rain. "So? What do *you* want, Rain? I'm game with however you want to play this out." And Matt meant every word, as his intention was to give Rain the kind of experience he might've wanted for ages but had never asked for.

NEVER in a million years had Rain expected Matt to ask him that, let alone offer him the opportunity to top. Sure, Matt wasn't as tall as

Rain, but he was more masculine and virile, not to mention more muscular, though not robust to the point of being hefty. Rain's head was swirling with the many imaginings of being the one doing the fucking instead of being fucked. Sure, Rain did want Matt to do that to him—*with* him—but this proposition was too good to pass up or to refuse.

Yet his nerves were a wreck at this sudden change in his typical course for sexual gratification, and he blushed with acute shyness. "It's been so long I doubt I even remember how...," he confessed with a whisper, embarrassed at the admission despite the fact that Matt himself had asked for Rain's reply.

Smiling with encouragement, Matt chuckled a little, caressing Rain's cheek. "Practice makes perfect—as you so kindly pointed out to me a while back." Matt emphasized his case with a suggestive grin and obvious waggling of eyebrows that caused Rain to let go of his nervousness and laugh out loud.

Still, he stopped soon and bit his lower lip anxiously. "Matt... are you sure?"

His smile deepening, Matt nodded. "Yeah, babe. I'm sure. Go for it."

Unable to even remember when he'd topped last, Rain returned to his former position between Matt's legs and resumed kneading the man's ass cheeks and slowly caressing his lover's tightly puckered dark hole with his slicked index finger. Being slightly scared that he'd perform poorly or would fail to make Matt come dispirited him a little, but bravely he ventured forward—literally and figuratively. Gently, Rain pushed his way past Matt's ass-muscle ring into the narrow dark heat and then pulled out his lubed-up finger. He was consumed by the intoxicating feel of his lover's inner workings as Matt's restless hips bucked up and then shoved down to get more of the invading finger in. The gripping muscles within Matt clenched and contracted in waves, and Rain felt it all.

Matt moaned loudly when Rain's finger worked around in circles, curling to make contact with the inner walls of his back passage. "Oh, fuck, yeah. Oh, Rain, so good."

"Mmm...." This was the extent of acknowledgement Rain gave, as he desired to have more of Matt. So he surrounded the thick blunt crown of Matt's dick with his lips, suckling and tasting. The slit on top was glistening with precum along with a thin coating of his saliva as the tip of his tongue lapped up the emerging creamy drops that had a peculiar blend of salty bitterness and sugary sweetness. Every man had a unique taste—but at the moment, Rain wasn't thinking about other guys. To him, Matt's rich flavor was akin to the nectar of the gods and the stuff of wet dreams. Unless Matt specifically ordered him to desist, Rain was going to keep at this through his lover's blazing orgasm—and beyond, all the way to round two, and maybe more if their energy and enthusiasm held.

All the while fingering Matt's hole, Rain moved his lips lower to wet his lover's erect shaft to ease the process. Coming up with deep suction, he flicked the tip of his tongue over the bundle of nerves just under the ridge of the crown, delivering excruciating wet pressure. Matt's whole body jerked and his whimpers turned to groans as his left hand bunched the sheets while the right raked through Rain's red-golden curls tenderly and lazily, without effort or force. Rain found he really liked how Matt massaged his scalp softly and tugged his curls a little amidst his fits of passion.

"Oh, baby, you make me so fucking hungry," Matt murmured in between pants.

Rain let go of Matt's cock with a rather obscene wet plop and grinned up at his lover. "I'm feeling quite ravenous myself, sweet thing." Keeping his green gaze locked with Matt's blue glazed-over eyes, Rain licked a few more pearly drops oozing out of the little slit. "Not to mention thirsty for your juices, lover. Mmm, so sweet, so briny." Making a sound of enjoyment, Rain took all of Matt's hard hot cock into his mouth, all the way down to the hilt until his face was buried in light-brown pubic curls. Matt had a sizable package and a noteworthy dick that, when fully erect, easily reached the back of Rain's throat and even slipped past it, giving Rain ample opportunity to relish his skill at deep throating due to his practically missing gag reflex. Despite his unassuming appearance, Matt was seriously hung, and Rain found every reason to be over the moon at having accepted his lover's offer of a date. Not that sexual intimacy was everything in a relationship, but Rain knew that shared passion, desire during the act, and two positive sexual outcomes were vital for the successful continuance of it. Without those essential feelings of interconnectedness, a romance would turn out as nothing but a wet blanket.

"Oh, for God's sake, Rain," Matt cried out in pleasure. "I'm dying here. Please."

Without a verbal response, Rain slipped another finger into Matt's cramped hole and jiggled them about until he found the soft spongy mass he'd been looking for. Alternately caressing and poking the prostate for his lover's aching delight, Rain increased the speed and curvature of his fingers. He kept hitting the sweet spot within Matt with his knuckles, and he vigorously sucked Matt's rock-hard, fiery-hot cock. His lover's husky voice clamored in reply to Rain's sensual stimulation, and his body shook and convulsed violently in spasms.

"Rain, please," Matt's hoarse voice pleaded. "Need you now. Need your cock."

Nothing cryptic about that statement, Rain thought, pulling out his fingers before placing a pillow underneath Matt's lower back and butt, and he readied himself quickly by flicking on one of his pre-lubed condoms. Yes, he rarely had a need to put on a condom for anal sex since he didn't do the fucking, but he used them for oral sex, which, despite the rumors, wasn't 100 percent secure from possible infections. It was considered low-risk by some and high-risk by others, but like everything fun, it carried with it a potential for danger. So as a result of years of practice, Rain was able to sheath himself fast and aligned the head of his cock with Matt's dark rosette.

"Ready or not…," Rain whispered, feeling quite out of his element but daring to proceed when Matt looked up at him, smiling softly, thus emboldening Rain to make the final plunge. And Matt's expression was nothing short of blissful expectancy.

At first, Rain's cock couldn't get into the tightness past the snug ring of muscle even though he pushed. Frustrated, Rain grabbed the base of his cock to keep it steady and rigid while using his other hand to spread Matt's ass cheeks more, and this time he slid in without resistance. Oh, Matt's enclosure was so hot and tight Rain was almost unable to thrust forward due to the sheer overwhelming pressure that surrounded him completely. As Matt exhaled slowly, the tension eased and his muscles relaxed, allowing Rain to shove in until his pubes nestled against Matt's ass.

At that point he had to stop. The sexual urgency weighed on his strained body, and his hips jerked in tiny spurts, almost of their own volition. "You okay?" Rain asked, panting, studying Matt's face closely for any signs of discomfort or pain.

Matt's blue eyes were closed, but they fluttered every once in a while. A satisfied smile tugged the corners of his mouth, like a tic. His back arched and the slight sheen of sweat covering his tough figure described his aroused state explicitly without words. "Uh-huh..." was all the sound Matt seemed capable of producing—which made Rain grin contentedly. Oh yeah, he was giving it to his lover *good*.

Rain's first shallow thrust made Matt's thighs ripple and his stomach quiver as he let out a low moan, his head falling back against the pillow, his mouth open to take in quick gasps. A few fast, small shoves at first, but then Rain pulled out as far as the rim—keeping only the crown of his cock inside the tight-fitting tunnel—and sank in fast, hard, and deep. With a sharp cry, Matt bucked his hips up forcefully, and Rain knew his cock was pressing against his lover's prostate. Repeating the move intently, Rain set a rhythm of heavy-driving thrusts, gliding over and pushing against Matt's sensitive spot over and over again. Pretty soon Matt had his hands placed against the headboard and he was pushing back with force, impaling himself on Rain's cock more and more every time.

Rain had forgotten how amazing it was to give this type of pleasure to a lover. Rain felt heated pressure and wet friction all along the length of his shaft, compressed in Matt's inner vise that milked his precum out and worked his cut cock with unseen muscles. The fierce grip was pushing Rain toward the edge of delight, toward the release he was nearly dying for.

"Oh, Rain." Matt's hushed voice barely reached him over the sound of blood thrumming in his ears. "Harder. More. Please, Rain. Need it harder."

Rain was holding onto Matt's hips, his fingers digging into the flesh almost violently as he began to lose self-control. He'd forgotten a lot of things about anal sex as the giving party. Frowning, he became aware of the difficulty of letting go in this position, kneeling between Matt's legs, his lover's feet pressed against the mattress to aid him to meet Rain's thrusts. Yes, he could use his own weight as leverage, but he wanted more full-body contact.

"Pushy bottom," Rain growled—but again, it sounded more like a purr, which was more than mildly annoying. "I'll show you harder."

In a fit of adrenaline and irritation, Rain pulled out of Matt entirely, and, grabbing his lover's legs in a firm hold, he flipped the man around onto his stomach in a swift, almost elegant move so domineering that it surprised even him with its intensity and aggression.

With a huffed grunt, Matt landed flat on his face on the mattress and shook his head as if confused, but Rain allowed no pause. Parting his lover's ass cheeks, he pushed his way back inside Matt with a single harsh thrust. Matt groaned, burying his face in the pillow. The searing, crushing heat welcomed Rain again as he regained his former tempo and momentum, working Matt's hole and passage with energetic eagerness.

"Oh, God, Rain. Yes...." Matt's low voice dragged out the final *S* until it turned into a husky whisper before trailing off entirely.

Placing his hands on the mattress on both sides of Matt's flanks for leverage, Rain put his back into it—or his hips, more like. For a good long while, nothing could be heard but the slap of skin on skin and heavy panting and grunting from both men. Rain could swear he had not been this potent and rigorous during sex in ages, but Matt had asked for it, so Rain gave it his very best in a spectacular show of dedication. It would have been an Olympic medal-winning performance—if they gave Olympic medals for bed sports.

Propelling his steaming-hot, steel bar-hard dick into his lover's cramped passage again and again, Rain felt the tingling of imminent climax at the base of his spine, beginning to speed up along his nerves, tendons, and muscles, and reaching every inch of him within and without. Yes, there was satisfaction to be had here, and Rain could feel from the deep judders racking Matt that he was close to coming as well. His ass muscles convulsed and undulated around Rain's stiff, ready-to-blow dick, nearly yanking the discharge out of his still resisting body, which longed for more selfish pleasure despite the need to come.

"Still... want to... give me... directions... you... cocky... twat?" His rhythm broken and, his arms losing their strength, Rain landed heavily over Matt's sweaty hot back, all the while entering his lover as his hips continued to move with a primal will of their own.

Under him, Matt was choking with laughter, which had the added effect of bouncing Rain over his body and shaking him along with his lover. Matt's ass also took part in the fun, pulsating around Rain's cock and twitching in a way that both grabbed and released Rain's dick at the same time. Rain decided that if they ever did this again with Rain on top, he'd make a serious effort to send Matt rolling on the bed beneath him with a continuous string of chuckles.

"Now... who's... pushy?" Matt laughed in exasperated gasps, clearly with the intention of taunting Rain into another show of force— and fun.

But, drowning in waves of pleasure, Rain could no longer think of a quip smart enough or fast enough to silence his teasing sex partner. He had to come—right now. "Matt," his ragged voice pleaded, and even though Rain was topping, Matt's climax was absolutely necessary for Rain to believe he'd done a job worthy of future remembrance. If his lover didn't come, Rain would always suspect he was the cause of Matt's displeasure.

"Coming, babe," Matt mumbled then, almost incoherently, fisting the sheets and tossing his head on the pillow, pressing his forehead against it and murmuring something inaudible and unfathomable. "So close... so good...."

Closing his eyes with a sigh, Rain felt ecstasy sweeping over his consciousness, dissipating all fears and doubts like mist vanishing in the stark morning light. Matt seemed to be just waiting on the precipice of pleasure for Rain to give him the nudge to tip over and climax. Rain, too, was ablaze with desire and felt like his anxieties were lifted because Matt was feeling just as plump and ripe for the plucking as he was. They would come together, and it would rock both their worlds.

Pounding into Matt with all the remaining strength he had, Rain fucked his lover within an inch of his life. "You... like... this... precious?" he muttered, wanting to hear Matt say the words that his newfound experience was fulfilling them both.

"Oh, fuck, Rain...." Matt gasped out his utterances in thick, raspy huffs of hot air. "Your... cock... feels... so... fucking... good." His back was slick with sweat just like Rain's chest, and Rain kept sliding off him. Only Rain's weight on Matt's body held them in place. Yet Matt did try to move, surging his hips up to get more of Rain's dick inside him and fill him to the brim. Rain tried to comply as best he could, but they'd been at it for way longer than he normally lasted. This hadn't been a race to the finish but a long arduous climb to the peak of pleasure. Rain was all but exhausted, and his reaming of Matt's ass was beginning to take its toll on his muscles.

"Matt, gotta come," he begged.

"Yeah, me too," Matt admitted breathlessly.

Matt's body trembled all over, taking Rain along for the ride since he clung to his lover's back like a monkey. Using his toes for traction, Rain grabbed beneath Matt's shoulders for support and, holding his breath, began with relentless fury his final onslaught toward triumph. Under him Matt panted hard and heavy, groaning between inhales and exhales.

"Matt, please," Rain whispered in the man's ear, begging. "Please, come."

Barely registering the nod, Rain felt Matt's body ricochet off him to the mattress as his violent spasms caused him to writhe as if in agony. Shouting out his release, Matt shook, and Rain could do nothing but hang on as Matt's fiery hot channel clenched around his dick, torturing and milking him to his own release. Slamming into Matt two, five, ten more times with a need stronger than his tired body's aches, Rain felt his balls tighten painfully. Rain shot his load into Matt as he came and came, stuffing the condom full with the eruption of his heated liquid. Matt's ass continued to pump him dry with involuntary convulsions. Shaken to the core, Rain remained draped over Matt's vibrating frame, both men gasping for air.

Trying to regain the full use of his lungs, Rain pressed his face to the hot and sweaty skin between Matt's shoulder blades, unable to shift an inch as his muscles quivered without his consent or control. The only thing that still seemed to work worth a damn—despite the lack of functioning mental faculties—was his running mouth. "Oh, Matt... you can be... my pushy bottom... whenever you want."

As Matt began to quake with winded laughter, Rain grinned so wide he felt his face might split. He wiggled and pressed against his lover to get more comfortable over his backside, having zero intentions of moving away anytime soon. "Insolent ruffian," he scolded with his usual drawl that he was too tired to resist. "Wait till next time, and I'll show you who gets the last laugh. Just... you... wait."

Rain let the exciting threat sink in to his lover before closing his eyes, all weary from the toil, and fell asleep faster than Matt could reply with a snide remark. In his dream he wondered if he remembered to remove the used condom—or even pull out of his lover's perfect ass before dozing off.

MATT, however, was all too aware of the limp, spent cock still trapped inside his ass. Squirming to get free from under his lover, Matt managed to slide the fast-asleep Rain off his back and flop him laboriously onto the sheets next to him. As he did so, Rain's cock slipped out of Matt, and for a moment Matt felt strangely empty and alone.

The soreness was there, the consequence of his inner passage having gotten used to the long cock sticking it to him, and now tried to readjust to the reinstated void. Gently, Matt massaged the edges of his anus, making the pulsing ring of muscles settle back into its regular configuration. That done, he felt the wet spot beneath his groin turning unpleasantly cold and annoyingly sticky.

Groaning with fatigue, his muscles shrieking and joints popping all in protest, Matt got up and with wobbly legs made his teetering way to the bathroom. He switched on the fluorescent light, which flickered a couple of times before releasing its full intensity in a cool bluish tint. After taking a clean towel from the rack, Matt returned to the bed and cleaned Rain, himself, and the sheets as best he could before going back to the bathroom for a glass of water.

While sipping the cool water, Matt had a chance to peer at his own reflection in the mirror. He stared at his flushed cheeks, sweaty skin, bed-tousled hair, lustful, glowing dark eyes, a few drops of come still on his figure. A blind man could've seen that here stood a man who'd just been fucked royally. Oh, yes, had he ever!

Closing his eyes and sighing deeply, Matt found himself exhilarated and energized regardless of the need for sleep drumming behind his eyes. He was glad he'd been right about Rain's proclivities and secret desires—and having offered his lover the opportunity to indulge in them to his heart's content. Yes, Matt still wanted to fuck Rain's brains out. But there would be time for that later. Matt didn't have a single regret about tonight's proceedings as his body hummed and vibrated. He felt like his body was a finely tuned and well-calibrated instrument—and Rain had played him like a masterful virtuoso, bringing him to a smashing and mind-blowing crescendo.

There was no need to feel like he'd missed out on something. In fact, Matt had gained an experience he knew he'd relish for a long time to come. His previous experiences of being on the receiving end of anal sex had left much to be desired. Not that sex in itself was ever boring, but sometimes styles and inclinations just didn't mesh. Add to that being in an unaccustomed sexual role, and you had all the makings of a night of pleasure soon forgotten—or a disturbing physical ordeal.

Tonight Rain had showed him that when two people's chemistries gelled, every part in their joined lovemaking could be a delightfully fulfilling experience. Matt couldn't remember the last time he had come so hard. He'd felt like the orgasm had been ripped from inside his soul and he had emptied every last drop of his heart's blood through the slit of his cock with his pearly-white cum. It had been, for Matt, the orgasm of a lifetime. His body might recover but would never forget, and his heart absolutely would not. Matt was certain that the two of them would engage in this form of love play again, sooner or later.

Draining the last dribbles of his glass of water, Matt sneaked back into the bedroom, slipped naked under the sheets, and gathered Rain's lithe body close, spooning him and kissing him softly on the nape of his neck, just below the wet-with-sweat red-golden curls. Burying himself in the sweaty, musky, and fruity scent of his lover, Matt drifted off to dreamland, both his heart and body sated to their fullest extent. In all his time with past lovers, Matt had never slept comfortably in another man's bed—or even in his own when there was a strange albeit handsome man next to him. This was the first time Matt felt so comfy and relaxed with a lover.

And in his heart, Matt knew the reason was Rain. At this epiphany, Matt fell asleep.

Chapter
Five

"CIRCLE your hips slowly but firmly, lover," Rain taunted him, laughing low and sensuous. "Like this."

And Rain showed Matt how to really dance the merengue, from the simple march in place to the swinging pivots on the balls of his feet and the lingering twirls with his butt swaying like a bubble-shaped instrument of torture existing for the sole purpose of driving Matt crazy. It was like Rain was dancing the song of the siren while Matt was bound by the restrictions of convention and law not to jump his lover in public and make sweet love to him.

Matt's restraint was tested time and again with Rain, who danced closer, teasing, and wound his arms around Matt's waist. "Be cautious, babe," Matt whispered in his ear. "That butt of yours is going to get more exercise later on, so don't wear yourself out."

Rain just laughed, freely and enthusiastically, with his head thrown back, his red-golden curls dancing and gleaming under the warm lamplight, and his whole body doing the tantalizing shimmy.

Yes, that had been another excellent date, Matt reminisced with a grin.

Since their first night together, they had settled into a dating routine, and Matt had spent most weekends with Rain, who made him laugh and moan, sometimes at the same time. Matt hadn't expected Rain to be comfortable with routines and predictability, but for some reason, he'd taken to it like a duck to water. Every Friday and Saturday, Matt sat in what had become his usual seat in front of the small stage at The Sultry Sound and listened to Rain's dreamy songs that set him on fire. As the slow burn took him over, Matt waited impatiently for their date afterward.

They went dancing—ballroom dancing, slow dancing, clubbing— whatever Rain was in the mood for. Rain loved to dance, especially the tango and rumba, and his physique and presence performed an endless dark seduction of Matt.

"And now... the tango," Rain murmured beneath his breath, his green eyes twinkling, and his arms shot up toward the sky as his body took the striking model-like pose of a dancer about to begin his number. As the melodious notes of the Spanish guitar filled the club, Rain danced, beckoning Matt with his lithe figure, tempting him to all manner of sins, and yes, Matt followed, grabbing the giggling Rain by the hips and yanking him close to his body and his heart. "Dip me...," Rain whispered into Matt's ear, his warm breath with the delicious aroma of squash tickling Matt's sense of touch and smell simultaneously.

Spinning Rain around like a whirlwind while he tittered in amusement, Matt felt Rain's leg bend around his own leg, and he dipped his lover so low that the tops of his red-golden curls brushed the parquet floor. Upon getting up, Rain was flushed red, and his hand glided down Matt's cheek in a wanton gesture Matt relished with the sensory memory of every one of his fired-up nerve endings.

Slipping out of Matt's hold, Rain closed his eyes and focused on the dance. Matt followed him across the dance floor, where Rain's hips, hands, head, and feet moved in quick snatching motions, almost smooth jolts, before the rest of his beautiful flexing body followed his popping joints in the slow, sensual steps of the tango. Gliding across the dance floor, Rain danced on air—and soared up high along with Matt's adoring heart.

"Come, lovey...." Rain smiled lopsidedly and, with an extended hand, entreated Matt back into his awaiting embrace. His long arms

encircled Matt in a ring of tenderness and love, and Matt hugged that willowy stem to his heart's content. "Dance with me."

"Oh, Rain," Matt mumbled against his lover's throat, where, with his lips, he could feel the quiet thumping of Rain's heartbeat quicken its pace with his lover so near. He felt it as distinctly as he felt his own start to beat faster for Rain—every time.

That had been the first time Matt had physically and emotionally swooned for Rain, but he knew it wouldn't be the last.

They walked together in the park in the early evenings, holding hands and taking their time amidst the mixed smells of nature and city. Rain loved walking in the great outdoors and often spoke of traveling somewhere where the sound of people wouldn't exist.

"Surely you're not scared of horses?" Matt ribbed tenderly, incredulous and having a hard time picturing Rain frightened of anything or anyone, but Rain still took to an efficient sprint to the other side of the park at the mere sight of approaching park mounted police as the equestrian police officers leisurely trotted along the park pathways on brown quarter horses so docile a bunny rabbit would've seemed rabid in comparison.

While Matt was busy not only following Rain's rapid stride but holding back a wild laugh, Rain's narrowing eyes took on a dangerous glint. "There's only one kind of stud I allow between my *legs, thank you very much. And don't call me Shirley." The pompous huff of righteous indignation only acted as the straw that broke the camel's back, and Matt roared with laughter while Rain's gait put distance between them startlingly fast.*

After running to catch up, Matt surrounded Rain's waist with his arms from behind and halted his lover's escape. "I'm sorry, babe. You know I meant nothing by—"

"Say what you mean, darling, *and mean what you say," Rain snapped back and wiggled to break free from Matt's hold, but Matt*

held on tighter to the sinewy perfection he couldn't wait to feel writhing against him.

"Don't snarl so viciously, babe. It'll ruin your lipstick—and that's my job."

Rain stopped resisting but remained uncooperatively stiff. "Is kissing me so taxing, sweetie, that you label it as work?" That time Rain was just baiting Matt, sounding almost peevish.

"Snobby queen," Matt murmured into Rain's ear and showered his neck with swift sloppy kisses.

"Bourgeois bully," Rain shot right back—but breathless and blushing, and Matt grinned with happiness so potent that it threatened to split his face in half.

They ate out in restaurants Matt found a little too pretentious and expensive but that made Rain feel like a queen—and he wanted to offer this experience to his lover, who satisfied the needs and wants Matt hadn't even been aware he had. Like being adventurous.

"Oh, don't be so frightfully tedious, darling," Rain sighed with struggling patience, his tone reaching an alarming volume in frustration and catching the unwanted attention of a few nearby fellow restaurant occupants. "I dare you to try it," he continued with a lower murmur, batting long eyelashes intended to entice Matt into immediate supplication—and succumb he did. After taking a bite of the blowfish— which had a surprisingly mild flavor—Matt expected to choke and keel over dead at any second, and he wondered if he'd feel his heart stop one beat before it actually did. Stupid fugu, Matt cursed silently while chewing the meat of a fish—which he never thought of as meat at all because it was fish. Sure, Matt had no problem with the occasional sushi, but poisonous fish, cooked or not....

After swallowing the piece and gulping a few more times for good measure, Matt shrugged impassively, keeping a level expression, and said, "Tastes like chicken. Bad chicken."

Harrumphing, Rain shook his lovely head, pursing his lips, dissatisfied. "Oh, sometimes you can so bourgeois, sweetie. It's not going to kill you to live a little." Matt was about to raise the rational point that with fugu, the chance did exist, when he caught on to the humorous glint in those pale-green eyes, and that mischievous man of his was almost showered with the remnants of Matt's pinot noir.

"Next time we go out, we're going to McDonald's," Matt said without pause to let his lover know he'd only take so much needling before dessert—in or out of bed.

Snickering, Rain leaned forward and bussed Matt on the cheek gently. "Whatever you say, precious."

And what had indeed sounded more like a promise than a taunt had been carried out to its fullest extent once they'd gotten back to Rain's place that evening. As far as dates went, that—their ninth date— had not gone exactly as planned with the choice of meals, but afterward in bed, Rain had acquiesced to all of Matt's feverish desires.

Matt found out early on in their relationship that he couldn't get enough of Rain and his beautiful sylphlike body that writhed and twisted beneath and on top of him in sexual ecstasy, filling the silence in between Matt's heartbeats with his low groans and high moans.

Yes, the sex was awesome—and so was the foreplay.

"Stop it, you fiend!" Rain cried out in between giggles and wiggles.

Frustrated, Matt held himself motionless, sighed, and counted to twenty. "Come on, babe. It's just a massage—not the Inquisition."

Whining, Rain squirmed even harder. "At least then there'd be song, dance, and Mel Brooks to entertain me," he sneered. He was wriggling so fussily that Matt bounced around on Rain's naked butt like he was stuck in an earthquake. The whole ordeal was so tricky that Matt had to press his hands firmly on Rain's shoulders to hold him still.

"Are you kidding me? I'm just trying to make you feel good, for fuck's sake."

Coiling and puffing, Rain managed to push himself off the mattress enough—no mean feat considering Matt was sitting on top of him—to turn around to lie on his back. A lascivious grin tugged the corners of his lips as he licked them so suggestively that it could no longer have been misconstrued as mere suggestion by anyone with half a brain. "You know what would make me feel good other than this ghastly form of physical torment you've chosen to inflict upon me, sweet pea?" Yes, Matt had discovered the hard way that Rain was indeed ticklish when he was touched in a way he wasn't mentally prepared for. So very, very, very annoyingly and completely ticklish that a simple massage had become a raging battle of wills and bodies. "A good, long, hard fuck would do me wonders, darling."

Those accursed pouting lips, that smut-ridden potty mouth, those damned batting eyelashes, those infernally twinkling pale-green eyes....

Just like always, with a resigned sigh, Matt relented and succumbed.

And Matt had never regretted a single act of submission to date.

Sometimes he admired his own patience when it came to dating Rain, whose schedule worked so dead against Matt's timetables. Sometimes the mere anticipation of being with Rain nearly drove Matt insane.

The music-filled foreplay lasted from morning when Matt woke up right up until the first time he embraced Rain after his performance and their dinner, and whatever entertainment they'd chosen for their date night. From that initial full-body contact, all the desires and passions came out clearly, demanding satisfaction. Rain was not only an inventive lover but a torturous one as well, because he could drive Matt crazy with a mere touch—and then leave him hanging, gasping and dying for more, as Rain just moved on to something else, wherever his mood took him. At least there was the consolation prize that Rain's moods, lips, and hands took him all over Matt. Where Matt adored and worshipped Rain's body with a kind of loving reverence, Rain craved Matt with an intense, fiery passion that Matt only skimmed the surface of and barely understood.

"When the rain is blowing in your face, I could offer you a warm embrace...."

Even in between gasps, Rain always miraculously managed to keep his singing voice level and harmonious, but that night it annoyed the shit out of Matt because he knew Rain was doing it to deliberately push his buttons, like he did at times just for the sheer fun of it.

Matt actually growled. *"I'll show you who blows who, you little minx...."*

Matt tried to turn the tables but quickly failed when Rain's chuckling mouth closed around Matt's cock. He hummed while sucking the crown, licking the length, and taking in all there was to be had until Rain's lovely lips brushed against Matt's pubes and his nose skimmed his pubic bone. Unable to contain the need, Matt bucked up, thrusting blindly into that wet heat he worshipped with every drop of blood gushing through his veins.

Coming up, Rain swiped the tip of his long pink tongue over the slit of Matt's dick and murmured teasingly, *"Can you feel the rain blowing on you now, lovey?"* There it was again, that taunting tone that drove Matt bat shit crazy, and he snarled again in frustration. Rain just chuckled some more. *"Yes, I think you can... lover."*

The smart quip on the tip of Matt's tongue evaporated when Rain's mouth moved in for the kill, drowning any and all retorts that were there. Rain's red-golden curly head bobbed up and down, his sweet, sweet mouth sucking so intently that Matt grimaced with pleasure so extreme it bordered on pain. The ragged, torn sound that emerged from his throat had nothing whatsoever to do with anything rational or controlled.

But just when Matt believed the satisfaction of climax lay ahead, Rain got up, straddling Matt's hips and lowering his mouth to cover his own, and Rain's fruity taste mixed with Matt's own saltier precum-laced flavor. That snakelike tongue of Rain's could do wonders in and out of Matt's body—and with any orifice. Rain's hands were everywhere, his body rubbing against Matt's in sweet delicious friction and pressure, and that divine mouth....

"Nothing I wouldn't do, go to the ends of the earth for you, to make you feel my love."

Those words Rain sang into Matt's mouth, and the breathy vibrations were unlike anything Matt had ever experienced. It boggled his mind, changing Matt into a feeble-brained idiot who sought his lover's pleasure from every arousing touch, every teasing word, and every lingering presence.

And that had been the first inkling Matt had received that his dalliance with Rain had become so much more than a mere game of who-can-come-last-and-most-this-time.

One of the signs of the seriousness of their relationship came in the form of friends. Matt had not met the friends of most men he had gone out with or had affairs with. Rain was not like them, and Matt was certain that an impish part of Rain delighted in having the two ends of the spectrum—Matt on one end, and Norma on the other—come into contact, like opposing poles of a magnet.

And true enough, Matt had blundered from the get-go.

"Isn't she lovely?" Rain crooned to Matt as soon as Norma set foot in Rain's apartment. Then Rain bussed his best friend on the cheek.

Norma was looking rather dazzling that evening, wearing a wig with long pink tresses, a pink satin corset that narrowed his waist to an hourglass, a hot pink mini skirt that showcased his long legs clad in silk stockings, and pink pumps to finish off the ensemble. Norma had glitter on his face—pink, of course—and pink lip gloss and fully made-over eyes, the massively long fake pink eyelashes crowning the display. Matt surmised that pink was his favorite color.

"Darling," Norma responded in kind, kissing Rain's cheeks in an exaggerated continental manner, and speaking in a curious high-pitched tone that Matt simply had no name for. It wasn't really feminine, but it was a far cry from masculine. Glancing at Matt with mock bashfulness, he smiled seductively. "Well, hello, gorgeous."

Before Matt could utter a single syllable, Rain laughed. "He is quite adorable, isn't he?"

"Yes, he is," Matt confirmed with a polite nod and a courteous smile.

When both Rain and Norma turned to give Matt the god of all glares, Matt realized Rain had actually been talking to Norma about Matt. He felt as if his cheeks went up in flames, and he opened and closed his mouth repeatedly in an effort to say something. Yet nothing intelligible came out.

Well, that explained the "she" Rain had used earlier, Matt thought dismally.

"I'm so sorry," Matt finally managed to say humbly, almost crestfallen. "I thought Rain meant... Norma, I didn't mean to insult you in any way."

Suddenly Norma swished his hand through the air, with a new, understanding smile on his face. "Don't feel bad about it, deary. That is by far the least *insulting thing anyone has ever said to me." He giggled girlishly, and Matt dared a sigh of relief at the deflated situation. "And I am quite pleased you think me adorable." Batting his eyelashes, Norma looked positively cute in Matt's eyes.*

"I must be behind on my gay terminology 101," Matt said, chuckling in a self-deprecating fashion, rubbing the back of his neck self-consciously.

That gave Norma pause, and then he was really laughing, the manliness in him apparent in his voice. "No worries, sweetheart. I'll educate you. We'll start at the bottom and work our way up."

It was amazing how Norma managed to make even education sound downright dirty; Matt just had to laugh at that. "I meant to say that you look very beautiful as a woman—just like Rain does—but I don't really want to forget that he's a man under those clothes. Consequently, I can't forget that about you, either. I mean no offense by it."

Norma seemed amused. "My goodness, darling." He was addressing Rain, while watching Matt intently. "Does he always use such big words?"

"Yes." Rain's glare had also vanished, and now he was beaming again.

"How utterly delicious." Matt felt like he was listening to one person speak, only from two mouths. Rain and Norma sounded so alike, it was eerie. Snaking his arm around Matt's elbow, Norma proceeded to direct them both to the living room couch. "I honestly do not care if you call me he or she, Matt," Norma said as they sat down side by side. "Depending on my mood, I can be either, both, or neither." Matt hoped his expression didn't give away his confusion at the last word. "It's true I wear my drag queen persona more often than not, precious, unlike my lovely Rain, who prefers to keep that restricted to work, as it is mainly a profession, not a whole lifestyle."

Norma blew a kiss at Rain, who made a kissy-face in return. "Love you too, honey," Rain remarked, and Matt bit down on his lower lip to stifle any laughter that threatened to erupt.

Norma continued. "The truth is I love being a man, physically you know, especially under these beautiful clothes, so I'm not transitioning. And as a proper queen and a bottom, I love to get fucked by men, so I am a gay man too. You see, whatever Rain calls me, or I her—See how easy it is?—we are men. Men who love men—and women's clothes."

Matt nodded. "You're transvestites, not transgender."

Norma chuckled. "There you go again, sweetie, with those big words of yours."

"Matt likes to make sense of things," Rain cut in serenely, planting a soft drink in front of his best friend. "But he doesn't make the same mistake twice." Sitting down on the coffee table, Rain winked at Matt, who just had to smile back. "When he gets all puffy with that gay social reform wind in his sails, I do get an earful of rhetoric."

Matt ignored the playful scolding that was directed more at Norma than him anyway. "I do think we should talk about things with their proper names—"

"And what if these names are inadequate to describe people?" Rain interrupted, his green eyes ablaze. "Words are labels, and people don't always fit within prescribed categories."

"I hate being labeled, as if only with a factory seal will I be approved by society," Norma said with a disgusted tone, wrinkling his nose disapprovingly and shuddering theatrically. Rain was nodding in agreement, so Matt felt it was time to throw in the towel.

"Terms aside, for what it's worth, ladies, I feel like a very lucky man, getting to spend my evening with, not one, but two beautiful women—and two handsome men."

If people could purr, that's what Rain and Norma would have done right then.

After that conversation the evening had been a veritable success in Matt's honest opinion. And meeting Rain's closest friend had reaffirmed Matt's image of the direction their relationship was headed. Long-term. Since that day he and Rain had spent pretty much all their available free time together.

Tonight was the night of their two-month anniversary, and Matt was nervous. The anxiousness didn't arise just from the fact that tonight Rain would see Matt's loft apartment for the very first time. Since they'd begun dating, they'd only spent evenings and nights together at Rain's place. No, there were other reasons too. Matt had cooked—a first for him, since he'd never had a relationship that lasted long enough for him to prepare a whole meal for a lover. Matt knew Rain preferred a vegetarian diet but was not above the occasional protein or carbohydrate snack. Still, tonight Matt had made an effort to please Rain, unsure whether Rain even remembered that this was a special night for the two of them. He hoped so.

He'd asked Rain to take the night off from his nightclub stint even though he knew how important singing was for his lovely lover. Admittedly he'd been a little surprised when Rain had agreed to his proposition without argument.

It wasn't that they fought often, but they did have their share of disagreements and rows. The biggest hurdle had not changed since their first meeting, namely Rain's flair, his flamboyant appearance and sassy attitude. Rain refused to budge from his stance that he had the right to be who he was no matter where or when he was.

"Why do you want me to change if you were initially attracted to me the way I am?" Rain's cool voice might have asked the question with enough clarity and precision to silence any ambiguity, but Matt heard all the unsaid questions beneath the surface. Those inquiries would've led down a dangerous path on the topic of brave personality vs. brutal reality.

"You know that's not what I mean," Matt replied, keeping his voice just as steady as Rain's, who, by the fiery glint in his pale-green eyes, had every intention of provoking yet another conflict. *"Why is it so wrong for me to want you to be safe?"*

Rain scoffed dramatically, cocking his hipbone and tossing his head back in flashy way. "Please, sir knight, save the chivalry for the damsels in distress."

"Funny how that statement is right on the money when it comes to you." Matt knew from the microsecond the utterance left his lips that he'd catch hell for that.

And he was right too, unfortunately. "Did I say chivalry? I meant to say rudeness, presumption, discourtesy, cowardice, and...." Rain shook his head furiously. *"Oh, Matt, sometimes you can be such a...."* Rain's rare struggling with finding the right words to suit the occasion told Matt in no uncertain terms just how angry Rain was. *"Such a closet case."*

That was new. "I'm not in the closet, Rain," Matt exclaimed, barely holding on to his patience and calming thoughts—but he was so preoccupied with managing his tone and emotional state that he forgot to censor his wayward tongue. *"Just because I don't parade around like a peacock—"*

Rain let out an appalled gasp, his sparkling eyes going wide and his full-lipped mouth hanging open. The shock lasted only a breath or two before Rain froze from top to bottom. "A peacock, eh? Well, they have a hundred eyes on their tail. Only my eyes are real—and they've just opened up to see what kind of man—"

"Rain, I'm sorry," Matt backpedaled as fast he could. "I didn't mean it—"

"No, no. You've made your feelings on this matter crystal clear."

Rain started for the door—curiously of his own apartment, so where on earth did he think he was going?—when Matt closed the distance between them, blocking his lover's exit with his hands up in surrender. "I'm sorry, Rain. I've grown to care so much for you I hate the idea of you getting hurt—"

"How can you say you care for me if you want me to change who I am?" The fact that Rain had stopped to speak meant he'd stopped to listen too, and Matt took the opening offered.

But suddenly all the fight left him, and Matt sagged against the door, maudlin and fearful. "I don't want you to change, Rain. I just... I like you. A lot. And I... I'm afraid."

There were a number of emotions flashing across Rain's face. Then he relaxed as his full lips pursed. "I guess, sweetie, this is going to be one of those things we'll never agree upon." Matt had been so worried that this conversation would be the deal-breaker, that he'd actually heard the words already playing in his head. Rain telling him good-bye. But then.... "If you ever call me a peacock again... Matt... I'll expect nothing less than a full drag on stage at The Sultry Sound from you as recompense." Rain only ever used his name when he was serious—and Matt knew without a shred of doubt Rain was dead serious. "Got it... darling?"

The sigh that broke free from Matt's chest then shook him to the core, and he smiled with relief. "Got it... babe."

Then Rain stepped into his arms and just like that, the fight was over.

And that was how Matt had learned that Rain didn't hold grudges or revive old quarrels but always looked straight ahead toward the future—even if they both knew they'd have this same argument again.

No, that had not been their last row or even the fiercest, but it pretty much summed up the way they talked past each other on this subject. They argued over the same thing—only not. Like talking about potatoes and potatoes, only with a different accent.

It wasn't like Rain was wrong in his wish and his right to be who he was, Matt grudgingly admitted, but Matt wanted Rain safe and sound, which was hard since he stood out even in the gayest of social circles. Matt had had zero influence on Rain's overflowing femininity and brilliant queerness. Matt was torn between wishing to keep his lover free and safe, and he hated that the two didn't coincide more.

Regardless of their differences of opinion, they had a great time together. Matt found he disliked sleeping without Rain's warmth next to him during the week, when he couldn't go to sleep wrapped around his lover and wake up to stare at those green translucent eyes sparkling with life and love and sex. Rain's lips against Matt's were the perfect way to welcome a new day.

"Good morning, precious," the amused melodious voice whispered in Matt's ear, arousing him from sleep and to life too. "Or should I say... sugar?" The sweet tone drifted farther away, and then Matt's morning wood was enveloped by moist heat and smooth pressure. Rain tormented him with a slick slide up and down, fondled Matt's ball sac tenderly and caressed his smooth crease gently. Tight lips, a gliding tongue, and a hint of teeth all teased every one of Matt's senses to reckless abandon.

"Oh God...," Matt mumbled. In the instant between heartbeats, the drowsiness encompassing his head switched to a sexual haze enclosing his consciousness. Shudders wracked his body, and he gave in to the demanding advances of his lover—not out of weariness but out of the desire that began to pump through his veins from his heart to his groin. He stood up at attention for Rain, whose amused laughter

vibrated on the wet sensitive skin of his erect cock as clearly as club music, beating through his skin into muscles and down to his bones.

"Mmm... I should stop now, snookums," Rain said in a nasty ribbing tone, lifting his head to kiss Matt's taut belly with such an airy touch it only registered because Matt's skin had become sensitized to sex.

"Huh?" Matt protested so shrilly Rain laughed loudly into the Sunday morning silence. "No, don't stop... please...?"

Rain got up to sit on his heels with his hands set on his hips in imitation of a steadfast pose, a berating look in his eyes. "Why should I have proper manners to finish what I start, sweet pea, when you don't even bother to respond to my good morning wishes?"

Matt braced himself on his elbows so fast that his still sleep-filled muscles protested furiously. "Oh, babe, I'm sorry. Good morning." In a conciliatory gesture, Matt got up, wound his arms around Rain, and pulled him down on top of him. "With you, every morning is so damn good, babe. I should never forget," he added lazily and gave a profoundly intimate smack on his lover's lips, to which Rain chuckled amusedly.

"Prove it, handsome," Rain taunted, and he slipped his tongue into Matt's mouth deeply and deliberately, curling that long tongue around Matt's own, licking and savoring with the same intent. When Matt wrapped his arms around Rain tighter to roll his lover over onto his back, the talking was definitely over.

Sometimes Matt found himself praying he'd have this bliss for the rest of his days.

Well aware that he might be letting his emotions run amok too early into their relationship, Matt steadied himself against the sink as the familiar heady anticipation of Rain's company sent his knees buckling and stole his breath away. On Mondays and Tuesdays, the scent of his lover's fruity perfume still clung to the pillow cases he always swiped from Rain's place just so he could keep his lover's fragrance near, and Matt buried himself in them on those lonely mornings he wanted to see the end of. He was tired of being alone and feeling this lonely when he'd found someone he really liked.

Glancing briefly at the clock on the wall of his loft apartment's open kitchen—6:40 p.m.—Matt shook his head to clear what he knew were premature thoughts. Not only was it still twenty minutes before Rain was to show up, it was too soon to bring up the conversation about having an exclusive affair or settling accounts with ex-lovers or maybe even shacking up together. Or was it? Perhaps the timing for a talk about their exes was wrong, but surely the expectation of exclusivity was not far-fetched after two months. Matt had realized a week or so ago that he wanted these things and, more importantly, wanted them with Rain. The epiphany had caught him off guard, since initially he'd surmised they were just both having fun and their casual arrangement didn't hold any guarantees or demands on either of them. Still, Matt wasn't prepared to dismiss these awakening feelings so easily and decided to analyze them to the deepest detail when the right window of opportunity presented itself.

That, however, was not tonight. For their two-month anniversary, Matt wanted them both to just relax and enjoy their special night together over a fine home-cooked meal and a hundred-dollar bottle of white wine, some music and dancing after, and then, maybe, some vigorous bedroom calisthenics. Yes, that sounded good, Matt thought euphorically.

No, better than good. He smiled as he checked the fruit salad in the fridge and the noodles simmering on the stove. Dinner would soon be ready—but it could easily wait if their other appetites took over before food and wine were served. After verifying for the fourth or maybe fifth time that the dining room table was set to perfection, topped with flowers and candles, Matt reviewed the clean, polished state of his flat, going over every inch with a fine-tooth comb, fluffing the couch pillows, opening the windows a bit for ventilation, and smoothing out the wrinkles on his bed coverlet.

He was so busy at all this rechecking that the clock face said 7:15 p.m. before Matt even thought to look at it. Frowning and biting his lower lip in a fit of anxiety, Matt dug out his cell phone from his jeans pocket, but there had been no missed calls or texts. *Where is Rain?* Focusing on calming himself, Matt sat on the couch, placed his hands in his lap, and waited.

DRAGGING his dysfunctional leg, Rain tried to limp his way to the door but failed and landed flat on his face on the dusty floor of his boudoir slash dressing room at The Sultry Sound. He heard himself sob in pain and blinked away burning tears, but he couldn't manage to get up again, for his shaky arms offered no leverage. Panting, he grabbed his leg, and even through the white denim, he felt the moisture there. The metallic tang of blood mixed with a fruitier and more putrid smell he didn't recognize. Looking at the stain, he saw it was darker than red with a tint of brown.

A temperate yet determined knock came from the door. "Rain? The cab's here. If you don't come out soon, you're going to be late, and guys like Matt aren't going to—"

"Norma…," Rain whispered, discovering to his dismayed surprise that his voice was hoarse. It was impossible to get a louder peep out, as if he had a cold with a sore throat. *Why?* Rain was rarely if ever sick. Good genes, good immune system.

Norma had apparently heard something even through the background noise of the club, because he knocked again, this time more firmly, and asked in a worried tone, "Rain? Are you there, sweetie? What's wrong?"

Thank God, Rain thought, when Norma tried the door that to his relief wasn't locked, and opened the door. Rain's head buzzed and he couldn't focus his gaze, so he only heard Norma shriek like a banshee before a rush of fast-paced steps advanced toward Rain. His teeth chattered as the waves of pain made themselves known to him when Norma grabbed the lapels of his formerly white leather jacket and turned him onto his back on the stone floor.

"Rain! Can you hear me?" Norma demanded, his voice painfully faint and trembling, and Rain felt guilty for making his friend go through this.

For this was Rain's fault—all the way.

"What is all this shouting—" Tiny's angry rumbling voice approached, was cut off midsentence, and then a flurry of movement, rapid footsteps, and powerful arms lifted Rain up to the cream-colored satin divan.

"Tiny, he's bleeding all over the place!" Norma screamed. "His leg—"

"I can see that, you twit!" Tiny cursed Norma into silence. "Make yourself useful and call the ambulance. Right now, you hussy, right now. Go!"

Shocked, Norma ran away—that much Rain could discern with his blurry vision.

"Rain, you stupid little...." Tiny continued to cuss incoherently and mumble under his breath, and Rain could hear the anger there— and he couldn't blame his friend. "You promised you would get that rusty nail scratch on your leg looked at by a doctor, you silly slut. You got that nearly a week ago, and this run-down rat hole has been here long enough to give you the bubonic plague if you don't watch those pretty little toes of yours. Goddammit, Rain!"

"I'm sorry, Tiny...," Rain whispered, slumping against Tiny's warm, solid side of rock-hard muscles. "I thought I could handle it on my own—"

"Right, with the imaginary doctor's license you've got," Tiny growled impatiently. "Damn it, Rain. How could you be so thoughtless?"

"You know me, sweetie." Rain tried for levity. "All hair and no brain. That's me."

"The ambulance is five minutes away." Norma's troubled tone pierced the air.

"All right, thanks," Tiny said and proceeded to wind his strong arm around Rain's waist. "Come on, you slut. Let's get you up on your feet and off to the hospital. I'll get you there even if I have to carry you there myself. And by God, if I have to do that, you're never going to hear the end of this!"

Usually Rain appreciated Tiny's growls a great deal because that meant he cared, but this time there was far too much anger and frustration to indicate pure concern. Rain had no doubt he'd catch hell for this for eons to come.

And then he thought of Matt….

Sliding to the ground again as his weak leg gave out, Rain thought only of how differently he'd wanted this night to play out. His two-month anniversary with Matt. Rain had spent the last night dreaming of the welcoming kiss on his lips, the coffee taste of his lover's mouth, those strong arms around him, the feel of his loving gentleness pressed against his naked body. Knowing in his heart he was falling for Matt, Rain cried out as the searing pain jabbed his leg, which felt like it was burning from the inside out. The one regret he had right then was that now he'd never get to tell Matt how he felt.

Tiny's alarmed tone rose, and Norma's shrill voice turned to cries near Rain, but he couldn't place exactly where his friends were. His vision went from flashing lights and colors to monochrome as the cold blackness swept over his consciousness. Then sights and sounds dissipated and darkness took him.

Chapter Six

"HE'LL be all right, Matt. He's been through worse. He's a tough little shit."

The warmth and kindness in Tiny's voice were blatantly obvious to Matt, just like the underlying love and affection. Tiny was Rain's friend, yes, but there was something about the way he refused to speak Rain's name. Just "he" this and "he" that. Matt knew why but didn't say it out loud. As long as you never said the words, it wasn't yet true, or real, or inevitably heartbreaking.

Waiting on the uncomfortable hospital couch—lumpy and raggedy from the hundreds, maybe thousands, of previous worried occupants—Matt felt worn out and worn thin. He felt like a shadow, without flesh and blood. Only the tears on his cheeks and the ache burning and freezing inside his heart were real.

The hesitant but intense grip on his shoulder was meant to be encouraging and reassuring, but all Matt wanted was to shake himself loose from Tiny's hand. He looked past Tiny at the openly weeping Norma sitting in an armchair by the couch. Sobbing an endless stream of tears, Norma shook with the power of his sorrow and pain. Murmuring something unintelligible, Norma kept swaying his blue satin dress-covered body back and forth, holding himself tightly as though the solace offered by his own arms belonged to someone else.

Matt could discern the discomfort of Tiny next to him as he too looked at Norma from time to time. Once Tiny had tried to console

Norma with a hand on his knee, but the horrified look on Norma's face had made Tiny remove his hand so fast it might as well have been on fire. Matt suspected that Rain's best friend took all forms of intimacy other than sex as an attack, and considering recent events like the gay bashing on Rain, Matt couldn't blame him either.

Wiping his cold, sweaty forehead with his trembling hand, Matt fought yet another pang of nausea threatening to tear his gut into shreds or bunch it up into a ball. It had been nearly four hours since he'd gotten the call from Tiny about Rain and his emergency situation. Apparently Rain had been barely conscious on the floor of his dressing room at the club when Norma and Tiny had found him and called an ambulance. When Matt had gotten to the hospital, the paramedics he'd spoken with had informed him that Rain had gotten a sharp gash on his leg that had gotten seriously infected and was now oozing pus by the bucketloads—naturally they'd used better language to describe the whole incident.

All Matt could think about was that he and Rain were supposed to be celebrating tonight.

Celebrating. Matt couldn't believe how happy he'd been waking up this morning, so full of hope and love at the prospect of getting to spend the evening and the whole night with Rain after not having seen his lover for a whole week. And now everything had gone to hell. In passing he wondered if he'd left the stove on or the candles burning or if he'd even locked the door, as he'd run out so fast he'd forgotten his coat. At least his home and car keys were jangling in his pocket when he moved around on the oh-so-fucking uncomfortable hospital sofa, his heart in unspeakable anguish.

"I should've been with him," Tiny mumbled to himself beside Matt, shaking his head and rubbing his hands together angrily. "I should've noticed that something was wrong with him. I should've escorted him to the hospital myself. I should've made sure he was all right. I should've been there for him to keep him safe."

On and on the self-recriminations went, and Matt felt powerless to stop him from prattling on. They barely knew each other, and he was too wrapped in his own pain to deal with someone else's. The wait was killing him, not to mention the initial description of Rain's injuries from Norma, who was blubbering his eyes out, mascara running down his brown cheeks. It had been hard to hear the miserable details of it and to know Matt was helpless to do anything about it. All he could do was wait and see. The paramedics had said so, the doctors had said so, and even Tiny had said so. Nonetheless, Matt was holding on by a thread.

And worst of all was the awareness that pain and sorrow weren't the only feelings festering within him. Matt was furious, positively steaming in his boiling juices. Never before had he felt such anger. Rain had kept his injury from Matt for over a week—that stubborn ass!—and now they were reaping the bitter harvest of the secrets Rain had sown. Matt didn't want to feel these dark emotions, but they entangled with all the other stuff in his head until he didn't know which way was up and which was down.

Still fidgeting in his seat, Matt almost missed the approach of the surgeon in his pale-green scrubs—which reminded him of the color of Rain's eyes—and felt a chill as he sprang up from his seat and stood there silently so as not to miss a single word.

"Mr. Burton?" the doctor inquired with a quiet reverence, his gaze jumping from Matt to Tiny and back again.

Tiny nodded. "I am. How is he?"

The doctor smiled, but it seemed hollow to Matt. "Mr. Deveraux has sustained a serious external injury that, left untreated, has resulted in severe septicemia. We've repaired the laceration and given antibiotics intravenously for the bacterial infection, but you should know that the situation is grave. It will be at least a day or so before he comes around. The next few days will be critical. We will continue to monitor his condition closely, and we should all hope for the best."

Not only did Matt despise the habit of doctors dumbing things down for laypeople, but he also hated how doctors always said *we* instead of *I*. He guessed it was a liability issue or an I'm-the-next-best-thing-to-God type of delusion. In any case, Matt was certain he might strangle this man if he didn't provide any assurances—even though he knew he'd never hear those words unless Rain made a full recovery. Then this doctor would step up to take all the credit.

"Can we see him?" Tiny asked, his voice surprisingly frail for such a big beefy man.

The doctor shook his head emphatically. "Not at this time, I'm afraid. We'll see how he is tomorrow, yes? In the meantime, I suggest the both of you, errr, the three of you"—he took a curious gander behind them at Norma, still sobbing away in the armchair in his pretty dress—"take this opportunity to go home, get some rest and something to eat. It would also be helpful if you got some of his things. I'm sure he'll need them when he gets back on his feet."

The doctor smiled with encouragement, and Matt knew that was all they were going to get from this man. Providing Rain with his clothes, toiletries, and makeup would be helpful for all of them. A kind of psychological healing before the real thing. It had to be enough—for now.

When the nameless doctor left with a curt nod, both Matt and Tiny sank back down on the couch cushions. Boneless and weary, Matt couldn't find the strength to get up on his feet and start the slow march toward his car.

"I have his key," Tiny said quietly from his side, a question buried in his tone. "Wanna go there now?"

Norma's noisy sobs began to irk Matt, same as the incessant smell of disinfectant and the steady glow of impossibly hard overhead lights. With a silent nod, Matt got up and headed for the exit. Unable to recall his speedy walk to the car as anything but a rush through lights and shadows, Matt reached the car, unlocked the door with shaky hands, climbed behind the wheel—and let it all roll over him even as Tiny slipped into the passenger seat. Matt's whole body shook with the intensity of the pain and sorrow he'd been holding in tight for hours. His head hurt, his eyes were sore, and he could barely swallow past the hard lump in his throat. But beyond all that was the horrible pressure around his heart, squeezing the life out of him. Grasping at the steering wheel like it was a life preserver, Matt hunched with the weight of the emotions barreling over him.

Faintly he felt Tiny's hand on his shoulder, then moving across his back in a soothing manner. Yet the big lug said nothing, and Matt was glad of the companionable silence. They were both hurting, and words were unnecessary. Of like minds, they sat side by side in Matt's silvery two-year-old Toyota Prius and waited for the storm to blow over.

When he was finally able to turn off the faucet of his eyes, Matt eased into the slow night traffic, the pain not muffled in the slightest. Tiny turned on the radio as a welcome distraction, giving Matt the chance to focus on something other than the near-empty freeway and his somber thoughts. It worked until Patty Griffin began to sing on the radio, the heavy, sad mood settling over them again.

"Sometimes a hurt is so deep, deep, deep, you think that you're gonna drown.

Sometimes all I can do is weep, weep, weep, with all this rain falling down."

Since Matt had known Rain, he'd taken more notice of music all around. Notes, lyrics, the ambience evoked by rhythms and sounds old and new. Rain's love of all things musical had crept under Matt's skin too, into his life and heartbeat. Sometimes he even heard Rain vocalizing the songs on the radio or TV, his chant superimposed over the actual singers, often taking over the entire piece with his usual flair and style. Now more than ever, Matt feared that if Rain didn't recover, Matt would live out the rest of his solitary existence without music—and the sound of his lover's sweet, melodious voice. The thought was too hard to bear, so he tried to shrug it off and focus on the woeful song instead.

As the female vocalist repeated the mournful words "rain, rain, rain," Matt felt like punching a wall in frustration and fear and anger. Only negative emotions swirled in the mush of his head that reason had abandoned hours ago. The soft guitar mixed in his mind with the sight—provided by his overactive imagination—of Rain lying on an uncomfortable, steely sterile hospital bed in a room with white walls and bleeping machines. Matt could barely catch his breath as his vision blurred with a new veil of tears that he blinked hard to get rid of.

Cold fear gripped his heart at the awful end of their special day, which had moved past them over an hour ago. Never mind that—Matt worried he'd never have Rain with him again long enough to celebrate a single new anniversary. Tears rolled down his cheeks in burning silence as he drove through the terrible lonely night, feeling hope slipping away with each sigh-filled tear.

THREE days later, Rain still hadn't woken up. These things were unpredictable, as the previously anonymous doctor whose name was Doctor Clark told Matt and Tiny. At least on the second day they'd been allowed to see him, however briefly. Tiny had been so angry he'd thrown curses and threats throughout the visit, promising a murderous fate to Rain if he ever did anything this stupid and ill-advised again. Matt had felt physically numb, unable to move closer to Rain for fear of hurting him but just as unable to move away in equal fear of missing him waking up—or taking a turn for the worse.

Matt had taken time off work to come to the hospital every day without fail to watch over Rain, who lay there, unmoving, his pale face sometimes slack, other times frowning as if in pain. His dapper prettiness was a thing of the past. Matt would've placed a large wager on the likelihood of Rain freaking out when he woke up and found his colorless face without the proper war paint not only for protection but for effect. Almost able to hear the whining tone of Rain's plea as he set out to order either Matt or Tiny to fetch his beautifying implements, Matt smiled a little and held his lover's slender hand in his own, squeezing gently with a lazy caress.

"Come on, Rain," he whispered softly in the dimly lit room. "It's been forever already, Sleeping Beauty. It's time to wake up." Bowing his head over the warmth of Rain's hand, he stroked his cheek against the smooth skin he loved to kiss and arouse from coolness to a blaze. Quietly he inspected the disabling damage of the velvety bruise on Rain's torn leg, not so much swollen as puffy. Even after being sent home to recuperate, Rain would have a long healing process ahead of him, Matt mulled, depressing himself further.

Last night, like for a few nights now, he'd dreamed of Rain's pleased pursed lips and heard him breathing something into his ear ever so subtly, but Matt couldn't make out the words. As he awoke, startled and sweaty—and filled with dread—he'd thought that if he could only distinguish those hushed lyrics, he'd understand the Harmony of the Spheres—because it'd be Rain humming them.

"Shouldn't... the hero... kiss his heroine... awake?"

At first Matt believed he'd dreamed it.

Lifting his head and opening his eyes, Matt was suddenly wide awake.

And apparently so was Rain, who was tiredly blinking at him with heavy-lidded green eyes and smiling faintly.

Matt scrambled onto his shaky feet, reaching to touch Rain's silky red-gold hair like it was the most precious thing in the world—and to him, all of Rain was exactly that. "Hey, sleepyhead," he murmured quietly, his stonelike face feeling like it was cracking under the sudden pressure of recreating the thankful, hopeful, happy smile he never thought he'd be able to generate. "And here I was certain you'd sleep right through our special day. But alas, you didn't miss a thing."

The corners of Rain's full lips curled up a bit in a grin. "Oh, that's good news, darling. I was so frightfully worried." The ghost of humor drifted with his words, spoken drollishly slow, and just then Matt knew everything was going to be all right. Sure, it would take time, but this wretched episode would end and they'd get their second chance. It was right here in front of them, floating in a tinge of breath between them, caught in the silence between their fragile heartbeats. All they had to do was to grab it and hang on to it tight.

And that's what Matt did with a tender kiss on Rain's dry chapped lips.

"Oh....," Rain mumbled into the kiss, barely audible. "I dreamt of you, sweetheart."

"Me too." Matt spoke mildly against his lover's lips, then backed away just long enough to pull out a little blue vial from his pocket and squeeze a little dollop of fragrant lip balm on Rain's trembling lips.

Gratefully Rain smiled back at him as Matt traced the contour and shape of his lover's lips with his fingers, coating them with a heavy dose of the healing salve he'd gotten just for this moment. "Every night, every day. I missed you so much."

Frowning, Rain blinked several times, clearly confused. "Just how long have I been lying on this… horridly white, poor excuse for a bed, peaches?"

Curses. "Awhile, baby. Just like Sleeping Beauty." Matt tried to lighten the mood with a chuckle, but judging from the vexed pursing of Rain's lips, his lover wasn't buying it. "Three days." He'd dreaded saying the words out loud because then the time lost would be real. Now it was, and he hated the shocked expression rising on Rain's already worn-out face. For a second Matt worried Rain might not get over this. He swore to himself that he'd be around for his lover—no matter how long or what it took.

THREE days. Rain fought for breath and to lower his heart, which had jumped up to lodge in his throat. How on Earth could that much time have passed without him being aware of any of it? The interval between closing his eyes and opening them felt like a blink of an eye. What had happened—

Oh, right.

The rusty nail, the long gash, the fever, the putrefied flesh, the falling apart.

Tears broke through in a moist veil over his field of vision. Rain felt Matt's comforting hand clasping his own, and the sweet touch moved right through his body to caress his aching, stunned heart. So he'd lost three days of his life—when he could've died and lost everything he held dear. Like the loving man standing by his side right now, pouring his caring kindness over Rain without expecting anything in return but a mere look in his direction.

Nearly choking on his raging feelings, Rain nodded a little. "All right, then. Three days. It's all right." After letting his gaze rise to meet

Matt's blue eyes, Rain noticed for the first time the tiny slivers of gray mixed with blue, like sharp needles, steely swords, or brewing rainclouds. How beautiful his lover was—and what big dark circles he had under his eyes, how shaggy his appearance was, how stale his sleepy breath, and how shaky his teetering stance hovering over Rain's bed. Rain didn't know what forces held Matt together, but Rain longed to ease his burden. "I'm so glad you're here, darling. I would absolutely have *hated* being woken up by some other man's kiss."

Puzzled, Matt shook his head a second, as if trying to assimilate Rain's words, but they didn't sink in so well. Then all of a sudden he burst out laughing so hard he had tears running down his cheeks and his whole body juddered at the relentless power of all the pent-up emotions coming out at once. "Good God, how I've missed you, Rain." Leaning over him, Matt kissed him again, making Rain moan inside like there was no tomorrow—and that possibility had been far too close for comfort. Closer than ever before. "Don't you ever scare me like this again, Rain. Never again. My heart couldn't take it." Matt's voice cracked into a sob, and Rain had to swallow to hold his own feelings in check.

"Oh, sweet pea, come hither," Rain whispered, tugging at Matt's blue sweater, and his lover leaned down to kiss him again, first on the lips, then his forehead, and then raining kisses all over his face until Rain felt so warm within he wished to pull aside the annoying sheets covering his body, which was beginning to feel way too aroused for a bit of a tumble in bed. "Matt, easy," he murmured into Matt's sandy-colored hair, which had a hint of the lavender shampoo he used but also had the telltale stuffy scent of someone who hadn't washed in a while.

Hastily Matt withdrew with a panicked look in his wide eyes. "Did I hurt you, baby?"

Shaking his head with a chuckle that quickly changed into a pained grimace, Rain realized that was definitely a move he should avoid for the time being. "You never hurt me, sweetheart. That much I know without a doubt. So, precious, when can I leave this dismal excuse for an asylum? This place is a white shroud-clad succubus draining my blood—and not the drop-dead gorgeous gentleman vampire I'd wish. Quick, Matt, tell me. Am I paler than normal?"

RAIN sounded so earnest that Matt couldn't help but laugh. Yes, he had his Rain back, and since he was joking away, the pain must've been as manageable as the humiliation that Matt knew the humor was masking. The pain meds were probably culpable—and yet worthy of praise for his bright spirits. "If you looked any more attractive and downright sexy, baby, I'd pounce you right here and now." Matt was only half joking.

Rain seemed to get that, because he batted his natural light-colored lashes with a huge grin. "Oh, how I've missed those sugar lips of yours, honeybun," he drawled, causing enflaming shivers to run up and down Matt's spine. "When I get out of here, I'm going to eat you up." With an extremely suggestive wiggle of his eyebrows, Rain made a kissy face, inciting another hearty laugh from Matt, who felt like it had been ages since he'd laughed this much. He'd missed the act as much as the current cause for it—Rain.

But… Matt was still fuming too. "Rain… why the hell didn't you get that damn gash looked at? The infection could've killed you. They had to cut out some flesh, for fuck's sake. Jesus, Rain…."

An embarrassed and guilty flush colored Rain's pale cheeks. "I'm sorry, precious—"

"Oh, no," Matt cut his lover off, shaking his head furiously. "No way are you going to get away with this that easily—not with a mere kissy face and a couple of endearments." Rain's lips twitched, but Matt was merciless as the pent-up concern, fear, and anger all fought for control of the situation. "You stubborn piece of—"

Frowning, Rain cut in, "Yes, lovey, I know I made a mistake—"

It was then that the room door opened and Doctor Clark walked in before waiting for anyone to accept his entry. Matt wasn't happy to see this sterile-lab-coat-wearing intruder interrupting their first and only one-on-one time in well over a week.

"Oh, we're awake—finally," the doctor said with exasperated glee. "And how are we feeling today?" Matt winced at the repeated patronizing *we* but bit his tongue to keep from erupting into a sardonic litany of insulting cuss words.

Rain snorted in disgust he absolutely did not fake. "I'm wearing an ugly excuse for a dress with the backside missing—which would be absolutely fine if we were in a BDSM club. How do you think I feel?" The honey-dripping voice oozed disdain, and Matt was happier than he'd been since Rain had opened his eyes.

The doctor, however, didn't seem too fazed by the comment—despite blinking rapidly a few times. "Well, that's too bad. We'll have to provide some fashion amenities first chance we get." Jesus, was the guy actually making an attempt at humor at a time like this? Matt was about to interject, but Rain, as usual, got there first.

"Something pink and fluffy with satin and ruffles would be perfect, darling. Or chains, shackles, and whips, whichever you prefer. Considering the gothic vibes and horror castle appearance of this... *establishment*, I'd go for the latter." Rain barely got the word out without looking like he was choking on a piece of poison apple. "How soon can I be discharged? No pun intended, lamb, I'm sure."

Stifling what threatened to sound like an inappropriate chuckle, Doctor Clark nodded but grew serious fast. "I'm afraid you're stuck with us for a couple days at least—"

"I don't have insurance."

Matt flinched at the sudden admission, but from the steady unwavering stare Rain was granting the doctor, he was certain that Rain would've said the same even if he'd had insurance and/or money coming out of his ass. He didn't want to stay here, and Matt couldn't blame him—even though his conflicting protective streak demanded that Rain remain in the hospital where he was getting the care and attention his condition deserved and required.

"Mr. Deveraux," the doctor said—to Matt's surprise—chidingly, "I'm well aware of your financial situation. And according to *Mrs.* Deveraux's standing instructions, you'll receive top care during your stay at any medical facility."

Matt didn't have a clue as to what was going on, and all he saw was the decidedly displeased, almost furious, expression on Rain's face as he pressed his full lips together so tightly they were nothing but a thin white line.

The doctor continued, "Now, Mr. Deveraux, there are a few things we need to discuss. About your condition—"

"Give it to me straight up, lamb. I say the same thing to all my men. Except the actually straight ones, of course. Them I prefer to taunt."

Changing his outright laugh into a more discreet cough at the last second, Matt saw that the infuriated Rain was on a roll. Whenever he was nudged toward a direction he didn't want to go, he shoved right back. Matt had no idea who this Mrs. Deveraux was, but whoever she was, she was pushing all of Rain's buttons—simultaneously and absolutely the wrong way. Soon there would be a scandalous scene.

"Very well," Doctor Clark replied coolly. "Luckily you have sustained no permanent internal injuries. However, there will be soreness for several weeks to a couple of months—"

"I'm used to soreness of all sorts, little lamby," Rain interjected briskly.

"However," the doctor continued as if there had been no interruptions, "the deep laceration to your left leg resulted in profuse blood loss from a torn artery, which we were able to repair, and to septicemia, which is still being treated with antibiotics. The wound extended beneath the skin to the periphery of your thigh muscle—"

"Rusty nails be damned…," Rain murmured as an aside.

"Fortunately, while the skin was jagged and broken," the doctor continued, "the deep gash did not damage your thigh muscle beyond repair. We have applied stitches to the wound beneath the skin to rejoin the edges of the muscle and tissue, and the body will eventually absorb them, so they will not be removed. As you can observe, gauze and tape have been used to secure and protect the wound. You should not wet the bandages. Use cellophane wrapper or an alternative to keep them dry, and we will inspect your situation during your follow-up visit next week. The type of laceration in your leg, however, will be painful, so we will administer some pain medication as well as antibiotics to combat any further infections. This injury, due to the severity of the infection, will cause problems with your walking for several months—"

"You mean I'll have a limp, darling? If so, then say so. I'm a big girl." Rain practically snarled his words out, and Matt felt from the hold on his hand how angry he really was. Helplessness often carried that feeling along for the ride, and his Rain did love to dance.

"Yes." The doctor nodded, still calm. "Pain and stiffness will hinder your normal activities for weeks, so you should avoid any undue strenuous physical exertions for the time being. We will examine your progress during your follow-up."

"Will there be a scar?" Matt asked softly so Rain didn't have to, as his prettiness was important to him. He didn't want to ask but felt like it might be a relief for Rain to hear the truth from the sidelines, as it were. To Matt, Rain would always be beautiful—no matter what happened—because it was his inner beauty that had captivated Matt's heart, body, and soul.

"All lacerations produce visible scarring, yes," the doctor replied. "Skin damage in the form of scar tissue is an anticipated result, but there should be no permanent loss of motor function if you attend a physical rehabilitation program as well as take the time to do personal physical exercises. That way the effect should be minimized into a healthy recovery period of no more than six to eight weeks." To this statement, Rain stayed remarkably silent, which didn't bode well for the doctor or Matt, who realized they were all waiting for the worst news to come last.

And the doctor did not disappoint. "There is, however, another concern. Because the bacterial infection in your leg compromised your immune system, it seems your body has also become susceptible to a viral infection. Your vocal cords may experience dryness and soreness due to this viral infection, which may have damaged your superior laryngeal nerve. Symptoms of vocal cord paresis include voice changes such as hoarseness and airway and swallowing problems. If any of these symptoms of inflammation appear, Mr. Deveraux, you must return to the hospital for voice therapy and possible surgery. Despite your ability to speak now, your voice will tire soon when speaking. It is our strong recommendation that for at least a few weeks, you should limit the time you speak to no more than a few minutes at a time. And absolutely nothing strenuous like shouting or singing."

And there it was. Disaster struck the bull's-eye with one flash of lightning.

Matt had thought it wasn't possible, but Rain's haunted face grew even paler than before, and now—for the first time—there was true fear in his eyes. Matt closed his eyes, knowing full well that there couldn't possibly have been worse news for a man who not only made his living from singing but who couldn't live without music. A beating or an accident didn't take anything away from Rain—unlike losing his voice.

At that moment, when despair and sorrow took him as effortlessly as they did Rain, Matt felt it might've been better if this jinx of a doctor had yanked Rain's heart out of his chest with his latex-covered hands. The outcome would surely have hurt less and been one that Rain could've lived with instead of this.

Chapter Seven

"WHAT?" Matt asked, holding back a snide remark. "Is this too bourgeois and blasé for you?" Referring to his loft apartment he was actually quite proud of, Matt waited for the other shoe to drop.

"Big words, darling." Rain snorted. "Careful you don't choke on them."

Taking a deep breath, Matt fought the rush of anger, giving his lover the once-over. "Why? Am I giving you inadequacy issues?" To that comment Rain only shrugged, his green gaze inspecting every nook and cranny in the apartment. He clearly anticipated the discovery of something to point out and criticize. "You're really being a...." Matt bit his tongue and counted, first to ten, then to twenty, in Spanish, just for good measure.

Convincing Rain to stay at Matt's loft was way more trouble than it was worth, and settling the patient in for the duration of his recovery period was a pain in the ass. In fact, the process was far, far less comfortable for Matt than pulling out the hairs on his head and crotch with tweezers one stupid strand and curl at a time.

Yet Rain couldn't go anywhere else either. His condition required monitoring, and he couldn't get the attention he needed cooped up all alone in his own cramped apartment. Tiny's small quarters were situated above a garage where Tiny worked his day job as a mechanic. Norma's dinky flat was already shared by two roommates, both of them female impersonators—and not very subdued. Rain needed time to recover in relative peace and quiet.

Matt understood what Rain was going through, not being able to recuperate at his own place, where he undoubtedly would've felt more like himself. But Matt wasn't about to let Rain get his way this time, because he really wasn't up for taking care of himself alone.

"Oh, do finish that sentence, gorgeous," Rain provoked him on purpose, his hands crossed over his chest and his chin uplifted in defiance. "No need to roll with the punches on account of my precarious condition."

Closing his eyes, which had become so accustomed to being open due to lack of sleep that it actually hurt a little to try to close them after all this time, Matt reached for his inner fountain of calm—which unfortunately was bubbling in fiery frustration. "Rain...," he said finally, feeling drained to the bone, "I don't want to fight with you. I'll let you get acquainted with the place. The front door isn't locked if you want to make your midnight escape. I'm going to take a shower and try to sleep for two fucking seconds."

Getting all the way to the first steps of the winding staircase leading to the upstairs bedrooms, Matt felt more than heard the heartbreaking sob behind him. Turning around on his heels, Matt found Rain flopping down to sit on the couch. He had the distinct look of a deflated party balloon, sad and saggy, lifeless and dull—despite the bright pastel colors of his clothes. Like a week-old newspaper lying in the ditch in the rain, he leaned his arms on his thighs, his face like a death mask.

Sighing, Matt sat next to him, wrapping an arm around his shoulder. "I'm here, Rain. I'm not going anywhere. I'll be here for you no matter what."

Defenses down and self-control walls crumbling, Rain buried his silently crying face in the crook of Matt's neck and wound his arms around Matt's waist. "I'm being so horrible to you, muffin," he sniffed in unclear mumbles into Matt's skin, his voice raspy. "I'm sorry."

"You're mad about what's happened to you. I get that," Matt assured his lover quietly, stroking Rain's red-gold silky hair slowly, enjoying the familiar feel and gesture. "You're allowed to be angry. And sad."

Furiously Rain shook his head but didn't pull away. "Big girls aren't supposed to cry."

Smirking in slight irritation, Matt replied, "Poppycock."

For a moment there was a deep-echoing stunned silence. Then, all of a sudden, Rain's shoulders trembled with laughter. "And here I thought *I* was the Southern belle."

"I guess you're rubbing off on me," Matt said with a pleased, almost smug smile. "The next thing you know I'll be drinking those god-awful mint juleps."

Nuzzling him, Rain chuckled and spoke, exaggerating his Southern drawl. "How dare you, you loathsome infidel? Such an outrageous insult will not be tolerated. Now I'll have to spank you."

"Anything you want, my sweet Rain. I'll even whistle 'Dixie' for you while you do so."

Shoving Matt with his elbow, Rain laughed out loud before letting Matt wrap his arms around him and kiss him until he was left panting, breathless. "When I'm done with you, the only sound you will be able to accomplish will be a whistle," Rain threatened in gasps but surrendered to Matt's embrace, melting against him in submission, and Matt held his lover tighter, never wanting to stop. After too many days when he'd felt like every day was just another inward death, Matt was relieved that Rain was finally letting him into his personal space— inside and out. There was only one direction to go from rock bottom, and it was up.

MINT juleps were unknown to Matt, so he couldn't prepare one even if he'd wanted to, but thankfully Rain was more interested in chicory coffee, which had become popular enough for Matt to be able to acquire some. While Rain was sitting tucked into the corner of his couch, his legs underneath him—even the one that had been sewn and stitched together—sipping his unpleasant-tasting coffee, Matt was watching the news, but his attention wandered. Muting the TV, Matt leaned back on the couch, against Rain's warmth, and snuggled him closer.

Pursing his lips, Rain put down his coffee cup and, in repose, complied with the hug. "You feel good," murmured Rain softly, resting his head against Matt's chest.

Over the course of two days, Rain had mellowed and his anger and sorrow had subsided. He'd let Matt close again, and Matt relished every second of it—despite the distracting thought that maybe he had a right to be angry too. But how could he voice it now, when Rain was already suffering so much from the aftermath of the mess he'd made himself? No matter how much Matt wanted to lecture Rain's ass off, he could not be so unkind. Not now.

For seven days—three with Rain unconscious, two before the hospital was willing to discharge him, and two spent together at the loft—this peaceful moment had been all Matt had dreamed of, and he was going to let nothing spoil it. "I'm so happy you're here, Rain. I'm glad you decided to give me—and this place—a chance. I know this isn't your home, but—"

Huffing a breath across Matt's throat, Rain snaked his hands around Matt's waist. "I was upset. Not with you, peaches. You know that, right?" Not waiting for Matt to say anything back, Rain resumed speaking. "I feel it inside of me, struggling to break free from the confines of this feeble flesh, now bruised and broken. I want to let it fly again. It's been only two days since I got out of the hospital, but I can't stand this." The tone of his voice had dropped to a depressing low.

"What do you mean?" Knowing the answer clear as day, Matt needed to hear Rain articulate the problem. Only then could he try to find a way to resolve it and make peace with the reality that it would take time to heal. There'd be no instant bouncing back from this.

"The music," Rain whispered, and his whole lean body shivered as if he were freezing. "I feel it inside my heart, aching and crying. I feel so alone and hurt. Like I'm drowning. I can see the surface above me, but I can't reach it. I miss it, Matt. I miss the sound, the hum, the rhythm, the beat, the song—all of it. What if I will never get better and I lose it forever…?"

The fear resonating in Rain was palpable. Matt could sense it, as real as the touch of his lover next to him, but it wasn't soft and cuddly. It was overbearing and hard and cold, and he didn't want this feeling anywhere near his heart—or Rain's already tormented spirit. "Music will always be in your soul, Rain. Nothing could ever take it from you. Not even this. You'll get better, and pretty soon you'll be singing my pants off me—again. Just you wait and see."

THE strong assurance in Matt's voice lifted some of the anguish from Rain's twisting gut, and he could breathe again. Closing his eyes, Rain slipped into Matt's welcoming hug, and his lover's arms encircled him in a cocoon of comfort and ease that separated him from harsh reality. Right now, right here, Matt was all Rain needed and wanted, because he didn't push for a speedy recovery or expect a miraculous change of attitude. Matt let Rain take this at his own pace—and that really was all he required at the moment. That, and sleep.

"I'm going to nod off for a bit, sweet pea," Rain mumbled into Matt's chest and curled up in a bundle under his lover's consoling arm.

"Go right ahead, love," Matt whispered back and kissed his temple gently. "I'll be here when you wake up."

Even in his dream Rain heard the word—*love*—letting it soothe his soul with its balm, until he felt like he was lying hot and naked on a tropical beach of silvery sand while the sun shone down its golden rays, covering him in a blanket of heat and light. That was what Matt felt like to him at times, especially now, when Rain was in the darkest place he'd ever been. Matt equaled refuge and solace—and love.

He loves me. To the echo of that last conscious thought, Rain fell asleep—with a smile of his own tugging the corners of his lips.

WHEN Rain stirred next, the shower was running. In all the time they'd known each other and been together, Rain had never heard Matt singing in the shower. He never even hummed. Rain thought that was a complete and utter waste of perfectly tiled acoustics, but Matt insisted he had a terrible voice, and on that opinion he wouldn't budge.

Wondering if he was well enough to join his lover under the hot stream of water made Rain anxious and angry—one out of want, one out of fear. He longed to be all right, to stand next to Matt and allow the physical need to sweep him off his feet to the sweet release that awaited beyond the intimacy of skin and flesh. But he knew that day was far off. Sighing in a blue mood that normally would've given him cause to sing, Rain was now kept company by silence alone.

Pressing his leg as he got up and groaning painfully, Rain slouched—or hobbled with his stiff left leg—over to the master bathroom at the back of the loft. Just as he entered the steam-filled room, the shower stilled and Matt stepped out of the stall, yanking a pure white towel to cover his dripping naked body—and his bulging groin. Looking up to find Rain standing in front of him, Matt grinned. "Missed you washing my back, love."

Smiling ruefully, Rain nodded. "I miss everything about you too, precious." He let the natural lilt in his voice hush down to a drawl to hide how sad he felt about missing their anniversary and not being able to succumb to the passion—and love—they both felt. Because of the ache in his bones and the pain in his body, Rain couldn't even for a moment lose himself and give in to the desire—and he wouldn't for weeks on end.

With a wicked smile, Matt closed the distance between them and lifted Rain's chin until their eyes met. "So we won't be able to do some of the really adventurous stuff we usually do—but that doesn't mean that there is *nothing* we can do."

Oh, I love the way he thinks. "What did you have in mind, darling?" Rain barely contained his rising enthusiasm—and his equally up-to-the-task cock. Surprisingly there was no pain in getting an erection, for which he was supremely thankful.

Winking, Matt said, "Well, since you can't exert yourself too much, I'll gladly offer my services to please you. I guarantee you will be fully satisfied with the attention I intend to lavish you with." Wrapping his still wet arms around Rain's waist, Matt gazed up and kissed Rain softly. "There's kissing, of course, and some quality snuggling and cuddling. I think you will be happy with the multitude of methods I will employ to give you as much delight as you can possibly handle. How does that sound, love?"

His imagination running wild as it was, Rain could only swallow and take a deep breath to calm himself since rapid breathing caused his throat to pulse with a wrenching feeling he wanted to disguise from his eager lover. "I'm putty in your capable hands, darling," he replied hoarsely, hoping Matt wasn't discouraged by the faintness of his smile.

Apparently, however, Matt was oblivious to Rain's physical plight, since he hugged Rain a little tighter, the moisture of his heated, showered body seeping through Rain's clothes. "You will be by the time I'm done with you, babe."

TEN minutes later Rain was lying contentedly on the electric-blue bedsheets of Matt's king-size bed, watching as his lover knelt between his outstretched legs and hovered over his naked frame with fiery hunger in his blue eyes. Rain had washed too, as much as he could manage with his leg covered in white bandages that sort of made the carnal lust fly straight out the window and practically made him limp with a mere glance at it.

As if reading his mind, Matt bent down to kiss Rain on the lips, brushing their contour as softly as a feather. "Don't think about it, love. Just close your eyes and let me do this for you."

At this sweet plea, Rain shut down his overactive brain and fell into the sea of sensations Matt surrounded him with. Tender kisses rained over his skin; wet pecks landed on his body; hands glided and fingers smoothed; weight landed on him and then lifted, granting him little dustings of warmth and then leaving him goose bumpy after. It was all very arousing in a teasing kind of way, and Rain melted into his lover's affection.

Through his skin, Rain heard the drowsy saxophone of Bohren & der Club of Gore's "Painless Steel" vibrating in a sensuous delectation that swept his heart away and lifted his soul to dance and soar with the dusky gloom of the bluesy sound. Like a sleepy breath and a slow heartbeat, the echoes of the music escaping from him filled him with the pleasure of knowledge that the score of his spirit had not been dulled by what had happened to him. He was familiar with these notes, and the ebb and flow of them washed through his hazy mind as he yielded to the probing touch of his lover.

Nuzzling Rain's neck, Matt traced his mouth down the column of Rain's throat and the line of the collarbone, kissing and suckling with a mellow craving. Rain didn't move a muscle, allowing Matt to take his time with his languorous re-exploration of his lover's body. Placing light kisses over his lover's skin, Matt made Rain fall in love with every passing second of pleasure, and at each airy contact, Rain sighed in expectation of yet another brush of lips and caress of hands. Rain felt like he was gliding through blue skies and floating in a cool pond, all the while listening to the ethereal sounds emerging from his memory, coinciding with Matt's every soft move and gentle action. He lay in a bubble of pleasure where lust had dimmed into a sunset, the trance giving so much but with a languid ease that dissolved all his resistance and regrets, the tormenting images of mistakes made and beatings taken slipping away into the night beneath the smooth jazzy sounds of his soul.

The epiphany that the music locked away within his injured self could be released through lovemaking with Matt caught Rain off guard, and he gasped at the newfound freedom of letting himself fall in love with the music Matt was awakening within him. "Oh, Matt...." Whispering, Rain wrapped his arms around his lover's strong shoulders, tugged on the hairs on the back of his neck, stroked his bare nape, and tickled his throat with his lips. The scent of lavender soap filled Rain's nostrils while the clean flavor of Matt was replaced by the growing musky taste of man and sexual arousal.

"Feeling good, love?" Matt inquired blissfully, lowering his exposed neck closer to Rain's searching mouth.

"Mmm..." was all the sound Rain made as he fastened his lips to the thin skin of Matt's neck and suckled softly, knowing that tomorrow his lover would sport a fancy hickey. Entangling his lithe figure and agile limbs around Matt, Rain felt the urge to find fast release burning within his groin, and his hips were bucking off the mattress. The pressure within was quickly quelled by the pain striking his leg muscles, and his body fell flat on the sheets as he moaned not out of pleasure but out of pain.

"Baby, be careful," Matt chided softly, placing his hand firmly on Rain's stomach to hold him still and down at the same time. "You lie back, babe, and let me do everything. I promise you'll get a chance to reciprocate when you're all better." Rain looked up at his lover, saw the flush of dull red coloring his cheeks and neck, felt the heat emanating from his lustful body, and heard his heaving breath.

"Well, get on with it then, dreamy," he scolded a bit impatiently, pursing his lips as the twinge of pain drifted away and the pleasure resumed with his lover's tender touch.

"Anything you want, baby cakes," Matt replied with a naughty grin, causing Rain to chuckle a little. It seemed they were taking turns finding the most ridiculous terms of endearment that anywhere out of bed would've sounded so awfully out of place that the ground might've actually opened up and sucked them in just for the awkwardness of it.

Every caress Matt made echoed within Rain in the form of lingering reverberations of the smooth sounds of a tenor saxophone. It was like synesthesia—only instead of colors, Rain experienced every touch created by Matt as an equivalent sound, as notes of internal music, some from memory and others from his heart, as original and unique as his breathing. As far back as Rain could remember, he had interpreted the world through music and sound, but he'd never known it to become so inextricable from a lover and sex. Rain understood, however, that Matt was the cause of it. Rain's hips began bucking again as the need within grew, and Matt played his instrument like a true master.

"No, baby," Matt scolded him again, pressing his stomach down on the mattress firmly. "Are you going to stay put, love, or do I have to restrain you?"

Didn't that just make Rain's day? All of a sudden, his breath compressed tight in his chest. Rain could only look up at his lover's laughing blue eyes and nod silently.

But Matt just shook his head as if well and truly serious—almost parental. "That was what you might call a rhetorical statement, baby love. Your ass is already in a sling. Pain is the restraint here. You will obey me. I will pleasure you, and you will just accept and take it. Got it?"

"Mmm...," Rain hummed, pleased, squirming a little under Matt.

"That's my girl," Matt complimented, winking. Rain was ready to give the arrogant dick his comeuppance with a hearty slap—probably two, and not necessarily on the face.

His designs were brought to a halt when Matt kissed him, gliding his tongue along the shape of Rain's lips, nibbling on his lower lip and then sliding his tongue into his mouth. With a moan, Rain ate the man up, wanting everything but not being able to do anything because of his own aches and his lover's determination that Rain not exert himself in any way, shape, or form. So Rain resigned himself to letting go of what he wanted and surrendered to the unequivocal enjoyment Matt showered him with.

KEEPING Rain still was a feat the success of which would be comparable with the actions of the gods, and Matt set out to hold his lover's enthusiasm at bay. Breaking the kiss, Matt felt breathless while moving down Rain's pliable body to his crotch, which he had to pin down on the bed to get the guy to lie still. His lover's pubic hair was a groomed nest of dark-gold curls, their underlying red hue revealing itself only when light shone on them at just the right angle. The sight caused Matt to gasp with awe and hunger. He had a pretty damn good idea what he was going to do, and it was all about giving his lover delight and release without extraneous exercise.

Admittedly the thought of using restraints on Rain, of having his way with him while Rain was unable to prevent it, was an overwhelming turn-on, but Matt kept up his composure with a firm resolution that they'd try that another time. Instead, he placed his hands on Rain's slim hips and narrow waist, pressing him down hard on the mattress so he couldn't do anything but lie there and receive Matt's attentions.

Caressing Rain's hard dick against his cheeks, Matt lapped up the wet, hot drops that accumulated on his skin and on his parted lips. Not knowing what precipitated Rain's sweet taste—his diet, a mix of soap and skin, or his natural zest—Matt relished his lover's taste, and tonight he was going to indulge himself in it and gorge on an all-out buffet of Rain's unique flavor and feel. Once he got started, there'd be no stopping him.

Rain's cut cock was standing up in ovation, hot and hard like a burning steel bar, the color dark red, angry and fiery. As Matt smoothed it across his face, it kept smacking him on the chin and cheeks and then slamming down on Rain's abdomen. His dick was so hard and heavy, so long and silky, that first Matt's mouth went dry as a desert and then he began to drool, like a hungry dog with a bone.

Rain kept wriggling and trying to reach Matt to pull his full weight down on him, annoying the hell out of Matt, who realized he'd have to find a way to bind his lover's movements that wouldn't hurt him further and slow his recovery.

"Babe, you're twisting again," he chided.

The cheeky look Rain flashed him with was driving Matt crazy. "So what, dove? What are you going to do about it?" Bold as you please, Rain stuck out his tongue like an insolent child.

Matt had to laugh. "You can be such a brat sometimes." Then his amused laugh turned wicked when a mischievous thought occurred to him, and he observed Rain's own impish smile fading when he detected the roguish resolve and determination in his lover's eyes. "Two can play at this game, babe."

Biting his lower lip, Rain suddenly lay very still, waiting slightly nervously. "Matt...."

Kissing his lover softly, Matt grinned as he backed away just a bit. "Here's the name of the game, babe. *Lips on—hands off.*"

Chuckling, Rain waited to hear more, raising his eyebrows in an amused query, so Matt pressed on.

"You and I can kiss. In fact, that's all we are allowed to do. Just lips, teeth, tongue, and mouth. No use of hands at all, or any other limb." At this Rain laughed wholeheartedly, thrashing his head back against the pillow, and the sound Matt had been dying to hear filled his heart—and he knew everything was going to be all right. "If your hands or feet touch me on purpose, as in deliberately attempting to fondle, grab, or caress, you lose."

"What does the winner get, precious?" Rain teased, shifting around on his back to get comfortable.

"The winner gets the loser," Matt replied, grinning ear-to-ear. "To be blunt, the loser must do whatever the winner desires."

"In bed?" Rain clarified, his green eyes narrowing. "That is to say, sexually?"

"Yes." Matt hovered above his lover, biding his time for an agreement to the terms laid out.

Rain didn't disappoint as he smiled cryptically and, with a simple nod, accepted the name, the rules, and the purpose of the game. Oh, yes, they were going to have all kinds of fun, all right.

"You ready, love?"

When Rain spread his legs farther apart and laid his arms out beside him until he was spread-eagle on the bed, Matt rose up even further and held his weight a few inches above his lover's body so they weren't touching. Yes, their hot, hard cocks kept bumping against each other, but that was to be expected, and without words, they both accepted that irrefutable fact.

Lowering only his head, craning his neck to do it, Matt licked his lips to wet them and kissed Rain, who returned the kiss with equal passion. Raising his head from the pillow, he opened his mouth to deepen their intimate contact. When Matt's tongue slid past Rain's and into his lover's mouth, Rain whimpered, and even without touching him, Matt could feel him quivering all over. Matt's breath caught in his throat as the sensations of his lover's sweet exhale became the air that he breathed.

Pulling back, Matt was thrilled to hear the disapproving sound arising from Rain, and, smiling, he glided his lips down to his lover's throat, scraping his teeth by the jugular vein first and then nibbling his way to the dip below the Adam's apple. He bit the skin all over Rain's neck, bringing the blood to the surface and causing his lover to tremble and moan.

"No... fair...," Rain murmured incoherently, shaking his head from side to side. Matt had no trouble understanding the significance of that gesture when the hot tip of his lover's dick brushed against him, leaving wet kisses everywhere. It was a peculiar feeling that, even though only his mouth and his cock had any sort of contact with his lover, Matt's nerve endings were tingling, humming, and buzzing all over his body, on his skin and beneath it.

"Oh, it's fair, all right," he chuckled breathlessly against his lover's skin. "I never said we'd be limited to kissing on the mouth." He dipped his head to press an openmouthed kiss to Rain's chest, licked his way to a now angry-red nipple, fastened his lips around it firmly, and suckled fiercely. Rain's back arched up against him as he drew a sharp breath, moaning loudly, and to Matt, it was the soulful sound of an angel sighing. Yes, a lewd kind of sylph, but still a beautiful angelic fairy enraptured.

"Cheater...." Nonetheless, Rain's feet and arms remained firmly grounded against the mattress, unwavering, which caused Matt a bit of disappointment. He'd wished that in his weakened state, Rain would cave in easily and effortlessly and thus, as soon as he were well enough to play rough again, he'd owe Matt his prize.

Facing up to the unrelenting truth that maybe Rain was strong enough to hold Matt off and keep his cool at the same time, Matt kept up the constant pressure of his mouth on the now hard nub. He encircled it with his eager tongue and lapped up the taste of Rain's skin, sweaty and musky and sweet with its tinge of honeydew and watermelons. Yet despite the fruity scents and flavors, Rain had a base odor that was all male. In this, Rain was anything but effeminate. It was a contradiction that intrigued and captivated Matt; it had ever since the first time he'd become aware of it. It was a kind of sexy mystery without a ready-made solution—and it kept Matt coming back for more. He wondered whether he would ever get his fill of Rain, or if he would forever be held prisoner by his own desire and passion for the uniqueness of his lover?

Swiping his tongue across the hard plane of Rain's sculpted marble-white chest, Matt relinquished one nipple and moved on to the other, and Rain writhed frantically beneath him, panting. Sucking hard, Matt waited for Rain to scoot up closer, and he did—but not close enough to touch in the full-body contact Matt had been hoping for. Apparently his lover's self-control was extraordinary—or he was getting tired again.

Pulling himself up, Matt inspected Rain's beautiful face for any signs of discomfort or fatigue. But there was only the pleased little curve of a smile and the blissfully ecstatic expression, enhanced by his closed eyes and shivering lithe figure that drew Matt in like a ravenous moth to a seductive flame. "You okay, babe? You wanna stop?"

Pale-green eyes like clear turquoise tropical waters shot open in a flash—gleaming with dismay. "Are you insane or just torturing me within an inch of my life, you cad?" Rain growled, displeased. Practically jumping up, Rain claimed Matt's mouth in a show of force the slender man had never displayed before. It took Matt by surprise, and it was fucking arousing and exciting—and so completely out of character for Rain that the raging passion unnerved Matt a bit. But he didn't break the kiss. Yes, he'd make sure that his lover wouldn't injure or strain himself further, but other than that, Matt was ready to hand over the reins to Rain.

For a heartbeat Matt feared his tongue might snap at the intense suction Rain displayed by drawing it into his mouth. Matt could barely breathe, and his arms began to tremble and falter. Soon he'd come toppling down all over his lover—and lose the game. And Matt wasn't about to give up that easily. Not with a single kiss, no matter how divine.

But he couldn't dislodge that tangling tongue without using his hands to push his lover down, so impassioned was Rain. Matt had never been kissed so fervently, as though he were being devoured by a voracious beast.

And, fuck, his hands wobbled even more, not to mention his hips beginning to do their grinding dance even in midair. He was on the verge of his sexual need overriding his rational control—and also on the edge of wanting to recklessly abandon his pursuit of victory. Practically lamenting in sensual agony, Matt fought to break free—and fought himself back in order to remain inside Rain's mouth. Undecided, he struggled for dominance of the kiss, dueling with his tongue for a swift conquest, causing a soft whimper to emerge from Rain.

"I love the little sounds you make," Matt murmured against Rain's parted lips when he finally got the chance, without moving away, when Rain had to retreat for a blink of an eye to catch his breath.

Indignant, Rain snorted disapprovingly. "Just who are you calling little, you villain?"

Matt chuckled amusedly. "I was referring to your sweet little whimpers, cupcake, and not any other part of your delicious anatomy."

His growl mutating into a purr, Rain said, "Watch it, you loathsome heel, or I'll play patty-cake with you—with good hard slaps, and I won't be clapping your hands."

Pulling up, Matt trembled with laughter. "Don't you mean patty-*buns*-cake, buttercup? For you, I'll have it trademarked and patented. And by the way, I'm game if you are." Wiggling his eyebrows, Matt grinned salaciously, and yet he was being absolutely serious. If Rain liked a little slap with his tickle, who was Matt to argue?

With a huff, Rain feigned outrage, and his lips thinned into a thin vexed line. "That's hardly the point—"

"Yes," Matt interrupted with a raunchy grin. "There are other *hard points* that should be taken in hand at the moment, love." Emphasizing his meaning by simulating Rain's long southern drawl, Matt provoked Rain.

And it worked like a charm.

"Oh, I'll show you the back of my hand—on your backside, you lascivious scoundrel," Rain huffed, all miffed, grabbing Matt by the nape of his neck, tugging the hairs there, and dragging Matt down on him, smashing their lips together in a deep, crushing kiss.

Oh, yes, victory tasted so good.

But Rain made good on his threat and, with his healthy hand, gave Matt's buttocks a series of good hard swats, making the skin burn and his flesh underneath sting. "Hey, watch those hands there, cutie pie," Matt scolded his lover but got an infuriatingly impudent laugh back for his efforts. Tilting his head to the side, he gave Rain a sign of what was to follow, remaining calm and composed. Rain's eyes narrowed with suspicion, and Matt chuckled. "Yeah, I advise you to tread lightly, baby, because I know all your games. You can't make a move without me getting on top of you."

Surprisingly, Rain burst into a hearty laugh, and Matt figured out in a flash of insight that Rain had wanted to lose. Matt had only won the taunting match because Rain had given up on purpose—given himself up for his lover's prize. Well, Matt decided he wasn't going to waste this opportunity.

"Looks like you're all mine, baby," he murmured softly, kissing Rain.

"Mmm…," Rain mumbled against his lover's lips. "That's… kind of funny… because you… seem to be… all talk, talk, talk, and… no play."

Matt knew Rain was busting his chops deliberately and pushing him to making a move—just so he could make his countermove. Like Matt had said before, two could play this game, and the play was definitely more fun with two participants. "All in good time," he teased, just like Rain had teased him their first time together.

Backing away to sit on his heels, Matt beheld Rain's lovely nude figure as he grabbed his lover's cock with a fierce grip at the base, and Rain's hips shot up while he moaned. Matt pushed Rain back down on the mattress and leaned down to lick a long wet line from the base of his cock along the pronounced vein underneath all the way up to the flared head that was beading precum in thick, creamy white rivulets. Suckling intently on the crown, Matt flicked his tongue over the slit, never quite stopping in one place long enough to bring Rain over the edge. Rain's body shuddered and he whimpered, thrashing his head on the pillow.

Then, all of a sudden, Rain cried out, and it wasn't a joyful noise.

Matt looked up and saw Rain's face contorted with pain. Matt quickly moved over his lover's body and kissed Rain on the lips, barely brushing against the soft, hot surface. "Baby, are you—"

"No, Matt," Rain sobbed. "Please, don't stop. I need you." His words rang true as a plea from a man who longed to be released from his agony, and Matt didn't have the heart to make him suffer anymore. He'd just have to be cautious.

Pressing his palms against Rain's slim hips to hold him firmly in place, Matt sucked Rain's weeping cock deep into his keen mouth, delivering a furious storm of pleasure. The hot flesh throbbed in his mouth, the weight heavy on his tongue, and Matt hummed against the sensitive skin, adding a sensuous vibration to the experience for his lover to enjoy. His ravishing tongue was everywhere, his suction and licks showing no signs of mercy. Determined to bring Rain to a swift yet satisfying release, Matt set out to tame the beast bouncing in his mouth.

After slipping his right hand down from Rain's hip and past his cock to fondle Rain's tight-drawn balls, Matt rolled them in his fingers and squeezed them in a sturdy clasp between his thumb and index finger, slowly introducing his other fingers into the tenacious mix. Surrounding his lover's balls with his entire palm and tugging gently again and again, Matt heard Rain moan and felt him trying to back away down the middle of the bed to escape his hold, but Matt secured his lover firmly in place with his left hand on Rain's stomach.

Never once giving a moment's pause to Rain, humming and chuckling at once, Matt staked his claim, driving Rain to the edge of release and, by applying solid pressure with the tip of his savage tongue directly to the sweet spot under Rain's cock's ridge, pushed him right over.

With a sharp cry, Rain came, his cock twitching violently with volcanic spasms, filling Matt's mouth with salty bitter fluid that washed over his tongue in steaming hot waves. There was a backwash and, as Matt was unable to swallow fast enough, fresh cum trickled down his jaw and neck. Lapping at and wiping up every drop, Matt didn't relinquish Rain's trembling dick until it went soft and limp in his mouth, still hot and heavy.

Pulling away, gently letting the wet cock slip from his mouth, Matt sat up on his heels and stared at Rain, whose half-lidded eyes were glazed over and drowsy, though a small contented smile tugged at his lips. Matt didn't wait for Rain to fall asleep. With a vigorous grip, he took his own hard cock in hand and began to pump vehemently, all the while keeping his gaze locked on Rain, who got up on his elbows to watch the show so as not to miss a moment.

Taking advantage of Rain's undivided attention, Matt grinned wickedly. "When you get better, I'm gonna fuck you on every conceivable flat surface, from the kitchen counter to the bathroom sink. I'm gonna fuck you until you can't walk for a week."

Rain's smile was both sated and hungry at the same time as he nodded with newfound excitement, licking his lips, his eyes bright and wide. "Can't wait, honey."

"Yeah, sunshine," Matt reaffirmed his intentions, edging closer to his orgasm, which was rolling toward him with every stroke and pull. "I'm gonna fuck you on your back, on your stomach, and on your side, in every position known to man—and all of them twice on Sundays. I'm gonna fill that tight pretty little ass of yours with my cock until you taste me at the back of your throat and are thirsty for more no matter how many times you or I come."

The bright light in Rain's pale-green eyes dimmed to dark lust until they shone almost evergreen, and he breathed low and shallow. "Oh, darling, guess what? When I'm better, I'm so gonna let you do whatever you want to me. Anything… you… want…."

That was all Matt needed to hear to bring himself to climax.

Roaring out loud, he felt his balls tighten, and he shot his white-hot spunk all over Rain's chest and belly. Before Matt's pleasurable involuntary convulsions had even ceased, his dazed eyes concentrated on Rain, who slid his fingers across his cum-covered skin, scooped up some of the splattered warm drops, and sucked his sticky fingers into his mouth.

If Matt hadn't already been coming like a geyser, he would've come again at the delicious, sensual sight. "Oh, baby…," he crooned, his voice hoarse and his chest heaving. "Now look at what you've done, dollface. You've gone and made a right old mess of yourself, baby. All that muck and grime...." Shaking his head and giving Rain a reproachful mock glare, Matt smiled mischievously. "Now I have to give you a thorough sponge bath and wash clean all those secret and hard-to-reach places."

The anticipatory look on Rain's face revealed a nerve-racking euphoria that caused Matt to hiss in excitement and his cock to twitch back to life—which surprised him, since he hadn't been able to get it up again this fast since he was fifteen. Nor had he found the mere vision of his lover tasting his cum to be such an aphrodisiac that he came like a fountain, spewing his cum all over the place. Rain made Matt feel young and reckless and rejuvenated. He liked that feeling, instilled into him through their act of love—and liked Rain even better because of it.

"Well, darling," Rain teased him mercilessly, "are you just going to gawk at me? Or are you going to carry me to bathroom and do all those wonderful things to me that you promised? I've been a very, very bad and dirty girl," he added, batting his lashes and pouting his beautiful lips in a taunting manner that drove Matt crazy. Rain often employed that tactic to get what he wanted, and Matt always let him get away with it. Well, almost always.

"Oh, baby," Matt acknowledged, grinning impishly. "Your body's not all I'm going to wash. That trashy mouth of yours is going to get a soaping for good measure too. That'll teach you to behave."

"Oh, darling. Like a good-hearted rogue of a space captain once said, 'I aim to misbehave.' Consider that my motto, precious." Rain giggled when Matt chuckled and hooked his arms under Rain's back and knees, lifting him tenderly from the bed and carrying him toward the bathroom. But Rain said nothing more, only stared into Matt's eyes with his green eyes with an almost starstruck admiration that gave Matt shivers up and down his spine. Matt held Rain in his embrace and knew that at that very moment, he was happier than he'd ever been in his entire life.

Chapter
*E*ight

"WHERE is he?"

The sight that greeted Matt in the wee hours of his day off, while he stood in the doorway of his loft wearing nothing but his black boxers and a white T-shirt, still scratching sleep dust from his half-lidded eyes, was anything but welcoming. The woman in her late forties or early fifties was beautiful—and must've been more so in her heyday. Tall and slender, she had an air about her, commanding yet sophisticated. Dressed in a simple but elegant businesslike suit with a tight prune-colored jacket, a white blouse underneath, and slim trousers—and black high heels too—she was the very picture of a well-bred and cultivated upper-class matriarch. Everything about her screamed generations of affluence and high-tier connections.

Green eyes flashed at him, almost fuming, checking him out from head to toe in a less than friendly manner. "Did you not hear me, young man? I asked, where is he?" Her voice was not quite shrill but definitely not low either. What it absolutely was, was standoffish and chilly.

"Uh…." Matt brushed the hair off of his forehead, as if that move would suddenly clear his head from the drowsiness. "Um, who are you again…?"

She took a deep breath, obviously unaccustomed to such blatant inquiries. However, she didn't have an opportunity to answer before a miffed voice behind Matt spoke quietly. "What are you doing here?"

Turning around, stunned, Matt saw Rain standing there in his long flowery pajama bottoms, barefoot and bare-chested. It had been a week and a half since he'd been released from the hospital to Matt's care, and his pale skin tone looked better, healthier. His leg, however, had yet to show noticeable signs of improvement. His voice was still hoarse and became a raspy whisper if he spoke too long, so his singing days were still far off.

Right now, Rain's face held fury and frustration as he scowled at the lady at the door.

"Now, now, dear," the woman rebuked him, patient and calm as you please. "Is that any way to address your only mother? And I do believe the good Dr. Redding warned you to watch your blood pressure, so mind your tongue and see about those manners of yours."

Numb and dumbfounded, Matt watched silently in awe as the lady simply sidestepped him and entered the apartment proper.

Rain, however, was neither amused nor stunned, his lips forming a stern line. "You can't just barge in here willy-nilly like you own the place, Momsy. It's Matt's home. Have *you* no manners?"

The middle-aged lady stopped in midstep, blinked as if confused, and spun around to face Matt. Her expression was a bit befuddled, and her cheeks reddened, but the smile on her face seemed genuine enough. "Oh, I do apologize. I fear whenever my son's health and safety are concerned, I tend to lose my composure, not to mention every last trace of my civility. Can you *ever* forgive me?" Though her words were somewhat exaggerated, her countenance suggested she was sincere— and she *was* embarrassed that her son had scolded her in public. Now Matt knew exactly where Rain's sugary sweet persuasion skills originated from. For a moment Matt just gawked at the one and only family member and blood relative of Rain's he'd ever had the pleasure of meeting.

"Um, sure, I guess…?" His head was still trapped in cobwebs of dreams, and he hadn't even had his morning cup of coffee. His brain was pretty damn slow on the uptake in instances like this. At least *he* hadn't forgotten his manners. "Would you like some coffee, Mrs. Deveraux?"

"Oh, that would be just darling," she chirped, all anger and annoyance gone out of her. "Thank you very much, young man. Matt, was it?"

"Uh, yeah, Matt Wetherton." He extended his hand, all of a sudden extremely aware that he had precious few clothes on, and coughed a bit nervously. At least he wasn't blushing all over.

She took his hand with a warm and firm grip. "Charlotte Deveraux. It is *delightful* to finally meet you in person. I've heard so much about you." Nudging Matt just under the ribcage with her manicured hand, she giggled like a conspirator. "Nothing bad, I assure you, dear."

Smiling politely, Matt nodded and made his way to the kitchen, leaving Rain to deal with his mother. But immediately he heard the tap of her shoes on the parquet floors following him to the kitchen. She sat in a chic pose on one of the black leather barstools by the kitchen island, flopping her Hermes handbag onto the seat next to her in a carefully planned-out manner that exposed the brand to anyone around. Talk about product placement, Matt thought dryly, focusing all his attention on the coffeemaker—and getting his head around to a waking state.

Rain's smooth, sultry voice oozed displeased disdain and dripped indignant agitation as he spat out, "You didn't answer me, Momsy. What are you doing here?"

Busier with the coffee machine than he strictly speaking needed to be, Matt heard the heated voices behind him clear as a bell. "Don't be upset, dear. You know Dr. Redding said—"

Charlotte Deveraux was coldly interrupted by Rain, whose tone held more than a tinge of anger. "To blazes with the doctor! It's none of your business!"

From the way mother and son spoke, Matt deduced Redding was a family doctor, although of all of Rain's physicians, Matt had personally only met Dr. Clark. It seemed the Deveraux name carried a lot of influence if the good doctor had deemed fit to divulge confidential medical information about the son to the mother.

Or perhaps he hadn't, and she was just guessing.

In any case, this was a family argument Matt wanted to stay out of.

"I'm your mother," Charlotte said emphatically, her voice just as stubborn and intransigent as her son's. "Do you have any idea how long it took me to learn what had happened to you in the first place, let alone the... incident before? I was so worried and—"

"Did I disturb you in the middle of cocktail hour or a tea party, Momsy?"

"That was completely uncalled for, dear," she said, hurt. "You know that I love you."

"Only if I don't interfere with your busy social schedule," Rain replied, slightly uncertain now and his voice more than a little shaky.

Matt turned around with his cheeks red, embarrassed to witness such an emotional family scene—only to see Charlotte place her hand very gently over Rain's arm. "To heck with social engagements. You are my only son, Rain, my love and my life. I would die if anything...." Her voice trailed off, and she bowed her head, fighting off tears and sobs, fishing out a monogrammed silk handkerchief from her designer bag. "Never in a million years would I...."

"Momsy...," Rain whispered, his fury dissipating and concern taking its place. Soothing her with a touch on her shaking shoulder, he regretfully said at last, "I'm fine. I'll be all right. Matt's taken such good care of me." Rain looked up at Matt, his green eyes moist and pleading.

"Uh, yeah, that's right, Mrs. Deveraux," Matt hurried to add. "Rain's injuries weren't that bad after all, the doctors all agreed on that during his last checkup. He's mostly fine now, and it won't be too long before he makes a full recovery. You have nothing to worry about." He wasn't 100 percent sure he meant everything he'd just said, but it was true, nonetheless. Other people in addition to Rain seemed to be of like mind about Rain's rapid recovery and good prognosis, so Matt had set his own fears aside and decided to believe both professionals and his lover. Now the trepidations of Rain's mother brought back some of the uneasiness Matt had been able to dispel over the past week or so.

Charlotte looked up at Matt too, with teary eyes, blinking them away fast and correcting her pose on the seat, as if not wanting Matt to see her in such a state. "Well, if the doctors say so, it must be correct." Before she'd even finished her sentence, she was in full control of her emotional state again, doing a little ladylike touch-up of her hairdo—where there wasn't a single strand out of alignment. "I'm glad to see you up and about, dear. I guess you must be on the mend, then."

Reluctantly, Rain nodded and grunted something unintelligible. "I am, Momsy. You didn't need to come all this way." To Matt, Rain sounded an awful lot like a child who'd been caught doing something wrong—and, being fully cognizant of it, accepted and took the scolding with the appropriate amount of guilt.

Standing up, Charlotte Deveraux embraced her son wholeheartedly, and after a second of consideration, Rain hugged her back just as enthusiastically. Though the exact nature of their relationship had not yet revealed itself to Matt, he saw the true caring these two had for each other, despite their very recent row. Matt understood both of their positions: Rain didn't want people to meddle in his affairs, and Charlotte wanted to watch out for the continued safety of her only son. Matt was well aware that Rain could be recalcitrant and intractable when it was suggested that he might be wrong about his approach to something, and these were characteristics he'd seemingly inherited from his mother.

"Yes, dear, I did have to come," Charlotte replied, her voice trembling just a tad. "You know how I worry."

Pulling back, Rain pursed his lips disapprovingly, shaking his head. "If it had been truly life-threatening, I'm sure your little spy would've informed you of all the gory details."

"Now don't be crude, dear," she said, wiggling her index finger in front of her son in a chastising manner. "You know as well as I that Norma—like me—only has your best interest at heart."

Sighing resignedly, Rain surrendered to what appeared to be the inevitable defeat to a mother's care.

"Now, why don't you tell me all about your handsome young man here. I'm dying to hear all the latest gossip—in and out of the bedroom."

While Matt was busy blushing, Rain laughed. "Oh, Momsy, you're so droll."

Mother and son both sat down on the barstools, and Matt dug a couple of mugs from the cabinet above the sink, filled them with fresh coffee, and offered them to the two. "It's not chicory coffee, I'm afraid. It's orange-flavored coffee," he added apologetically. Rain preferred coffee brewed from chicory root, but Matt hated it. Still, he usually had both on hand. Right now, unfortunately, he had run out.

Charlotte's eyebrows lifted in surprise, but she sipped her coffee, smacking her mouth just a little to indicate the conscious activity of her taste buds. "Oh, dear, it's quite good. I'll have to make a mental note to purchase some of this back home. We hold so many social and political functions at our estate that something new and sweet like this will absolutely be adored. Thank you, Matt, for introducing me to this."

Functions? Estate? Matt was teeming with curiosity. "You're very welcome," he replied courteously, nodding a bit and feeling so much better now that he'd had his morning coffee. He took a deep gulp from his own mug to awaken his head and yet lull his emotions at Rain's mother's unexpected visit to a dead calm. With coffee, he could handle anything that came his way—even Rain's mother.

Rain grimaced but, glancing at Matt, smiled bashfully. "It's hot," he said, shrugging, as if Matt hadn't noticed the real reason behind his dislike. Matt replied to the comment with a low chuckle, not fooled for a second, and caused Rain's high cheekbones to blush pink.

But like the paragon of obstinate defiance, Rain refused to verbally admit he'd done anything to be embarrassed about, either coffee-wise or by keeping his apparent social standing a secret. "Um, darling, don't you think you should finish getting dressed, like, right now?" he suggested whimsically, nodding his head toward Matt's underwear.

Suddenly, after a moment of domestic comfort, Matt noticed again that he was terribly underdressed to entertain guests. Clearing his throat nervously, he nodded and set out toward the stairs up to the mezzanine floor where the loft's three bedrooms—the master bedroom and the two smaller guestrooms—were all located.

Charlotte stepped adamantly into his path. "I do beg your pardon, Matt, for my horrendous conduct earlier. I was so abhorrent and beastly toward you." The sincere remorse in her voice came through loud and clear to Matt, who found it hard to get past the weirdness of the antiquated speech patterns and fanciful vocabulary both mother and son apparently employed in their everyday lives. "Sometimes I can't see sense when it comes to my son."

To that truth, Matt had to chuckle amusedly. "Oh, I know *exactly* how that is, Mrs. Deveraux." Living with Rain, Matt knew there was more than a grain of truth in that statement. Looking over at his lover, whose green eyes flashed with annoyance, Matt grinned and winked at Rain.

"Please, Matt," Charlotte said, doing her best to contain her own smile, "call me Charlotte. I imagine we will be getting better acquainted soon." Looking over her shoulder, she pursed her lips in a custom very similar to Rain's. Then she turned her attention back to Matt. "I must say, Matt, that you have a very lovely apartment," she cooed like an infatuated teenage girl, surveying the loft with an attentive gaze.

"Momsy...." Rain's eyes widened and his mouth pressed into a grim line as he shot Matt a warning look.

"Hotels can be so dreadfully impersonal, not to mention noisy and crowded, don't you think so, Matt?" Charlotte continued as though there had been no interruption.

"Momsy...." Rain's voice dropped a few octaves, his dangerous tone more crisp.

"Norma tells me you have not one but two accommodating guest rooms here," Charlotte proclaimed, her green eyes big and innocent.

"Momsy!" The unflattering word coming from a grown man so steadfast and set in his ways sounded veritably puerile to Matt, and the infantile effect was only compounded by the constant repetition.

"My word, dear," Charlotte huffed. "I'm sure that a gentleman of Matt's stature would hardly object to—"

Rain sounded equally peeved. "You should wait until you're invited, Momsy, and not expect that just out of the blue—"

"It's all right, Rain," Matt interjected, raising his voice above the others like a schoolteacher commanding hellraisers. "I know what you would like, Charlotte, and I don't mind one damn bit. You're more than welcome to stay here for as long as you want—as my guest."

"Oh, aren't you positively a dear," Charlotte declared with glee, giving Matt a smooch on the cheek. "Ah, yes, the more the merrier, I always say." Taking quick inspection of the irate Rain, she quickly added in a more conciliatory tone, "My son regards me as presumptuous as a door-to-door salesman who, once getting a foot in through the door, does not take *no* for an answer. Matt, I by no means wish to cause you any trouble...." She trailed off purposely as she peered at Matt, batting her lashes, and waited for a decision on her fate as calmly as if she were taking inventory of her shoe rack.

"Like I said," Matt said, "you're more than welcome here, Charlotte."

At that she beamed like a kid at Christmas, practically bouncing on the soles of her high-heeled feet.

"Matt...." Rain's pale green eyes flashed—he was pissed off. "Can I talk to you for a second—in private?" He waved his hand theatrically toward the large open living room, not even bothering to hide the emphatic gesture from his mother.

Not a chance, love. "Sorry, babe. But as you yourself pointed out, I should probably go put some clothes on." Matt deflected the impending verbal assault quite tactfully by withdrawing from center stage and making a quick escape to the exit—or, in this case, the master bedroom. Yes, he'd catch hell for this later, but for now Matt wasted no time in letting things cool down on their own—and the only way that could happen was for mother and son to have some quality one-on-one alone time. Climbing up the stairs in hasty hops, Matt just prayed the two didn't manage to strangle each other before he had a chance to return to the scene fully clothed.

DOWNSTAIRS, standing in front of his mother, Rain did his best to simmer down from his fuming state. Yes, he knew his mother well enough to be aware that despite her meddlesome nature, she meant no harm—and loved Rain more than anything else in the world. That thought was sufficient to reassure him that the reins were still firmly in his grip.

Regardless, he couldn't resist another jab. "Are you happy now, Momsy?"

Charlotte smiled softy, came over to him, and bussed him on the cheek. "Very, dear."

Dang, she could be disarming when she set her mind to it. Rain grimaced but was already well on his way to being fully placated. "How did you find me?" It was a silly question, to be sure, Rain knew, since the answer wasn't a deep Southern mystery. He didn't begrudge Norma for keeping Charlotte in the loop about Rain's life—and love life. It just meant that Rain didn't have to—which was easier all around for all concerned. And the number of those concerned with Rain was pretty small to begin with. Apart from Charlotte and Daisy, most of Rain's blood relations tended to view his flaunted queerness as something shameful to be sheltered from, as if his gayness were contagious or lethal. This was especially true with his male family members from uncles to cousins, with whom he had zero interaction. Good riddance to bad rubbish, Daisy had scoffed and mumbled something not very civilized about foaming-mouthed bigots and so forth.

"Is Norma seeing that incredibly huge lug of a man, that Little John person?" Charlotte inquired, pouring another mug of coffee for herself, and from the happy smirk on her face, Rain realized she really liked Matt's choice of orange-flavored coffee.

"Tiny," Rain corrected automatically. "No. They're just...." No, Norma and Tiny were not friends. They knew *of* each other, but weren't acquainted or intimate in any meaningful way. Sure, they hung out a lot in the same places, clubs and back rooms, but as far as Rain knew, they had no personal relations whatsoever. "Just pals, I guess."

Charlotte looked suspicious. "Hmm, I don't think that's right. There was something going on there, if I do say so myself." What could Rain say to that? Charlotte had an uncanny eye for the fun and games people played—and what was brewing beneath the surface of civil upbringings. If she said there was something there, then there probably was. Rain tried to imagine Norma and Tiny together but couldn't for the life of him make the picture work.

Shaking his head, he dispelled the image. "Where's your luggage? Only one handbag? You'd surely die." That wasn't a joke either. His mother did nothing small.

"Oh." Charlotte waved her hand dismissively, as though she'd forgotten all about it. "I'll have the chauffeur bring them up at some point." Rain was about to comment on the indecency of leaving a driver waiting in the car—most likely a limousine, if he knew his mother—for what could be hours on end. But he knew it would be to no avail. Charlotte would take care of things in her own time, in her own way. There was little Rain could do to persuade her differently.

"How long will you be?" Unable to hide how tired he felt all of a sudden—the weariness attacking him at the oddest hours and most awkward moments—Rain couldn't keep the aggravation out of his tone.

Charlotte's observant eyes filled with worry. "Are you all right, dear? You look positively pale. Come, sit down." After ushering Rain toward the couch, Charlotte shepherded Rain to sit, and he sighed deeply, his whole body quivering with fatigue. His eyes felt incredibly heavy and his leg began to burn and ache with the thumping of his heart.

"I need my pain meds," he managed to whisper as his voice tired too.

"I got them, babe."

Turning to see Matt rushing down the stairs, Rain was starstruck as his mouth went dry and his heart raced at the delicious sight of his lover. It wasn't the stylish charcoal dress pants or the white buttoned-up dress shirt with silvery cuffs that did him in, per se, but the bright lavender-colored tie Rain had bought Matt on their one-month anniversary, telling him to liven his mundane drudge-filled life with some much-needed color. *He may be wearing those clothes for Momsy's sake, but he's wearing that tie for me.* Never had Rain seen Matt display such poise and elegance in the short time they'd known each other. It was such a turn-on that Rain felt the massive hard-on tenting the thin fabric of his pajama bottoms almost to the point of embarrassment.

If Matt spotted his aroused state, he said nothing, only placed a glass of orange juice in Rain's right hand and a pain pill in the left. "Here, love. I'll make you some breakfast after, if you feel up to it." Rain was about to say that what he really wanted was some shut-eye, but when he noticed the playful glimmer in Matt's eyes, he realized exactly what the man had insinuated—right in front of his mother. *Great.*

His brain, however, didn't feel like playing, and a smart retort eluded him as he swallowed the pain medication and took a swig of juice afterward, falling back on the sofa cushions with a slow sigh. Barely aware of Matt slipping to lie next to him in a protective and possessive manner and his lover's tender hand stroking his hair, Rain nodded off to dreamland.

WHEN he managed to pry his eyes open to half-mast next, Rain heard Matt and Charlotte talking softly by the kitchen island. They were engaged in a rather lively debate over politics and gay and lesbian rights advocacy groups, and Rain had no intention of interrupting them. The nagging pain in his leg had subsided, same as the fatigue and the sandpapery sensation in his throat, so Rain felt assured enough that he would be able to stand again. His bladder demanded some instant gratification, and even though he didn't want to interfere with his lover and his mother bonding, he seriously had to pee.

With a grunt like an old man, Rain pushed himself up to a sitting position, wondering how long he'd been out of it. The pain and the meds made him fall asleep faster than ever, and the time interval between his waking state and REM sleep couldn't have amounted to more than ten, fifteen seconds at most. So as a result of this zombielike existence, every day was a continuation of the annoyance of feeling like his head had been stuffed with balls of cotton. Though he was physically fit to move about again, his mind had trouble following him to consciousness, let alone igniting anything resembling common sense, logical faculties, and reasonable conversational skills.

In an instant Matt was there, picking Rain up by winding his arm around his waist, holding some if not all of his weight as he helped him first to the bathroom, then to the kitchen. At first Rain had hated Matt babying him like this, as if he were an infant or an invalid, but over time he'd sort of gotten used to it, knowing that Matt meant nothing by it but concern and caring.

"You okay, babe?" Matt asked, escorting Rain to the counter and setting him down on a stool, carefully smoothing the ruffles of his clothes and tousling his red-golden curls before moving away with a grin.

A loud rumble emerged from Rain's belly. "Hungry," he murmured, blushing, massaging his empty stomach. The meds made him woozy and eradicated his appetite, but sometimes the needs of the body outweighed the nausea.

"Bacon and eggs with fresh-baked pumpkin bread. How does that sound, love?" Matt was already making his way around the kitchen: he fetched ingredients, put an empty plate in front of Rain, turned on the stove, fished out the frying pan, and poured a liberal dose of extra-virgin olive oil into it.

Actually, though Rain preferred a vegetarian diet, right now Matt's offer sounded just heavenly. His stomach agreed with a low growl.

After glancing at the clock on the wall, which read 11:02 a.m., Rain turned to Charlotte, who sat next to him with a radiant, happy look on her face. "All settled in, Momsy?"

"Oh yes, dear." His mother beamed, the glow making her look ten years younger and far prettier than ever. "Matt has been a tremendous help. Such a kind, polite, and obliging gentleman he is. I'm quite taken with him." She winked at Rain, who had to laugh—and surprisingly there was no following twinge of pain. His leg and throat gave him only a little grief anymore, and usually as a result of stress, excitement, and too much exercise.

"Sorry, Momsy, but he's spoken for."

As Matt turned around briefly to face Rain, his blue eyes shone with love and laughter, and at that moment, Rain honestly didn't believe he could love the man more. And that his mother seemed to adore Matt just as much made his heart flutter. At best Rain had wished Charlotte would try to get along with his lover—and it wasn't like Rain brought guys over all the time to introduce them to his mother—but this amicable association was above and beyond his hopes and dreams. Especially since Rain wanted Matt to stick around. For a very, very, very long time.

Would he, though?

"Well, my word," Charlotte huffed, pleased, directing her comment at Matt. "I do hope that you, Mr. Wetherton, intend to make an honest man out of my son, as he is—"

"Momsy!" Rain shrieked in quite an unmanly manner, sending his mother nearly toppling over her chair in shock. Oh, this was just what Rain needed while he was convalescing: an eager beaver mother who had weddings on the brain.

Then he heard Matt chuckling and saw him leaning back against the sink, relaxed, his arms folded across his chest, his blue eyes sparkling with humor. Shrugging smoothly, Matt said coolly, "Well, Momsy, you never know." Then, returning to his chores, he turned his back on the joyful Charlotte—and Rain, who was stunned into silence, staring at his lover's strong back like he'd never seen it before in his life.

What the blazes had just happened?

Faintly he caught his mother rambling on about flower markets and party fashions and Southern culinary wonders, but Rain couldn't wrap his dozed-off brain around what he'd just heard. Did Matt just suggest he might… propose marriage… to Rain? No. No, that was just insane. They'd known each other barely three months, having lived under the same roof for just a week and a half since the injury. And Matt had not been with Rain constantly—just for the first week—since he *did* have to go to work. All in all, they had been seeing each other for two and a half months now. Certainly not enough time to think about walking down the aisle—of the state registrar's office instead of a church, unfortunately.

MATT could see how Rain was completely dumbstruck and totally teeming with curiosity, and it made him chuckle inwardly. No, he hadn't intended to spill it out in quite such an innocuous way—and with Charlotte in attendance, no less—but, all in all, Matt did have plans for the future. And they definitely involved Rain.

Right now, though, his only project at hand was finishing Rain's breakfast. Rain had not eaten much lately due to the pain, the meds, and sleeping, and he had lost quite a few pounds. The doctors had said that he needed to eat and keep up his strength. And for once Matt agreed with them 100 percent. So he prepared a full-course meal that left little doubt that he intended to stuff his lover full—with food, at least.

After carrying the food to the island counter and laying it all out on a huge platter, Matt served Rain his breakfast-brunch-lunch. Along with the previously mentioned bacon and eggs and fresh pumpkin bread, Matt had prepared a bowl of fruit salad and a dessert of orange-chocolate mousse with whipped cream. After Rain ate all this, he'd be in a food-produced comatose state for the rest of the day. Lately Matt could count Rain's ribs with his fingers and feel his hipbones clearly. Rain could use some beefing up, and Matt was up to the task with his gastronomical skills.

"If I eat all this, I'll blow up," Rain whined with a low voice, eyeing the many foods with apprehension, moving the food around with his fork.

"Go right ahead, babe," Matt laughed. "I'll protect you, princess," he added with a feigned courageous voice, banging his puffed-up chest with his fist, wearing an exaggerated barbaric expression. Stifling a bursting giggle, Rain nodded and set out to perform the magic trick of making his meal disappear.

All the while, Matt and Charlotte kept chatting about anything under the sun, from politics to the weather, and the chatter was a soothing sound for Rain, a familiar background noise that dulled the sharp edges of his headache. Of course, the mere fact that she was so talkative about casual topics meant she was avoiding something big, and Rain fully expected to get an earful of glee later about the possibility of upcoming nuptials between him and Matt.

As Rain was finishing his last few bites and starting to dig into dessert with a hungry luster in his green eyes, the doorbell rang.

Matt rushed to the door. Norma and Tiny burst in with bags and boxes.

"Oh my God, I'm sure that if I had to carry these one more block, I'd simply keel over right here and die," Norma stated, huffing and puffing like a balloon being filled, dropping the bags down on the living room couch with a theatrical toss. He had on tight feminine jeans with fake jewelry and ornaments along the seams, and a white blouse with bright-colored flowery lace around the amply giving neckline. Norma's favorite wig—resembling one of Lil' Kim's—flowed down in large curls so very pink it nearly hurt the eyes of onlookers. With a garish air, Norma would've appeared almost cheap if he'd been a woman, but as a man he made the outfit work like a charm. Actually, if it weren't for Norma's narrow hips, one might've mistaken him for a skinny, flat-chested girl.

"We parked out front," Tiny—dressed, as always, in black-on-black, from his jeans, sleeveless T-shirt, and leather jacket to his combat boots—explained from the hallway, giving Norma a deprecating glance before lowering the three boxes he'd been carrying to the floor. "And then we just put this stuff in the elevator, for fuck's sake."

"It's called artistic license, sweetie," Norma replied, indignant, as if mortally wounded by Tiny's accusations. He cocked his hip to one side and delivered an angry stare to the man—in a style very similar to Rain. The two friends copied each other to a tee sometimes, and their friends didn't always know who had started what mannerism or gesture. If it weren't for the color of their skin and their different physical type, one could've assumed they were twin brothers rather than best friends.

"You mean prevarications, don't you?" Tiny kept on pushing Norma's buttons, giving him a glare of his own from under his strong masculine brow.

Norma was about to raise his voice to start the mother of all arguments. Matt knew his moods well enough, so he hurried to interject, "What's all this, then?"

"Rain needed some stuff from his flat, so we thought we'd help out," Tiny stated simply and curtly, as was his style in all things. "Clothes, makeup, things like that."

"Oh, ladies," Rain cried out joyfully and clapped his hands. "I love you both. Thank you so much." After skittering over to the boxes on the floor, Rain bent over—and immediately sprang up again, pressing his leg with a painful grimace on his face.

Matt grabbed him so quickly a lightning bolt would've ended up in second place. "Babe, you okay?"

"Quite," Rain snapped, trying to break free from Matt's hold.

Reluctantly, Matt let go, swallowing hard with disappointment, and moved back slowly. He knew Rain hated being too weak to do things on his own and people making a fuss about his injured state, since he'd been independent from his midteens, and that he would refuse even his lover's assistance was hardly surprising. Still, it hurt that Rain had to make such a big deal about Matt wanting to be there for him—especially in front of people, and in this, Rain had the pride of a stubborn man for sure.

"I'll put these on the table over there," Tiny said, lifting the boxes and taking them to the living room coffee table. Matt didn't miss him giving him a sidelong glance that told him just how well he understood. Tiny had known both Rain and Norma for a long time and was familiar with their quirks, moods, and attitudes. Sometimes Matt hated that another man knew Rain better, emotionally more intimately, than he did, but there was nothing he could do about it.

Without even noticing the tension Matt was sporting and the empathy flowing from Tiny, Rain sauntered over to the couch, sat down, and began opening the boxes. "Oh, my music." He giggled—and sobbed—at the sight of the contents, crushing his beloved CDs to his chest like they were puppies yearning for his adoration. "Love you, ladies."

Tiny had moved to stand by Matt, and Matt heard distinctly the disapproving growl he made. Being an ex-military man, Tiny did not like being referred to as a lady in any sense or situation, and Matt wondered why he tolerated it from Rain without so much as a word in edgewise. But inside he knew why. Matt wasn't the only one who loved Rain.

"Thanks for bringing this stuff over," Matt thanked Tiny, who just nodded in reply, his gaze never wavering from Rain and Norma, who'd sat down on the couch beside his friend, and Charlotte who joined them from the kitchen. Now all three of them were cooing and giggling over every new discovery from the box, laying them out on the coffee table delicately as though they were the crown jewels. Well, if these homey items made Rain happy, then Matt would welcome them into his home—which he'd lately begun to secretly hope would be *their* home soon. His and Rain's together.

After skipping over to the CD player, Rain flicked on his music. As the sweet harmonious tones swooped in and won the open space of the loft, Rain's face took on a blissful look that Matt adored. Brassy instruments, drum, and bass, all rounded together to perform a dark, sensuous jazzy melody that lingered in the room like a silk and velvet dress.

"You're some kind of mystery, sweet kind of mystery.

Gotta getcha close to me so I can figure out what this mystery's about."

Swaying in place with his eyes closed, Rain was in a trance, mumbling something like "I love Diane Warren." Matt had once hoped he could instill this look on his lover's face, but over time he'd realized nothing could hold such power over Rain as music. Rain was a willing love slave to the soft, dark rhythms of jazz and blues, and no one could ever compare, not even Matt—no matter how much he might love Rain. Either he could accept that he'd always hold second place in Rain's life, or he'd have to learn how to live without him.

Matt wasn't ready to throw in the towel yet, if ever. Even if Rain was just the kind of mystery to him that the female vocalist sang about.

Holding back a sigh, Matt took the dirty dishes from the counter, brought them to the sink, emptied the leftover food into the compost trash basket, and began to do the dishes. The simple domestic task settled some of his nerves but not the nagging, stinging feeling that he was deeper in the clutches of an emotional entanglement than the man he loved. As though he was alone in his feelings, like they were unshared and unrequited. He had to bite his lower lip hard to fight back the urge to cry.

"Wanna talk about it?"

Tiny had become a good friend to Matt over the past weeks, having let Matt into his small circle of trusted companions. His concern for Matt's well-being was genuine, of that Matt had no doubt. Still, Matt didn't feel like sharing at the moment. "No."

From the corner of his eye, Matt saw Tiny nodding quietly and leaning against the sink with his arms folded across his chest, never taking his eyes off Rain, Norma, and Charlotte. "When he's better, things will return to normal."

The comment required little guesswork on Matt's part, and he snorted. "Yeah, with me fighting with music to get his attention." He couldn't keep the bitterness out of his voice and wondered in passing how the hell his mood could sink so damn low so fast from the dizzying heights of ten minutes ago, when he'd hinted about his intentions to Rain.

"You know, Matt, this is by far the longest relationship Rain has ever had."

Though he didn't question the veracity of Tiny's statement, Matt wondered if that mattered. Rain was his own man, and he didn't really need anyone. Was Matt only muddying the waters to the point where he himself had lost sight of the fundamental truth that once Rain was better, he would no longer require Matt's presence in any sense of the word? Maybe Matt would be a constant reminder to Rain of this horrible time in his life, which would lead to him distancing himself from Matt altogether. Deep down Matt knew that a relationship could not be founded on need alone—whether it was the need for sex or the need to help. What did he really have to offer Rain, aside from his heart?

These dreary thoughts were brought to a halt when the doorbell rang. As Matt's hands were soaped up with dishwater, Tiny went to the door in his stead. From the kitchen Matt could distinguish every quip of the verbal exchange clearly, despite the music rolling in and the cheerful chatter of Rain, Norma, and Charlotte from the couch.

"Who're you?" a man's voice asked.

"Who're *you*?" Tiny asked in reply.

"I asked you first."

"What are you? Five?"

"What are *you*? A bouncer?"

"Yeah, and if you don't answer me I'll throw your lily-white pansy ass out to the curb so fast you'll think you did a quantum leap."

A muffled chuckle echoed in the outside hallway. "I'd love to see you try to do that, pal."

"You'll see nothing past the black eye I'll adorn you with," Tiny growled.

It was at this point that Matt cleaned his hands in record time and rushed to the front door to stare at the man standing there, annoyance and amusement battling on his face, which was similar to Matt's, only more masculine and angular. When the man saw Matt, he let out a breath and shook his head.

"Just what kind of people are you hanging around with these days, baby brother, that you need bouncers on your doorstep?" Not expecting an answer—he never did—Mitchell grabbed Matt by his shirt and yanked him into a fierce brotherly hug that nearly cracked every bone in his body and shook loose at least a few kinks in his popping joints. "Hey, Matt. Good to see you."

Matt tried to breathe against his brother's massive athletically built chest, waving his arms around in a very unmanly way. "How can you... see anything... of me at all?" he huffed.

Mitchell laughed with all of his body, as was his style, and he let go of Matt, who took deep breaths into his burning lungs. He studied his little brother like he was a toad about to be dissected. "You've lost some weight, baby bro. Haven't you been eating enough?" It was easy for Mitchell to say since his diet was composed of meals it usually took a small town of people to digest. He was an athlete: huge, muscular, and bulky—and perpetually hungry.

"I've been busy," Matt defended himself, even though he was well aware it was a mistake. With Mitchell, contradicting his structured way of life and his health-nut views was akin to throwing gasoline onto a forest fire. "With work and stuff."

"That job of yours is going to be the death of you one day, baby bro," Mitchell criticized with the thorough conviction of a man set in his ways—happy and successful in his own line of work with zero misgivings about the choices he'd made or the path he'd taken. Sometimes Matt envied his brother's natural ease, and other times hated his light all-knowing tone.

"Who is it, Matt?" Rain came up behind Matt and wound his long arms around his waist in a manner that could not be misconstrued.

Mitchell lifted his eyebrows in a silent question while his blue eyes were preoccupied with examining the apparition before him. Undoubtedly Rain was doing the same, and Mitchell, in his clean blue jeans, sports jacket, white T-shirt, and sneakers, was the spitting image of an all-American sports hero. Mitchell could've stepped off the pages of a male model catalog at any time.

Matt set out to make the introductions. "Oh, right. Mitch, this is Rain Deveraux, my, uh, boyfriend. Rain, this is Mitchell Wetherton, my brother."

Rain let go of Matt to shake hands with Mitchell, but Matt knew better. His hesitation with the descriptive term of Rain's role had struck a nerve in Rain, probably pissing him off. *Great.* His mood sank even lower.

"It's such a pleasure to meet anyone from Matt's family," Rain flirted shamelessly, cocking his hip and giving Mitchell the once-over with a long-lingering inspection. "And, gosh, aren't you just the very picture of male perfection, darling." Matt winced at the feminine intonations of Rain's voice, for the first time feeling embarrassed at his lover's behavior. Immediately after, he was consumed with guilt over it, wishing for the earth to open up and swallow him whole.

Mitchell was rarely baffled, and this apparently wasn't one of those times, either. If he was surprised by his brother's choice of partner, he didn't let on. "Nice to meet you too."

Snaking his hands around Mitchell's left arm, Rain giggled and escorted the man inside the loft apartment, babbling about lunch, sports, fashion, health, even politics—all in a seemingly endless stream of keen speech without so much as a pause for breath. Mitchell kept nodding but, not getting many words in, glancing back over his shoulder at Matt. He didn't plead for assistance but winked at Matt with a grin. Matt couldn't misconstrue that either, since his brother was 110 percent straight—and here he was, being ushered around Matt's own place by the most feminine man Mitchell had undoubtedly ever seen. Matt knew what conclusion his brother would draw from this scene, which was turning bad in epic proportions.

"Sorry, Matt. I didn't know it was your brother when I talked to him like that." Tiny spoke quietly next to him, calming Matt with his mere presence, so solid and stable that for a moment, Matt felt like leaning against him for both moral and physical support.

"Mitch is a big boy. He can handle himself." Although against the steady onslaught of Rain, Norma, and Charlotte, any man would succumb. Mitchell was being pushed back onto the couch to sit. The two ladylike men followed suit by taking seats next to him, so close they were practically in his lap, with Charlotte taking a seat slightly further back in the armchair but being just as vocal as her son and her son's best friend. They were talking about music now, and Matt knew they'd be at it for ages if Rain's undying enthusiasm was anything to go by.

Walking back to the dishes he'd been cleaning, Matt couldn't believe he was actually jealous of music.

ENDING the talk with Mitchell and allowing Charlotte and Norma to take over the conversation, Rain saw Matt clearing the counter and sink in the kitchen, removing dishes and wiping the surfaces with a wet sponge. Tiny was with him, and the two of them were gabbing in low tones and small utterances, just like typical men. At least they weren't entirely cavemen, resorting to mere grunts.

Staring at his lover's hunched back and blank face, Rain felt a pang of remorse in his heart. As the days had gone by, Matt's jumps to his aid had begun to bug him more and more. He knew that Matt only wanted to help and be there for him should Rain need him, but it didn't matter. Rain was biting his tongue until it bled to stop himself from snapping at every little helpful gesture Matt made, but it was turning into a losing battle.

Rain hated their sweet thing turning sour—and knew it was hurting Matt too.

Yet he couldn't prevent what had become an almost instinctive response. Rain needed his own space and his music. Matt, Norma, and Tiny all tried to chip in and grant him that—and still keep a watchful eye out for him. It created a schism between them because the two goals tended to conflict. Rain felt well enough to return home and finish his recuperation there. The compulsion to just cut and run had grown exponentially lately. He knew his leg wasn't yet in any shape for him to be on his own, but their hovering just reminded him all the time that he wasn't well, and it exacerbated the already inflamed situation.

Causing misery and pain to Matt had never been, and would never be, what Rain had intended or what he wanted. He liked Matt. He liked Matt a lot. He more than liked Matt.

Rain got up to have a conciliatory talk with Matt when Charlotte intersected his path, smiling softly—but with a telltale gleam in her eyes. This look Rain knew well enough after having been what one might diplomatically call a troublesome child. Trouble had certainly found him at all hours—or he'd deliberately gone in search of it.

"You know, dear," Charlotte started in a hushed voice she used when speaking of delicate matters in mixed company, "if there is one thing I've always admired about you and been so very proud of you for, it's that you never run. You always face your problems, whatever they may be. Where lesser men accept defeat and head for the hills to bury their heads in the sand—not you. You have ever been the one in this family who isn't afraid to be who he is or to face the music. You are fabulous and victorious. And remember, sweetheart," she added, kissing Rain on the cheek, her lips warm and motherly, "we—your family and friends—will be here whenever you need us. Don't you ever doubt or forget that."

Without waiting for any kind of acknowledgement, Charlotte returned to the couch and engaged Mitchell in a debate about the long-term effects of public sports becoming infinitely more commercialized. Rain kept staring at her like he'd never really seen her before. Yes, she could be insightful and brilliant when she wanted to, but this little impromptu speech had hit the bull's-eye so dead center that Rain contemplated the possibility she'd been hiding telepathic abilities from him throughout his childhood years.

The exigent urge to go back to his own place and remain holed up under the covers of his king-size bed had faded infinitesimally. Other thoughts had risen to stand just as resolute next to it. Matt had been there for Rain from the start, but lately he'd become even more pronounced in catching Rain's attention. And Rain didn't run away from hardships or from who he was.

And who Rain was alone was far less than who he was with Matt.

Taking a deep breath, Rain sauntered over to Matt, mindful of his throbbing leg. Sure, he'd have no reason to dig out his dancing shoes from the back of the closet any time soon, but he reminded himself that this state of affairs wasn't permanent. Yes, they'd all get past this, and years from now, they'd look back and laugh at this memory of when Rain had tried to tear them apart with his cowardice and wayward anxiety.

Studying Matt's sad expression, Rain was aware that no other lover in his life had ever created such sweet symphonies and brought up more moody melodies in Rain than Matt. When they had made love, Rain had drowned in the mélange of sensuality and jazz that had been elicited from their shared passion. Music sprouting from sexual release had taken Rain by surprise, to be sure, but he craved more. The music of Matt had become the most important thing to Rain.

Winding his arms around Matt's narrow waist—a bit hesitantly at first—Rain rested his chin on one of his lover's quite strong shoulders. Matt was shorter than Rain, and there was a comfortable little nook at the juncture of his neck and shoulder where Rain could always make room for himself—and loved it. "I like your brother."

Making a small amicable agreeing sound, Matt nodded. "Everyone likes Mitch."

Caressing his soft cheek against Matt's strong stubble so that his skin tingled with the burn, Rain chuckled a little. "Do you mind terribly, darling, if I like his brother better?"

Scared, Rain noticed Matt's body tense up and stiffen. For a minute he feared he had lost the man for good with his silly antics. Then, suddenly, leaning backward into the embrace, Matt sighed deep in his chest. "My brother's a big boy. He'll learn to cope with the loss."

Oh, Matt had made a joke. Rain couldn't begin to phrase out loud how much it meant to him. He snuggled closer to his lover until the hug became a full-body experience that threatened to do away with his resolve of not luring Matt into a fiercely passionate sexual encounter that they'd both thoroughly enjoy. That might, however, aggravate Rain's wounded leg into a new spin of thumping, wrenching pain. That thought made him go wooden, and not in a good way.

Seemingly interpreting the silence correctly, Matt turned around to face Rain with a concerned look on his face. "You okay, babe? Need to rest?"

Again infuriated, Rain stepped out of the embrace, muttering angrily, "I'm fine." Not needing to see the rigidness returning to Matt, Rain made his clunky way to the stairs and the master bedroom, clearing up his scattered items of clothing on his way up. Whenever chaos entered his peaceful, fluffy little pink dream world, Rain succumbed to the impulse of cleaning, as though the mundane task could right all wrongs and smooth all rough edges—and clear away all the heartaches and messed-up emotions.

Rain got all the way to the bedroom before he began to sob, holding his hand over his mouth as though that could somehow prevent the sounds from escaping. Suddenly he was startled by his lover, who gently pulled him into his arms, rocking him in place ever so sweetly.

"I know you're fine, love. I wish I had a button that, like with a flick of a switch, could turn my worry on and off—for your benefit. I hate to see you upset."

Now his sobs came out in full force. Rain's whole body shook, and tears rained down over his cheeks. Matt was so sweet and perfect and wonderful. Rain didn't deserve him. "I'm so sorry, Matt. I'm so horrible to you all the time. I don't want to be. I don't mean to be. I just can't help myself. I want to be better. I want to be fine already. I want to be able to do things by myself."

"I know, baby," Matt soothed him, holding him tight, breathing soft and warm against his neck. "It sucks feeling helpless. Like you have to depend on others all the time. But, love, if this had happened to any one of your loved ones, you'd insist on being there for them too, throughout the ordeal. You take care of everyone, Rain. Let us, just this once, for just this brief period in your life, take care of you for a change. We all love you so very much."

Spinning around on his heels, Rain flung himself at Matt, locking his arms around the back of his lover's neck and pressing flush against him so hard he almost wished he could slip into Matt and stay within his solid strength forever. Burying his head in Matt's sandy-colored hair, Rain could only whisper, "I know, muffin. I'm sorry."

"It's okay, babe," Matt assured him tenderly, stroking his back.

"I feel like a prisoner inside my own flesh," Rain confessed in a harsh gasp, spilling out all the thoughts that had been driving him crazy. "There's nothing but the constant awareness that I'm not healthy. I can hear the music drifting in the back of my mind, but I can't reach it. Like a mirage, it taunts me and evaporates because I'm not well enough to dance with it. Without my music… who am I?"

Rain hadn't intended to admit all that, but he couldn't help but let it spurt out of him. Matt evoked those words with his steady composure by his mere presence, and Rain wanted the man to sooth his aches—even though he knew he was giving precious little back in return. Rain felt like a cad and a heel and a villain of the worst sort—selfish and self-indulgent, not recognizing the care and comfort his friends and family were kind enough to bestow upon him.

"Now, Rain, you listen to me," Matt started suddenly, his voice determined and steadfast. "It will be a while before we can go out dancing, yes, or for you to get back on stage and enchant us all with your lovely voice. But, baby, just because you have a dysfunctional leg and an uncooperative voice box doesn't mean there is no means for you to let the music out to play. You could, oh, I don't know, perhaps play the piano?"

Tears wet his long lashes, and Rain peered through them at Matt, who smiled encouragingly, maybe even wickedly. "The piano…?" How could he have forgotten about his piano? His most beloved musical instrument? All this wallowing in self-pity had morphed Rain into a dolorous moron who was so busy fending off the loving attentions of his fellow men that he'd completely set aside the fact that he had other means beside his tempestuous voice to let his music fly into spheres unknown.

"Now, we wanted this to be a surprise, baby," Matt said, regaining Rain's attention in an instant. "But while you were sleeping on the couch, Charlotte and I talked about your condition. Not your medical condition, love, but your emotional state. We all know you, and despite all that"—Matt winked—"we love you. Charlotte has arranged for a piano to be brought up here—to the living room, to be precise. It'll arrive tomorrow. I'll be at work most days, so you can play as long and as loud as you want. No neighbors here to attempt to squelch your mastery, my beautiful virtuoso."

His sobs of sorrow turning into sobs of joy, Rain kissed Matt and kept on kissing him everywhere across his face. In the short time Rain had known Matt, he'd learned that aside from his voice, there was the pleasurable discovery of the music of sex—specifically sex with

Matt—that had the power to give his music swift angelic wings and take off in flight. Now Matt had reminded him of yet another medium—his treasured piano—for releasing his music within. There were not enough words in the English language for him to thank Matt for everything he had given Rain.

And he'd repaid the man's love with nothing but fits of anger and snaps of frustration.

That was going to change, Rain decided firmly.

Unable to start making his much-needed amends right away, though, Rain found himself being swayed in his lover's arms, tantalized by music from the soul. It was then that Rain first heard it in his ears as Matt nuzzled him subtly—Matt singing, so softly it barely registered in his conscious mind.

"If you want a lover, I'll do anything you ask me to."

Crooning, Matt held Rain closer, and all Rain could do amidst the swirl of his raging emotions was hold on and partake of the splendid gift of music Matt was granting him. The slow, sensuous tones of Leonard Cohen's song drifted gently from Matt's mouth into Rain's ear, consuming him in a heady haze that dissipated all fears, doubts, and anxieties like clouds of rain dispersing with the dawning of the sun.

Matt had been honest about his poor singing voice and his apparent tone deafness, and as he sang, his voice trembled. He lacked the confidence of someone who sang professionally or had a genuine talent for it. Still, he sang from the depths of his heart, and the lyrics—though not originally his—came to life as he hummed his way forward with determination and fortitude.

"Here I stand. I'm your man."

As Matt fell silent, Rain could still hear the music in his heart, flowing from Matt to him, dancing between them and around them, holding them transfixed in a moment of pure delight and perfect harmony. *I belong here—with Matt.* Rain remained mindful of his hurt leg but allowed himself to swim in the sensations of dancing cheek to cheek and chest to chest with his lover. Rain breathed in his lover's lavender soapy scent mixed with a more masculine aroma that caused his cock to twitch with eager anticipation in his pajama bottoms.

"That feels nice," Matt murmured in his ear, obviously keenly aware of Rain's eager prick pressed against his hip.

"I'm sorry, Matt," Rain said, knowing he sounded an awful lot like a broken record—which was not good for a singing artist. In his confused heart and weary head, he knew he'd find a way to not only repay Matt for everything he'd done for Rain but to patch things up with his lover and to make good on all those unspoken promises he'd made. Rain prayed they hadn't become too estranged already to make things right between them.

"Shh…," Matt whispered, low and husky, and held Rain even tighter against him. They kept up their infinitely slow dance, their shifting legs intertwined by proximity and their anchoring arms grasping each other ardently. There was no rush, no urgency.

Hushing his keen cock down with his strength of will, Rain slipped into Matt's closeness, stepped into his body, and dipped into his embrace. Lingering as though they had all the time in the world, they shuffled their feet around in a dance, holding each other near. And for however brief a time, nothing and no one existed in the world but them.

Chapter
*N*ine

"WHY did you bring me here?" No gentle teasing, no terms of endearment, no tonal emphases, and no emotional exaggerations. For once Rain was utterly and truly stunned, Matt could tell, and he grinned mischievously.

Glancing around, Matt looked at the dimly lit, sparsely decorated public dance hall where soft moody jazz played through the discreetly placed speakers and people of all sexual persuasions had commandeered the dance floor in pairs. Fortunately the space looked more like a nightclub than a college gym. This spot, The Quick Step, was one of the places where they'd gone dancing on their dates, and tonight—three days after Charlotte and Mitchell had taken up residence at the loft—it held an air of comfortable familiarity.

"You brought me here to remind me of what I can't do anymore?" Rain's shaky voice was more sad than angry. He never used loving nicknames or lilting tonal changes when he was too confused or depressed to argue properly, and Matt rushed in to explain.

"No, baby. I brought you here for two reasons." Slowly Matt wrapped his arms around his lover's waist from behind and securely and steadfastly held Rain to him. "We're here to show you what you're struggling toward and will be able to do again in the not-too-distant future."

For a moment Rain said nothing, as if actually going over what Matt had said. Then he said, "What's the other thing?"

At that Matt chuckled low and pulled away to turn Rain around to face him. "Look at my feet." Whatever sadness, frustration, or anger had been there on Rain's beautiful face vanished in an instant when he stared down at Matt's cowboy boots, too surprised for words. "The other reason is that we're here to dance."

Rain had an expression that promised a swift and stormy confrontation, but then he just shook his head, baffled. "What on earth does that have to do with your feet... dumpling?" And right then, when Rain resorted to an endearment, Matt knew that whatever temper tantrum Rain had been about to have was no longer imminent.

"I'm wearing my cowboy boots. The ones Mitch gave me for my birthday. They're hard and sturdy and can take the weight of a bull if need be, so—"

"You're comparing me to a bull, gumdrop?" Rain said, his head tilting to the side and his red-golden curls dancing in the air, and he cocked his hip to one side in a defiant, flaming manner, daring Matt to retort. "I do *not* weigh—"

"I never said that, love," Matt quickly stepped in to deny any and all accusations and was overjoyed that Rain understood where he was going with this. "I merely said—"

"Yes, yes, heartthrob. I heard you the first time." Rain dismissed him with a theatrical wave of his hand and, holding his breath, glanced around as if disinterested, but Matt knew better. With a tiny cough and a dramatic pause for effect, Rain suddenly looked at Matt with a feigned bashful expression from under his long well-done lashes. "So, lovey, are we going to dance or what?"

Rain gasped when, without warning, Matt grabbed his waist tight and yanked him close boldly, and Matt whispered temptingly in his lover's ear, "Oh, we're going to dance, all right. And after... I have a surprise for you."

Rain responded to the low teasing tone like a raging bull to a waving cloth, and those green eyes glimmered as his lips pursed in feverish anticipation. "*Do tell*, muffin." He tried to coax Matt into revealing the surprise with a sweet smile and batting gold-tipped blood-red lashes, bursting with barely held back curiosity.

Matt laughed. "Nuh-uh, no peeking. Now...." Winding his right arm behind Rain's back and holding out his left for Rain to take, Matt nudged his lover's feet with his own gently. With a shy smile and blushing cheeks, Rain stepped on top of Matt's cowboy boot-covered feet with his own high-heeled leather ankle boots, as if he were a child being taught to dance by a parent. He rested his left hand on Matt's shoulder and took Matt's offered hand with his own right hand.

Despite his willowy height and sinewy musculature, Rain didn't weigh much at all, and he kept to his toes over Matt's boots. It was effortless for Matt to keep Rain in his arms. In his slim dark-red leather pants and a bustier of the same shade with gold trimmings and with a see-through long-sleeved shirt underneath it, Rain was definitely not underdressed. Next to him, in his formal gray slacks and blue button-down shirt, all spick and span, shower-cleaned and shaven, Matt felt way overdressed in a classy yet stiff-upper-lip sort of way. Nonetheless, he didn't let their clashing styles of attire separate them.

As the musical piece changed from a jazzy score to a leisurely pop song, Matt began to move in place, swaying gently like a bendy reed in the soft summer breeze, but mostly just moving around in place, shuffling his feet about. Rain in his arms felt too good to be true. Matt could feel how careful Rain was with his leg, timid and cautious, but also how he let himself go in the moment and allowed himself to be held by his lover.

Rain let go of Matt's hand and wound both of his arms around Matt's shoulders, burying his face in Matt's neck, cuddling. Sliding his arms up and down Rain's long lean back, Matt soothed his lover's aches and gave him all the comfort, support, and love he could muster. Matt was so excited about dancing with Rain again that his hands, which longed to touch Rain everywhere at once, trembled anxiously. Without a shadow of a doubt, Matt knew he could've looked at Rain the whole evening, the following night, and on until infinity. He was almost scared to blink and miss out on a curved smile, a wink from those pale-green eyes, a reddening of cheeks, or a lick of those plump lips waiting to be kissed. In his heart, Matt wondered if standing so close, Rain could feel that power of love surging and flowing through him. Matt was at once elated and afraid of the answer.

Then Rain began to sing softly along to the jazzy Alison Moyet tune that followed. So inaudible was his voice that Matt doubted it carried beyond the cocoon of intimacy they shared.

"It's that old devil called love again. Gets behind me and keeps giving me that shove again.

Putting rain in my eyes, tears in my dreams, and rocks in my heart."

Matt closed his eyes, letting the wave of pleasurable auditory sensations wash over him and drown him in a sea of contentment, delight, and love. Rain's voice was almost back to full strength, and that made Matt happy. Never growing tired of Rain's beautiful voice, so revealing in its nakedness yet so empowering in its hopefulness, Matt wondered if his life would ever feel complete without Rain in it in any capacity. At that moment Matt became fully cognizant of the fact that he was totally, completely, and utterly in love with Rain.

Matt wanted to kiss Rain more than he'd ever wanted anything in his life. Rain's sweet embrace and matching delicious husky tone caused Matt's arms to tighten around his lover in a fit of possessive passion. He was so intent that he didn't even realize it until he heard a smothered gasp as a puff of air against his ear and cheek. Quickly he loosened his hold on his lover.

"Sorry, babe, I kind of lost myself there for a moment," Matt apologized, embarrassed.

Surprisingly Rain chuckled against his neck—and tightened his own hold of Matt until it was Matt who was panting. "That's how I want you, lovey. Losing your precious self-control and surrendering to your passion." Emphasizing his meaning with a lascivious lick over the sensitive spot below Matt's ear, Rain pressed his groin and his now obvious erection against Matt's belly and ground down so hard that Matt's cock filled with red-hot blood so fast his head was left spinning, as all the blood there seemed to be rushing south to join the party.

"Careful, babe," Matt whispered, not daring to use the full force of his voice with the certain knowledge that a commanding, self-assured tone wouldn't fool Rain for two seconds. "Because I will allow you to make a spectacle of yourself this time, you sly hussy, and if you taunt me, I will make love to you right where we stand—even in front of all these people."

Rain's hips stilled and the sharp gasp that followed told Matt all he needed to know. No matter how flashy Rain could be, doing *it* on a dance floor amongst a crowd of strangers might be a bit too outrageous. "Y-you don't mean that, darling...." Clearly unsure of whether Matt's threat was a genuine one, Rain stammered, and Matt chuckled low, teasing.

"Don't test me, babe," he cooed in reply. "I dare you, Rain. I won't be bashful or show restraint this time. This isn't an empty threat." Directing his words straight to Rain's blushing ear, Matt spurred him on with a whisper. "Just... you... try... me." And surprising even himself, Matt knew he meant what he said. If Rain pushed him, Matt would allow himself to be provoked. He craved his lover more than he'd ever thought possible, and holding him in his arms was such sweet agony—more than foreplay, to be sure.

FOR a second Rain entertained the notion of Matt having his way with him in the dusky dance hall amidst a flurry of people, all minding their own business. It was a tantalizing and arousing prospect, he had to admit, and felt his cock hardening in his pants, which were his loosest pair but still too tight to make an erection a welcome guest.

But still... some propriety had to be maintained, right?

Lowering his left hand to his side and interlacing his fingers with Matt's, Rain rested his forehead on Matt's and smiled. "You're feeling particularly energetic and bubbling with delicious and creative ideas today, darling."

Matt smiled back, holding Rain tighter again. "You ain't seen nothing yet, babe," he drawled seductively and kissed Rain on the lips. At first the touch, though intimate, was just the pressure of soft, warm flesh against soft, warm flesh, firm and tender. But then Matt parted the seam of Rain's lips, a breath of coffee-flavored hot air fanning into

Rain's mouth and against his face, and upon the brush of a tip of a tongue, the kiss turned insistent, urgent, demanding, and passionate to the point of oral sex.

After what felt like an eternity and a single heartbeat, Matt pulled back a little, his moist, swollen red lips a mere inch away from Rain's.

"I do love these sugary lips of yours, lovey," Rain murmured, panting, and, with his fingertips, traced the curve of Matt's lower lip and the double curve of Matt's Cupid's bow before licking the same circuit with the tip of his tongue, catching Matt's lower lip between his teeth, and nibbling gently. Rain loved the way Matt's lips weren't too thin or too full but just right for Rain, just like the bear's porridge for Goldilocks, and the fact that those same lips could utter sweet vows of love and could smile brighter than the sun made Rain's knees buckle and tremble like a jellyfish.

He couldn't stand this torment for much longer. Abruptly he pulled away and stepped back off of Matt's cowboy boots to give himself some breathing room. He inhaled and exhaled several times to catch his strained breath. "A pox upon thee...," he mumbled quietly, not directing his words specifically to either himself or Matt but to the general way of the world.

In front of him, Matt chuckled amusedly. "I hope that cuss isn't aimed at me...."

"All right, precious, enough of this riling," Rain huffed, indignant, accentuating the final S of the endearment with a fierce hiss akin to that of a venomous serpent. "We've tiptoed far too long around the issue at hand already—literally and figuratively. What's the surprise, then, lovey?"

The surreptitious look gleaming in Matt's blue eyes forebode something wicked and exciting, and Rain could barely hold still, biting his lower lip in a fit of nervousness. "Follow me, babe, and I'll show you a world filled with music, dance, romance, and love—and a few teases to boot."

Now that was a promise that caught not only Rain's undivided attention but his breath in his throat too.

"OH MY God, how this takes me back...," Rain murmured in amusement, leaning back to snuggle more comfortably in the nook of Matt's arm, watching the musical playing out on the big screen through the windshield of Matt's Toyota Prius at the local drive-in movie theater, which wasn't exactly packed with people. There were only a few cars on the lot aside from them.

"Yeah, we're definitely going to end up in the back sooner or later, pumpkin. Don't you worry about that," Matt whispered stimulatingly in Rain's ear, earning a low purr and a contented giggle from Rain's plump pursed lips.

Resting his head on Matt's shoulder with his arm stretched out behind him, Rain shook his head slightly in gleeful bafflement. "How did you find out this movie was playing here?" With heady anticipation, Rain waited for his favorite scene in *Singing in the Rain*, the legendary musical comedy from Hollywood's golden era of musicals. The movie starred Gene Kelly, Debbie Reynolds, Donald O'Connor, and Jean Hagen.

"This year is the sixtieth anniversary of the movie," Matt replied. "I knew it's one of your all-time favorites, so I did a little digging—and persuading."

Rain's wide-eyed gaze shot toward Matt in a blink of an eye, and he couldn't believe what he was hearing. His heart pounded frantically in his chest. "You... you convinced this drive-in to show this movie... tonight... for our date?"

As Matt grinned from ear to ear, his blue eyes shone brightly. "I did, babe. Just for you."

All of a sudden, Rain couldn't breathe past the boulder-sized emotional lump lodged in his throat, and he had to blink fiercely to dissuade the tears from flowing. "Oh, darling... no one has ever done anything like that for me." He held his hand dramatically over the violently thumping heart in his chest, his voice cracking with impressed affection.

Matt shrugged casually, as if carefree. "Their loss—my gain."

Rain could barely hold back the teary hysterical laugh, and he glanced at the screen filled with Gene Kelly's magnetic good-willed presence and was enamored over both what he saw and what he felt—for Matt. "Oh, look at those tight buns…."

Matt sniggered, and Rain had a feeling his dreamy tone of voice was the cause. "Hey, I dare you to find someone with a more trim backside than Gene Kelly's, precious. Oh, to have those strong thighs and hard calves wrapped around my waist, or me bouncing up and down on those scrumptious buns—"

"Watch it, babe," Matt cut in, and Rain loved how Matt could be jealous over a film star who was no longer among them in the land of the living. Correcting his position on the seat by straightening up, Matt suddenly nodded eagerly toward the silver screen. "Hey, your scene's coming up."

Rain cuddled back against Matt's side, taking his lover's arm and wrapping it around himself, the weight and the warmth comforting beyond words, as he watched Gene Kelly sing in the rainstorm and dance and muck about in puddles, all the while with that insanely happy smile plastered all over his in-love face.

"I'm singing in the rain, just singing in the rain.

What a glorious feeling, I'm happy again."

"Singing *in* the rain…," Rain murmured and then hummed along to the musical piece with Gene Kelly until his voice began to tire a bit and grow raspy. "Do you think there might be a euphemism or a double meaning buried in there somewhere?"

Matt laughed wholeheartedly—and impishly. "For the two of us, absolutely." Glancing at Rain, Matt stuck out his tongue between his teeth and wiggled his eyebrows, and Rain burst into laughter too, shaking all over—and more when Matt's hands began to roam and tickle their way all over his extremely ticklish body.

Tears of joy dripping down his cheeks, Rain exclaimed shrilly, "Hey, you big oaf, I want to see this!"

"You can see *me* now," Matt replied smugly, pulling Rain into his arms and kissing the breath out of him.

Swinging his legs over Matt's thighs, Rain allowed Matt to angle him into his lap so he was sitting in between Matt's spread legs, and let the familiar scent, taste, and feel of his lover fill him up to the brim until his heart overflowed with the intensity of it.

When Matt finally released Rain's lips, his head was dancing and everything blurred in his field of vision. Only Matt's glowing blue eyes were crystal clear—as was the arrogant grin tugging at the corners of his mouth. "Oh, you...." Rain began to chuff, but when Matt's strong palm rested gently on the small of his back, smoothing out the tension and the kinks there, Rain couldn't stay even playfully mad at his lover. Caressing Matt's cinnamon-colored stubbly chin with his fingertips, Rain rubbed his nose gently across his lover's warm cheek, smelling his woodsy aftershave. "You kind of remind me of Gene Kelly...."

Matt chuckled low and shook his head, bemused. "How, exactly? With my suave grace on the dance floor or my award-winning singing voice in the shower?" he said in a self-deprecating, humorous manner, quirking an eyebrow.

Rain frowned. "Sometimes your belittling sense of humor leaves much to be desired, honey, as does your self-confidence."

Matt shrugged. "I guess I need you around to hone my deteriorating skill set and boost my self-esteem." But then there was a sheepish hint of a smile and a flush of cheeks, and Rain knew Matt was giving him a run for his money.

"Oh, that teasing tongue of yours is going to get twisted into a knot one of these days," Rain incited, trying to catch the slick tip of Matt's tongue with his fingers and failing.

"Are you gonna give me my comeuppance, babe?" Matt goaded with a grin.

Behind his hand, Rain giggled with feigned girlish bashfulness. "We'll see what comes up as the night progresses... darling," he murmured low and sexy and kissed Matt's jawline with serious intent, nibbling and suckling softly. "And if things get too heated, I'll be sure to blow on all your boo-boos and kiss them better."

Laughing, Matt shook his head and said, "Poppycock."

With a fake hurt huff, Rain slapped Matt's arm playfully. "For your sake, buns of fun, I do hope that *is* a reference to my addictively delicious love stick—"

Chuckling, Matt interjected, "What did you expect it to be, babe? A slanderous remark on your Southern heritage? When both your accent *and* your dick are, in fact, as sweet as molasses and as right as rain? I reiterate… poppycock."

"That seems to be becoming your favorite word du jour." Rain smiled contentedly.

Matt looked Rain in the eye with a deliberately provocative gleam. "Company is as company does, sweetheart."

"Smartass." Rain snickered and snaked his arms around Matt's neck, covering his lover's mouth with his own, kissing Matt until he felt his toes curl, his heart flutter, and his body crave his lover more than air itself. Finally he pulled back, panting, and he saw Matt's blue eyes darkened with lust. "Matt. Backseat. Now."

Matt might have been able to angle himself effortlessly into the backseat, but due to his leg, Rain had to climb out of the car to get in the back. But the moment Rain slid in and closed the car door, Matt attacked him, snatched him by the waistband of his pants, and jerked him forward to again sit in his lover's lap, only this time straddling his lover with his backside firmly planted against Matt's bulging groin.

"I told you we'd end up in the backseat making out," Matt laughed.

Rain chimed in happily, reminiscing about their very first date. "You did, honeybun."

When Rain began to wrap his long legs around Matt's waist, Matt's hand stilled his movement. "How's the leg?" That was the last thing Rain wanted to hear, and his body and mind both tensed in response. But all of that melted away when Matt chuckled low and intense and said, "Just ascertaining what positions I can twist you in, baby."

That seductive tone undid Rain, and he smiled tentatively at his lover. "I'll tell you if something's amiss with my silly little flesh wound, cupcake, will that do?" From the quick flash of Matt's narrowing eyes, Rain knew Matt wasn't overly fond of his dismissive tone concerning his injuries, but from the way Matt drew him closer, Rain knew his lover was going to let that one slide. Rain was glad about that because he didn't want Matt mad at him—not now, when a sense of profound intimacy was closing around them in a soft, warm cocoon of lovemaking. Not once since the hospital had Matt accused Rain of keeping his life-threatening secret, and even when he had mentioned it in casual conversation, he had never raised his voice. A part of Rain did want Matt to express his anger—even at the risk of hurting more than Rain's feelings. Just not right now. "My flesh is aching, Matt... I'm aching to be with you," he whispered and got a comforting lopsided grin from Matt in return.

"Oh, babe, you feel too good for words," Matt mumbled, leaning over Rain's body and burying his face in Rain's red-golden curls, which smelled like forest fruits due to his shampoo. Matt's lips attached themselves to the soft white skin of Rain's neck and suckled gently, the tip of his tongue teasing along the jugular vein, up and down, with occasional tiny love bites from his teeth. With that kind of attention being shown to him, Rain trembled all over, loving how Matt could touch him anywhere, even in the silliest of places, and get him so turned on he felt like his cock was about to take flight.

"Or too good for lyrics." Rain giggled amusedly, tilting his head and arching his back to give his lover greater access to his sensitive skin. And Matt took complete advantage, advancing on his neck like he was running into fierce battle, opening his mouth wider to encompass more ground. "Oh, muffin, that feels so good...."

"Mmm..." was the only sound emerging from Matt, who planted his hands on the arching small of Rain's back. Matt lifted Rain tighter against him, sliding his mouth lower to lick the little hollow of Rain's throat. The tip of Matt's tongue tested Rain's tolerance to the breaking point until he was panting so hard in his light-headedness he thought for a second he might actually faint.

"Listen, dove, I was thinking—"

Matt's head popped up lightning fast. "*Now?*"

The shocked expression on his face made Rain chortle. "What's wrong with now?"

Shaking his head emphatically, Matt growled, dissatisfied. "If you can still think, I must be doing this wrong."

Rain smiled tenderly. "You're doing it just right, hot stuff. Trust me." Matt's narrowing eyes flashed suspiciously, so Rain grabbed the man by the sides of his face, dragged his face down, and ground his mouth over his so hard that their dueling tongues could've done each other serious harm if Matt hadn't cautiously pulled back with a relieved grin.

"Good to hear, baby," Matt whispered huskily against Rain's mouth, their lips brushing in passing as he spoke, and Rain tasted the cappuccino Matt had drunk before. "So, what were you thinking?"

As Rain was about to answer, his voice died in his constricting throat when Matt tugged at the gold-colored silk laces holding his bustier together until they became loose and his hands were able to slip underneath to caress Rain's soft skin and sinewy stem. His heart pounding like a drum in his throat, Rain gasped, and as he wiggled, Matt's hands slid deeper beneath Rain's clothes, stroking his flanks and every inch of skin with the single-minded determination of distracting Rain from whatever he'd been about to say.

While Matt was busy feeling him up all over, Rain tried to squirm free of the clothes that had seemed to fit him so well a moment ago but were now too hot, too tight, too everything. Rain longed to lie nude in his lover's arms, and his whisper broke free. "Matt, please...."

Without a pause in his fondling, Matt liberated Rain from his decorative corset and the silk shirt beneath it and surrounded him with his arms, following the trail his fingertips had made over Rain's skin with his lips until he reached a rose-red nub of tender flesh and sucked the nipple like his life depended on it. A shudder ran through Rain's body, just under his skin, like little lighting jolts, firing him inside out, and he saw flashing stars behind the black curtain of his closed eyelids. Whatever Matt was doing to him affected Rain beyond his body until his heart was singing a sweet symphony of sex and love.

Suddenly Matt stopped everything, the caress of his lips and the touch of his hands, and sat up, giving Rain chills when the warm weight was lifted from his torso. Steaming, Rain was about to argue the case in point when he saw the look on Matt's face, and he swallowed nervously. Never had he seen Matt's face so tense and so relaxed at once. His blue eyes glowed dark with lust, and there was adoration, reverence, passion, and obsession, all potent and raging.

"Matt...?" Rain whispered anxiously, swallowing again.

Matt moved so hastily Rain cried out when Matt's mouth fastened around his throat, where his Adam's apple was bobbing frantically, and licked and bit a wet line down to his left nipple and sucked so hard—with sharp grazing teeth—that Rain's brain exploded in fireworks. He'd never been crazy about his nipples being touched, as it was just another way of pleasuring, but with Matt, every reaction was intensified beyond comprehension.

His lover's drastic need awoke the music within him again, which had thus far been only a low background hum, but now arose to do him in with the sweet guitar melody of Poets of the Fall.

"Do you breathe the name of your savior in your hour of need?

Come feed the rain 'cause I'm thirsty for your love, dancing underneath the skies of lust."

Just like in the song, Rain's lust grew and built until he couldn't stay in place and he writhed under Matt's ardent assault, feeling clearly how Matt's feverishly hot hands fumbled with the buttons of his pants, ripping them open so that Rain's erection sprang up, eagerly reaching for his lover and lapping up his attention.

But when Rain's weeping, wanton organ finally stood erect before him, Matt's hands moved away again, touching Rain's distinct ribs under his alabaster skin and caressing the winglike hipbones framing his totally flat, smooth stomach without an apparent six-pack but that held a dense inner strength nonetheless.

"You're so beautiful it kills me," Matt said suddenly, drawing Rain right out of his heady haze. "Since the very first moment I laid eyes on you, it's been like that. Like I can't get enough of you no matter how many times we make love or how often we spend time together. When you're not with me, I still see your infinite beauty with my mind's eye, and you take my breath away and make my heart miss a beat."

"Oh, darling…," Rain murmured, shivering. In that moment Rain truly believed that if he loved Matt any more, he would float away high up into the stratosphere and beyond with the levity and light of that emotion.

After shifting Rain beneath him, Matt hovered above Rain with his arms extended straight by his flanks. "Even when you were broken, there was a fire burning within you, and I was drawn to your flame like a moth—and I didn't care if you burned me to cinders as long as I got to spend my last moments with you."

Though he knew Matt had never lied to him, Rain also knew he'd never heard Matt speak so earnestly from the depth of his heart, for this was the voice of pervading emotions, sizzling flesh, red-hot blood, and sexual need—all pounding away to a primitive beat matched with that of a human heart. This was the music of his lover that Rain had grown to crave, yearn for, and love more than life itself.

"You found me at my most desperate hour, Matt," Rain said, hushed, threading his long fingers through his lover's thick sandy-brown hair. "With you I feel like no disaster can destroy me because you are there for me. You make me so happy…."

Lowering himself to rest on his elbows, Matt lay on top of Rain, chest to chest, heartbeat to heartbeat, hot cock to hot cock, and his face was serious but calm rather than stern. "I want to be here for you, Rain, whenever and however you need me—and to give you space should you want it."

"Matt—"

"I know I crowd you at times—"

"No, I'm over it, Matt. Because you gave me back my music. The other night, for the first time in what felt like ages, I was able to let the music out. Not with my singing voice or my dancing feet but through the notes of my piano. You gave me that." Rain stopped further interruptions from Matt by pressing his index finger gently over his lips, caressing the lower lip lovingly. "Oh, Matt…." Rain wound his arms around Matt's shoulders and craned his neck to reach his lover's lips, so perfectly shaped for him, so rich in the flavor of coffee mixed with his natural zest. "Sometimes I'm so afraid you'll leave me...."

Matt's head popped up again fast. "Never!"

"That you'll grow tired of my impatience and flashiness, and—"

"No, Rain," Mat declared, shaking his head furiously. "If ever I have given you cause to believe that... it's not for the reasons you think." As Matt leaned over Rain again, his hot breath mixed with Rain's own, he inhaled his lover's scent until it filled his lungs. "I adore you, Rain," Matt sighed into Rain's mouth. "Just the way you are, baby. I want you safe, yes, but I trust you to keep *yourself* safe—and ask for a helping hand or a shoulder to cry on if and when you need them. I need to let go of *my* fears when it comes to you—and I think I'm halfway there. Not all the way, babe, but soon."

Rain smiled warmly and nuzzled Matt's neck. "My brave hero," he cooed.

"Are you never afraid?" Matt asked, kissing Rain's soft cheek and smooth jawline, all the while searching for something from the space underneath the front seats with his left hand. The digging-in position caused the warm, heavy press of Matt's erect cock to poke against Rain's thigh, and for Rain it was a turn-on of galactic proportions to know he aroused his lover so.

"Of what *might* be instead of what is? No," Rain replied stoically. "As I said, there's only one fear I have—and that is losing you. That I could not bear."

"Lucky for you I've got no pressing engagements elsewhere—only the one lying underneath me right now," Matt teased and nibbled on Rain's earlobe until Rain felt as if the soft suction there had suddenly shifted to his groin—as if Matt had been sucking on his cock instead of his ear. As though there was an invisible tenuous line connecting the two sensitive physical spots with a live wire. "There's no need to talk about this any further, babe—and there are other and far more pressing needs to attend to, don't you think?"

"I—I can't think...," Rain mumbled vaguely, the rush of hot blood forcing his cock to stand upright, to leave a wet kiss on Matt's hand as it caressed Rain's belly. Matt's presence was rousing his dick to play—even though his leg throbbed, like his cock, both in a similar state, borderline pleasure and pain.

"Good...," Matt murmured with a grin and backed away again, leaving Rain cold without his lover's warmth. Rain was about to protest the cool treatment when Matt placed a light-green tin can on his bare stomach, the cold metal giving his hot, sweaty skin goose bumps, and all Rain could do was stare at the curious thing, frowning with a silent query. His lover was up to something... but what? "One hundred percent natural ingredients, this," Matt promised. "And the flavor is just up your alley, pardon the pun. See?"

Rain took the can and read over the description. "Lubricant. Warming massage oil. Watermelon-flavored. Sugar-free." Looking up in surprise, Rain gasped, "Edible body lotion?"

Matt chuckled, beginning to unbutton his blue shirt, licking his lips salaciously. "Of course. It'll get warm as we get warm, and it'll taste... well, tasty—either like you *for* me or what you like *on* me. Good outcome in both cases, don't you think?"

Blinking, Rain tried to wrap his brain around what Matt was offering him, and his imagination ignited like someone had thrown gasoline on the fire. "H-how do you want me...?"

Matt shook his head with a sly smile. "Oh, no, babe. You tell me what you want and we'll do that—within reason, that is. We'll be mindful of your leg."

At that, Rain had to really think. What did he want? Rain knew he wanted Matt and all that came with him—but how? In what position? And to what extent? With too many possibilities wracking his brain, Rain uttered the first thing that sprang to mind. "I—I want you to eat me up, lovey."

Matt grinned wickedly. "With pleasure, baby."

After rapidly divesting both himself and Rain of their remaining clothes, socks, and shoes, Matt shifted to kneel between Rain's outstretched legs. He pushed Rain's knees up against his chest, being mindful of his lover's injured left leg, which he held almost reverently over his own shoulder, gently caressing the area around the white bandage. That balmy thoughtfulness was like a sweet symphony in

Rain's ears, and he closed his eyes, relishing the intimate touch of his lover.

A very intimate touch indeed.

The darting tip of Matt's tongue encircled the rim of Rain's anus, flicking over the snug shivering hole in a playful and relaxing way, coaxing the tight ring of muscle to open up. Rain panted and his hips snapped up, but Matt tenderly pressed him back against the bench back seat—and then cupped the snow-white globes of his ass and lifted his hips up, almost folding Rain in half, all the better to devour him.

"Easy, baby," Matt murmured with a smile Rain could feel. "You asked me to eat you up, didn't you?" Rain almost protested that he'd been referring to his cock instead of this tongue bath of his ass. But then that warm, slick tongue licked around his hole and those luscious lips suckled his opening, granting him a lewd kiss, and Rain forgot what he was about to protest—and why on earth he should bother to at all.

"Yes….," he whispered inaudibly. "More…."

"I love how smooth and hairless you are," Matt huffed appreciatively, biting the soft yet firm white skin of Rain's buttocks in between determined licking and fierce suckling. "I love your rosy little hole and how it's calling out to me like a siren's song. Your song, Rain."

Certain that what was left of his mushy brain would short-circuit right then and there, Rain moaned when Matt ran his tongue up his silky crease to lap and suck his balls. The licking was one thing, but the intense suction brought Rain to tears, and his hands moved up to grab the door handle and the side of the passenger seat. He was unsure whether he wanted to drag himself away from the lusty invasion or push himself closer until he'd disappear into Matt's hungry mouth whole.

"Jesus, Matt…."

The vibrations of Matt's chuckle against Rain's achingly hard cock caused alternating hot flashes and chilly goose bumps in Rain. He shook and jolted when his lover's left hand smoothed his thigh while his right hand cupped his balls and jangled them in his fingers. Matt's mouth reattached itself to the rim of his hole and suckled vigorously. Then Matt's jabbing tongue penetrated Rain's loosened hole and entered him, and what had been stars in Rain's field of vision turned to dancing and exploding fiery stardust. Rain shuddered from his red-golden curls-covered head to his painted toes.

Rain reached for his erect cock with the serious intention of addressing his acute need with the spit-wetted palm of his hand, but Matt grabbed his hand and pushed it aside. Shaking his head, slightly vexed, Rain remarked, "You're being terribly overbearing tonight, darling, if you don't mind me saying—"

With a growl, Matt locked his mouth over Rain's opening and sucked—hard—and then began to torment him with licks and jabs until Rain was sure he'd come from this alone, without a single touch on his cock or any deeper penetration.

Only… Matt's tongue wasn't finished by a long shot, and he kept pushing his tongue in deeper, over and over again, until Rain was writhing and whimpering like a wanton love slave.

"So, babe, what was it you were thinking of, hmm…?"

Even with his mind erased by red mist and his senses overtaken by his lover's seductive advances, Rain could distinctly hear the baiting, and his blood roared in a mix of lust and fury. "Why you… flippant imp…," he huffed, indignant—and proud of the humorous banter Matt chose to unleash on Rain, who wasn't yet in perfect health. That gesture, more than anything, affirmed Rain's belief that everything would be all right—with Matt, with Rain, and in general.

Chuckling, Matt moved his lips in a series of soft teasing kisses until he reached Rain's balls, licked his way past them to his cock, and blew a gust of warm air on the sensitive organ. Matt surrounded the tip of Rain's cock with his mouth, suckling only the silky, spongy head until Rain believed he might actually die from too much pleasure. It wasn't the physical contact that undid him but the emotional connection he felt they shared, and Rain's heart jumped.

"Who's teasing who, baby?" Matt murmured low, still needling. "Aren't you going to tell me what was on your mind?"

A curse on that lover of mine. "You're… being… so… cruel."

Tracing endless circles on the ridge of Rain's crown with the tip of his tongue, Matt chuckled and then withdrew, getting up to sit on his heels, his head brushing against the roof of the car. "You refuse to tell me what you're thinking—and *I'm* cruel?" Matt said suddenly, his palm resting on Rain's belly, not really pressing down but not feathery light either.

Raising himself up on his elbows, Rain shook his head, baffled—and more than a little fuming. "Do you really want to have this conversation right now?" Matt's grin told Rain plainly that he'd heard the unspoken nickname buried beneath the furious sea. "Fine," he said, huffing and feeling almost outraged. "I was thinking that you're a mean bully and a self-satisfied ass—"

Matt laughed. "No, baby. It's *your* ass that's on the table at the moment—"

"Not anymore, you loathsome hoodlum!" Rain said, sulking, and tried to lower his legs from his lover's shoulders and wiggle his way up to a sitting position and then out of the car.

Laughing still, Matt grabbed Rain's hips, drew him closer, then moved on to seize his wrists and pushed them above his head. Unafraid that Matt would hurt him, Rain squirmed to shake loose, but Matt's hold and weight kept him confined. "Baby… stop twisting, or I'll have to restrain you permanently."

Rain was two seconds away from shouting. "Matt—"

Matt bent down and kissed him, and on his lips and tongue Rain tasted the musky scent of arousal and the masculine smell of himself. When Matt pulled back, Rain saw how dark Matt's eyes were, his pupils dilated and glowing with lust. "You tease me, Rain." Rain was about to point out that he wasn't, honestly, but his intentions were cut short when Matt shook his head to stop him, and his hardening jawline gave Rain shivers. "You tease me every single second of every achingly long day. I wait all day to be with you. It's nearly unbearable."

Rain's breath hitched in his throat, and as his heart leapt at the words of his lover, he was a little bit scared at the intensity of it all. "Matt—"

Snatching the can of watermelon-flavored lubricant, Matt kissed Rain again. This time his tongue slithered its way into Rain's mouth with a hunger Rain had never experienced with Matt, whose lovemaking was always saturated with adoration, worship, and reverence. This sudden shift overwhelmed Rain—and turned him on so much that he felt consumed by the flames of Matt's ravenous appetite.

And when Rain felt Matt's lube-smeared fingers testing the clenching snug opening into his body and breaching all resistance with ease, Rain melted. He fell back onto the seat, relaxed and wanting, his legs splaying as open as his heart for Matt's entry.

"I love it when you tease me," Matt murmured on his way down from Rain's lips to his jaw, neck, collarbone, chest, ribs, belly, groin.... "And I can't stand it. You drive me crazy when I'm not with you—and when I'm with you."

The joy that bubbled within Rain's chest came out in hoarse, breathless giggles. "Oh, how I love your sugar lips, honey."

"Is that what you were thinking?" Matt's lips reached Rain's cock and took it in all the way to the root, moist wet heat and slow suction covering every inch of him.

"No...." Rain shook his head, his eyes closed and his body trembling with desire. "I was wondering... what it was that you... liked about me when we first met... and what you were attracted to about me...."

"That's it?" Matt came up again, licking his swollen lips that, to Rain, looked like ripe, juicy apples, and he was dying to taste them, to lick, to nibble, to suck, to cover entirely and own for an eternity. "Don't you know the answer by now?" Suddenly Rain felt his cheeks flush with heat—and not with arousal so much as with embarrassment. And from his hovering perch, Matt could see it all, that much Rain knew. "Rain...?"

Never ashamed of who he was, Rain was, however, sometimes embarrassed over the many ways in which his relationships, both the social and the sexual kind, had gone awry. As reluctant to reminisce on those bad memories as he was, Rain knew he could confide in Matt. "The guys I've been with... some want sex, some want a show, some….” Hesitating, he searched for words. “There is always the question. Do they prefer me as a man… or as a woman.”

From Matt's severe blinking and fisting hands, Rain could tell this topic was angering his lover—but he was surprised to hear Matt say, “You're *not* a woman. You're a man who loves women's clothes. I'm *not* with a woman when I'm with you. I'm with *you*, Rain. Only with you.” After bowing his head again for a soft kiss, Matt said, “I prefer you as you are, baby. Any way you want. I adore you, Rain.”

And just like that, the unsettling knot in Rain's stomach unwound. The strange coveting need of Matt's also seemed to dissipate. What was left was love made manifest as Matt smiled tenderly and held Rain in his arms, and there was no pain in Rain's leg when he reciprocated and wound his arms and legs around his lover's short, stout frame. And what burned inside of him when Matt's lubed-up cock entered him was his heart, and he cried out amidst the ravages of pleasure.

The scent of fresh sweat and heating watermelon filled Rain's nostrils when Matt covered him with his body, slowly pushing into him, filling him with sex and love. Matt's hands ran up Rain's thighs before settling beside him on the seat for leverage. Matt's mouth ran a wet line from Rain's nipple up to his neck, where he sank his teeth in possessively and kissed the sharp sting away.

“Oh God, Matt…,” Rain moaned.

“Thanks for the compliment, babe,” Matt mumbled into his wet skin, the warm breath giving Rain shivers, and he could feel Matt's smile against his skin and feel his laughter in the way he breathed in gasps.

“More, Matt,” Rain was able to say between harsh pants as the hard, strong repetitive motions of Matt's cock penetrating and impaling him kept pushing the air out of his lungs time and again. “I'm dying to be yours. Always.”

Holding Rain's head between his arms, Matt kissed the breath out of him, moaning into the kiss, and all the while, he thrust in and out of Rain, who felt he might not only swoon but seriously pass out. With every cell in his body, Rain yearned to give his lover everything he had, and even more if Matt wanted it. Snaking his arms around Matt's neck,

Rain delved into the kiss, plunging his tongue deep and clinging to Matt fiercely to keep him exactly where he was, his fingers tangled in Matt's thick hair. They'd had sex before countless times, but this was too intense for him to ignore the implications.

"You're mine," Matt muttered into the kiss, and Rain agreed with a whimper. "Forever mine. All mine."

Rain wasn't about to argue the point, and he could only return his lover's maddeningly sweet kiss with equal or greater passion. Rain knew there was nothing he wouldn't do for Matt—in or out of bed—and whether he made a full recovery or not, whatever good came out of this situation would all be due to Matt's persistent love, compassion, and companionship.

Entwined around his lover, Rain let Matt set the pace because he knew his lover would see, listen, and feel what Rain wanted too, and Matt matched those qualities, styles, and preferences to a tee until they moved in perfect harmony. And pretty soon their movements settled into a rhythm, as Rain had expected, as the push and pull, shift and slide, and tug and thrust created a synchronized lovemaking of equals—regardless of who topped and who bottomed.

Flailing his hands frantically around, partly swiping the steamy windows of the car and partly digging his nails deep into Matt's broad muscular back, Rain felt the urgency of sexual climax begin to boil in his balls, which tightened to a near painful state of arousal. Matt's movements were hasty now too, and the only sounds echoing in the car were pants, gasps, and grunts, and the hiss and slap of skin on skin. Familiar noises of impending ecstatic release swamped Rain's consciousness, and he clung to Matt tighter, hearing only faintly his own keen cries of pleasure through the rush of blood deafening his ears.

"Honey… I'm so close.…" Rain groaned even as his hips began to snap involuntarily.

"Me too, babe," Matt uttered incoherently, and his thrusts increased in intensity, pace, and volume until he was pounding into Rain hard, fast, and deep—and Rain loved every microsecond of it.

"Matt, Matt…," Rain whispered over and over again, falling more in love with every breath he took, with every quickening frenzied heartbeat.

"Rain, I love you," Matt whispered in return—and that was all it took for Rain, whose pleasure peaked without him touching his cock once all night, and he came in beady creamy spurts between their writhing bodies. He'd never climaxed without applying some kind of pressure on his cock, but this was Matt, the man he loved, and Matt could do what no other man had ever done with or to Rain.

Nestled contentedly in his cocoon of love, joy, safety, and sex, Rain felt how rigid and still Matt suddenly became, having pushed all the way in, holding his stance and his breath. Even through the latex barrier of Matt's condom, Rain felt the red-hot splash within his constricting and twitching channel. It was proof positive that their bond had not been broken by Rain's behavior being all over the emotional map—and that the man Rain was head over heels in love with had found pleasure within him.

Finally Matt's quivering muscles caved in and he slumped on top of Rain, breathing heavily, his shaking body hot and sweaty, smelling of Matt, and Rain, and sex, and watermelons.

It was the best moment of Rain's life for a long, long time, and, holding his lover closer, he buried his cheeks, moist with a sheen of sweat and tears, against Matt's neck and wet hair.

He never gave a single thought to the possibility that someone in the other cars might have seen them or heard them—or might've run off to the manager of the drive-in and complained about the perverse indecency going on in a Toyota Prius. All he cared about was that the negative aspects of his recent past had been reduced to miniscule and irrelevant specks on the windshield as he and Matt drove off together toward a brighter and more positive future.

"Thank you, Matt," Rain croaked in a whisper, his emotions as bare and exposed as his body was in his lover's embrace and his voice as hazy as the windows of the car were steamy.

"You're very welcome, baby," Matt chuckled in his ear breathlessly, still recovering.

Somewhere in the background, the end credits of the movie started, and it was time for them to go before they got locked in the drive-in parking lot—or someone called the cops.

RAIN banged hard against the large windows of the loft as Matt leaned his hot forehead against the cool, smooth surface. No stars were visible behind the dark, puffy storm clouds that had rolled in soon after sunset.

Earlier, in bed, Rain had cuddled right into Matt's arms, getting comfortable and then falling fast asleep. It had felt good to have his lover back, Matt reminisced, enjoying the memory of that tender, intimate moment.

It was late now, after 2:00 a.m. After their dancing, film watching, and car-sex-filled date night, Matt was having trouble sleeping. Standing downstairs in the living room all by his lonesome to reflect suited him, and the rain outside matched his wistful mood.

"Hey, bro," a sleep-dozy mumble came from behind his back, accompanied by a loud yawn. "What are you doing up this late?" Mitchell leaned against the wooden frame of the tall window, raking his bed-tousled brown hair, his blue eyes glazed a bit.

"Or early," Matt clarified with a small grin.

"Yeah, whatever." Mitchell chuckled, staring longingly in the general direction of the kitchen, as if hoping that a huge pot of black coffee would magically appear if he wished for it hard enough.

"What's up, Mitch? You've been here for three days. Why the surprise visit?" It wasn't like Mitchell never did anything unexpected or wild, but he always kept Matt in the loop. "Is it Marian?" Mitchell's wife was, without much exaggeration, a saint of a woman. Any woman would have to be to live twenty-four-seven with Mitchell, whose very male and nearly bachelor way of life was never compromised or threatened by the existence or company of women—not even his wife, who'd been his high school sweetheart.

"What? Nah, Marian's fine." Mitchell waved a dismissive hand through the air, wrapping his woolly blanket around his bare beefy body tighter. "It's all you, bro." Mitchell gave Matt a poignant look. "You never take time off work, never a vacation or even a sick day. So naturally when we heard—belatedly by over a week, thank you very much—that you'd taken a whole week off to tend to a new boyfriend we'd never even heard about… Not to mention the fact that it took a personal visit by yours truly to learn that you and Rain have been together for over two and a half months. Hardly casual, that…."

Grumbling, Matt shook his head—but he wasn't really all that angry. "You guys can be such gossipmongers. It's none of your business what I do."

"Of course it's our business too, idiot. Don't be like that," Mitchell scolded, frowning. "We're your family, for God's sake. Not some band of strangers butting into your privacy." To emphasize his point, his brother elbowed him in the side, which Matt knew he had coming. His parents were good people, just like his brother. They knew who and what he was, and accepted him as such. "Intrusion" wasn't the word to use with them.

"I'm sorry, Mitch," Matt whispered, embarrassed, letting out a sigh. "I'm just… tired."

"Yeah," Mitchell chuckled. "I can imagine why, with that little firework of a spitfire in your bed."

"Jesus Christ, Mitch!" Matt slapped his brother on the arm hard enough to sting a regular person, but not enough to silence the laugh from his brawny big brother.

Mitchell just kept on laughing. "What? I admit that he surprised me, that little Rain of yours. But I do like him. He certainly knows who he is and what he wants. It's good to have goals and ambitions."

"You would think that, you lousy jock," Matt murmured.

"Well, you should have more of those too, unless you want to stay buried behind that crummy desk for the rest of eternity." Mitchell's voice may have sounded impassive, but Matt knew just how his brother felt about Matt doing work he had no passion for. Mitchell had had the good fortune of landing his dream job and making a huge success of it. He always said it was because of the inner drive that had steered him in the right direction, pushed him forward with vigor until he got what he wanted. Being one of the Denver Broncos had been a lifelong dream of his, and as proud as he was about it, his family— including Matt—was even more impressed about it. One of the reasons for it was that he remained down-to-earth through any and all ordeals, never giving in to the demands of fame and fortune to become high and mighty.

"My work again?" This was becoming a familiar topic with Matt's family, ever since he had hit the big three-oh two years ago. "It might interest you to know that I'm up for a promotion." It was true. What Matt left out was that he wasn't the only one competing for this coveted managerial position. He was up against some heavy hitters on this one—and one of them was Goodman, his arch nemesis in the gray-cream-white workplace.

"Well, hurrah, brother." Mitchell smirked. "Only took you, what, ten, eleven years to get there?"

"If all you want to do is to depress me, you can just get lost," Matt growled. "I like my job. I always have."

"I know."

Matt turned to stare at Mitchell, who was smiling back at him knowingly. "You fucking turd." Why was it that a brother could forever regress one to the level of a five-year-old in terms of vocabulary and hostility?

"Language." Mitchell employed his best imitation of their mother, and both of them laughed out loud until their stomachs hurt. "Anyway," he continued, wiping tears of laughter from the corners of his eyes with the back of his hand, "you've got things set, baby brother. You've got a great place to live, a job you like—though it's driving you to either madness or early retirement—and a guy you like as a boyfriend. You're all right."

Speechless, Matt swallowed the lump in his throat, blinking away fresh tears. "Thanks, Mitch." His voice was hoarse, but he smiled gratefully. He had a great brother after all, and a lot to feel good about. Figured that it would take someone like Mitchell to point it out. Oh, he'd never hear the end of this from his smug big brother, who'd rub it in every chance he got.

Next to him Mitchell grinned, knowing exactly what Matt was thinking. "So…." As he started, Matt got a sudden pang of queasiness in his stomach. "About Rain…."

"What about him?" Matt snarled, even though he knew he should've said nothing.

"Are you gonna snag him or what?" Mitchell chuckled amusedly, giving his brother a playful slap with his palm on Matt's shoulder.

"He's not a designer bag, and I'm not a purse snatcher," Matt snarled, turning to look at the rain outside instead of walking over to his bedroom to watch the Rain there.

Mitchell laughed. "You're not fooling me, little brother. I see that you like him a lot."

"So?"

"So… what are you going to do about it?"

Laying his forehead against the cold, damp glass for the second time, Matt sighed low but said nothing.

Mitchell smirked again. "Well, baby brother, you better decide soon, because guys like him don't stay on the market forever. If I weren't straight, I'd—"

"If you finish that sentence, I'll rearrange your face," Matt growled so low his words were barely audible, and his hands made fists at his side as he stared at his brother with an unspoken challenge.

Mitchell blinked several times, his brow shooting up toward his hairline. "Oh my God, you're already *in love* with him!"

He could've denied it. Here was his chance to renounce any and all feelings he had for Rain, emotions he hid in his heart. Smiling ruefully, Matt nodded. "Yeah… I love him. I love Rain to bits. I want to ask him to marry me." Saying the words aloud made the idea come alive and become real—and for Matt, it was the very heart of truth of his intentions.

"Bro…." Stunned, Mitchell was about to start bellowing happily—and loudly—when Matt shushed him quiet.

"Shut up, you doofus, or everyone will hear—and I'm not ready!" Matt let Mitchell pull him into a bear hug till his ribs cracked, and couldn't help the smirk attaching itself permanently to his lips. When his brother finally released him, Matt blushed a little, not having expected such a ringing endorsement from his closest friend and only brother. "I know Rain's not healthy enough yet, and I worry sometimes

that I'll never come first for him like he does for me. His music...."
Matt winced and sighed. "I love his music. Not just because I love him.
With him things are fun and light, and we have a great time together.
But... we don't have a lot in common, and he works late on the
weekends while I work early during the week, and—"

"Seriously, bro," Mitchell cut him off, scoffing incredulously.
"Can you hear yourself? Are you gonna break up with him because of
scheduling conflicts? What—the—fuck?" After taking a calming
breath, Mitchell continued more steadily, "Matt, you know I'm just
your straight older brother, and you think I can't understand what it's
like to have a gay relationship. But the truth is, most relationships are
fundamentally the same—regardless of the gender or sexual orientation
of its members. And the key to any lasting relationship is
communication. Man, if you have doubts, you have to talk to him about
whatever troubles you."

Matt smiled. "When did you become so wise all of a sudden?"

Mitchell shrugged impassively but grinned haughtily. "I've
always been wise. You just weren't paying attention." Chuckling, he
squeezed Matt's shoulder in a very brotherly manner, that simple
contact conveying the warmth of his feelings to his only sibling. "So,
my baby brother is going to propose to his sweetheart. God, I never
thought I'd live to see the day...." As Mitchell wiped an imaginary tear
off the corner of his eye, his shoulders shimmied with either feigned
crying or a pent-up guffaw.

Matt's eyes narrowed just before he lunged for his brother, who
roared in laughter. "Oh yeah? You sure you're gonna live that long,
you mouthy jerk?" And the two of them went tumbling down over the
back of the couch in a heap of arms and legs, both laughing their asses
off.

RAIN hadn't intended to eavesdrop on Matt and Mitchell.

Stirring awake, he'd found the bed cool and vacant, long since
emptied of his lover's warm presence. After wrapping a blanket around
his goose bumpy slim frame, he'd slipped out of the bedroom to the

mezzanine railing opening down into the two-story living room. He'd heard the two brothers talking in low voices by the large curtainless windows, but because of the openness of the space, Rain hadn't missed a single word.

Matt loves me and wants to marry me. Rain smiled.

He thinks I value my music more than him. Rain winced.

The day Charlotte and Mitchell had arrived Matt had hinted at the possibility of a wedding in their near future, a proposal straight out of Rain's fantasies—and that was the dream Rain wanted to cultivate to full bloom. Rain wanted to assure Matt that he came first in his life.

But how?

Rain didn't know about Matt, but Rain had intended to bring up the nature of their relationship the day after their two-month anniversary—the morning after their heated night of passion and celebration, to be exact, the one they had not been able to have. Rain had dreamt of an exclusive affair then and, just maybe, of moving in together to see where their path in unison would lead them. Now Rain knew they'd been on the same page all along, and the thought made him grin.

But if Matt now doubted Rain's feelings for him…. Rain grew serious, his brow furrowing. Rain didn't know how to convince Matt differently without his music—his native tongue.

Or did he?

The flash of insight hit him like he'd stumbled into a brick wall at full speed.

Yes. That plan was perfect. Smiling to himself, Rain retreated back into the safe harbor of the bedroom he shared with Matt, and while he slithered beneath the sheets, the plot was already forming. In the morning he'd have to talk with Charlotte and make the proper arrangements, and….

With a soft smile curving his lips, Rain fell back asleep.

Chapter Ten

His coffee was turning stale and cold as they waited for Mr. Griffin, their boss, in the conference room, and Matt tried to wake himself up. The monthly department meeting on Monday morning was already over half an hour overdue as Mr. Griffin was a no-show.

Early this morning, as Matt had been preparing for the meeting, he'd had the radio on, and the soft cooing in a husky voice, with the occasional high-pitched lilt, by the late Marilyn Monroe had greeted him with an effective downward spiraling mood-killer. He could relate to the singer, knowing he'd never love anyone the way he loved Rain—adoring the man to death.

"I'm through with love, I'll never fall again."

Matt was so in love with Rain it was tantamount to torment not to be with him every second of every day. It was Rain or no one for Matt.

For the past week, their apartment had seen a revolving door cavalcade of familial friends entering, staying, and leaving his apartment, only to return mere hours later. Charlotte and Mitchell had become permanent fixtures since their arrival over a week ago. And Norma and Tiny had a habit of making their occasional visits feel more like an occupying force that lasted for hours on end—and sometimes their visits stretched into the wee hours of the night until the two of them ended up sleeping on the twin couches in the living room. Matt was glad of their company, but it cut down on his and Rain's personal time.

Also, Rain's piano music echoed into every nook and cranny in Matt's loft apartment. Blues all the way, but Rain's music wasn't so much sad as it was riddled with what Matt could only describe as deep longing. The melancholy mood of the lingering melodies of jazzy desire was set from the moment Matt stepped back into his apartment after work, and the ambience lingered throughout the evening until he nodded off in his bed late at night. The blue notes of ennui followed him into his dreams, haunting him with images of Rain disappearing into the wind—even though at night, he held his lover as close as ever.

Matt didn't understand why Rain would be sad now that he was on the mend, both his leg and his voice improving at a swift rate that promised a speedy recovery. Matt heard the almost despondent tone of Marilyn's song, as if she knew exactly what she was singing about. Matt was beginning to empathize with her lyrics, and it caught him off guard.

"Why did you lead me to think you could care?"

At times Matt caught Rain looking at him with a soft loving expression, but as soon as he saw that Matt had noticed, he turned away, pretending that nothing had happened. Other times Matt found Rain staring far into the distance with a longing look in his pale-green eyes and a ghost of a wistful smile on his lips. This odd duality of behavior was driving Matt into the loony bin.

Every time Matt tried to bring the subject up, Rain addressed one of the others or just changed the topic with his bubbling voice until Matt was drowning in mindless chatter.

"Hey, babe," Matt said, leaning in to buss the piano-playing Rain on the cheek. "You play so well. I love your music."

"Why thank you, darling." Rain beamed, glancing at him from under his batting lashes, smiling so brightly it made Matt's day.

Matt sat on the piano stool next to Rain, and while his lover's long fingers skimmed over the keys, Matt kissed Rain. One simple gesture of intimacy lifted his heart soaring up in the clouds, and he'd almost asked the question then.

But soon Rain withdrew, and an odd introverted countenance took the place of the delighted look. "How was your day at the office, dear?" Despite Rain's recent tendency for reclusiveness, Matt was able to tell Rain had been saving that cheesy commentary for a while, and he grinned.

"No fun without you," he replied with a suggestive wiggle of his eyebrows.

"Then we'll have to do something fun now to make up for such a dreary day, and I bet can bring your mood right up, lovey," Rain whispered, nuzzling Matt's neck with single-minded purpose, and Matt surrendered to the heady high of making love to the man he loved.

Yes, Rain could use sex to avoid talking too.

Fidgeting in his seat, Matt felt his fingers brush the familiar bump in his pants pocket, where the ring box poked at him. Matt had been planning on popping the question for days now. He kept waiting for the right moment, but Rain's odd behavior made that impossible. With the others constantly around, they were never alone together—and even in bed, Rain insisted on sleeping instead of making love.

Was Rain preparing to leave Matt? The thought gave Matt cold chills up his spine.

"Taking time off your busy work schedule to tend to your *boyfriend* after such a terrible illness is commendable." Goodman's charming voice reached everyone in the room, which, before the comment, had been filled with the low hum of chitchat, and the room fell silent as people leaned back to enjoy the show or leaned forward to hear better. Matt waited in place—stiff and still, his flippant, anxious tongue glued to his palate—for the other shoe to drop. "Albeit time-consuming. I do hope for your sake, Matthew, it doesn't cost you a promotion." And there it was. The false sincerity, the feigned compassion, the barely held back sneer. Goodman was, contrary to the definition, no good man.

It was at that moment—with Matt seriously considering committing murder—that the elusive Mr. Griffin made his appearance at the scene. One of the two founding partners in the Griffin and Lyons

Law Firm, Charles Griffin was a grand, stout man in his early fifties, dressed in an impeccable steel-gray business suit with his still dark hair parted on the left. His equally gray eyes never left a stone unturned, whether it was about people or something else. He was a force to be reckoned with in the legal community and a merciless adversary in the courtroom.

With everybody taking their seats and falling silent, the monthly department meeting began. And never had Matt wished more to be anywhere else.

"MATT, stay. I need a word."

No one disobeyed Griffin's orders, and Matt was no exception. He stilled his steps, then moved back toward the head of the stylish oval wooden table where Griffin was organizing his legal papers and other documents into a leather briefcase that most likely cost a lot more than Matt made in a month.

Nervousness washed over Matt. "Sir, if this is about my recent absences, I can assure—"

Griffin's resolute stare rose and fixed on him. "Your boyfriend? How is he?"

It shouldn't have surprised Matt that Griffin knew about what had happened to Rain, since the man kept his ear to the ground at all times and in all matters pertaining to his firm. "Um, one day at a time, as they say, sir."

"Good, good," Griffin stated with the kind of confidence that could only come from a man who had an unwavering belief that things eventually sorted themselves out, like a miracle of heavenly proportions. "You know, Matt, I...." After hesitating only for an instant, he continued subtly, "I don't often confide like this, but under the circumstances... my younger brother, Carson, he is gay too. It was a shock to our family, I can tell you. But what can you do?" Though he sighed heavily, Matt suspected Griffin didn't really mind his brother's sexual orientation that much, or maybe not at all.

"Oh." His brain frozen, just like his body, Matt couldn't think of anything intelligent to say. What was there to say, really? He didn't know the people involved, personally or otherwise. He'd never even heard of them until today.

"Anyway"—Griffin shrugged the awkwardness off casually—"this is about the department head position. Both you and Goodman are up for it."

"Yes, sir."

"You're hardworking, loyal, and precise, Matt. Goodman's an ambitious little prick."

Don't you mean an asinine loudmouthed attention whore? Matt corrected his boss in his mind acrimoniously, doing his very best to stifle the ensuing wave of bitterness that followed. He was better than this.

"Despite his effective climbing of the corporate ladder, however," Griffin continued in his hard-boiled manner, "I'm inclined to offer *you* the position."

"Really, sir?" Though pleasantly surprised, unable to break the habit, Matt waited for the other shoe to drop.

"Yes. Guys with our kind of social network should stick together."

And there *it* was, Matt thought sourly. "With all due respect, sir... if I weren't gay and Goodman wasn't such a... uh, an unpleasant individual, would I still get the job?"

Griffin's steely eyes flashed and narrowed. "Goodman's a dickhead, yes, but he has strong leadership skills. He has a commanding presence. He's charismatic and socially engaging. He's always a solid boost to workplace morale—and, most importantly, he's on time with his assignments." Griffin paused only for a second. "You can work on those things, Matt."

Nodding outwardly but inwardly feeling like he'd been punched in the gut, Matt said, "So that would be a *no*, then?"

"Like I said," Griffin clarified, his tone sharper, "I'm inclined to offer you the job."

"But not solely on the merit of my work, sir?"

Griffin snorted. "Managers are never hired for that alone, as I'm sure you understand."

"I see, sir," Matt replied softly, and he did too. Goodman might have been a jerk, but he was a jerk who delivered. He knew when to brown his nose and when not to. He finished his work assignments on time or even ahead of schedule. He gave his fellow workers hearty laughs around the water cooler. Little did people suspect that he was a backstabbing horse's ass who'd sacrifice anyone and anything to get ahead. He fooled people with his Hardy Boy routine and good fellow act and always ended up getting his way. In short, he was the mirror opposite of Matt, who, despite his diligence, didn't have the guy's social obfuscation skills.

Griffin nodded, resolute. "You have until the end of the week, Matt. Give me your answer by Monday morning."

"If I decline, Goodman will be my boss." It was a fact that didn't really need putting into words, but Matt wanted to hear the confirmation nonetheless.

"That's correct." Griffin had finished packing his papers into his briefcase and stood in front of him, ready to leave. "Don't forget, Matt. This position has a lot to offer you—despite *some* of the reasons behind it. There will be a noticeable pay increase, a corner office, more flexible hours, more vacation time year round—"

"Yes, sir. Thank you, sir. I won't forget. Good night, sir."

As Griffin nodded his acknowledgement of Matt's well wishes and walked out of the room, Matt's stomach plummeted much like his sunken mood.

He needed something to lighten up his spirits, and he needed someone to talk to. And Matt knew only one person who could deliver both in one. The mere thought of Rain made his heart flutter and his lips curve into a smile, as usual, and his hope raised its head from the mire.

After reaching for his cell phone in his pocket and flipping it open, Matt saw he'd gotten a voice message during the meeting. He listened to it more than once, more confused each time.

"Hi, Matt. It's me, Rain. Listen, Charlotte's taking me back to Mobile to recuperate for a while. I'll be gone a couple of weeks. I'm sorry to spring this on you like this so out of the blue, but we're already on our way to the airport, and you had your business meeting that I didn't want to interrupt, so... I'll miss you terribly, darling. Kisses."

Toward the end Rain's tone had become flirtatious and high-pitched. It was polite and jolly, and it made Matt queasy and confused. The tiny pauses seemed to contain unspoken volumes, and Matt mulled over in his head the possibility that he might just have been dumped with a voice message. Well, better than with a text, he thought glumly.

Why had Rain left him? What had Matt done wrong? Had he waited too long to ask Rain to marry him, and Rain had gotten tired of waiting?

When he tried Rain's number, Matt found Rain had turned his cell phone off, as had Charlotte. Perplexed and anxious, Matt left both of them voice messages and asked them to call back as soon as possible. Then he tried Tiny's number, but the man had had no idea Rain was on his way out of town, and Norma was working a party gig downtown, so Matt couldn't ask him either.

Perturbed, Matt decided it was time for a stiff drink. Wandering aimlessly out of the meeting room, he undid the lavender-colored tie he'd gotten from Rain as a gift. He wasn't about to toss it in the bin, because apparently it was all he had left of Rain.

Chapter Eleven

"GOD, Rain, I miss you so much...."

Lying spread-eagle in bed and staring at the white ceiling of his bedroom late at night, at the end of yet another day that sucked ass in the wrong way, Matt couldn't remember why his life had gone to shambles. The one thing he did know was the exact moment when it had happened almost a week ago.

After flipping his cell phone open—again—he listened to the voice message—again—and felt confusion, fury, disappointment, sorrow, and pain wash over him—again.

And still nothing from Rain, or Charlotte, or Tiny, or Norma. After closing the phone, he dropped the cell on the nightstand.

Getting out of bed, taking a shower, going to work, eating breakfast, lunch, and dinner—it all seemed pointless, and he barely managed to drag his sorry ass through the daily routine. It was Saturday night, and he couldn't find enough inspiration to go out and actively do something about his depression. What was the point without Rain? Matt sighed.

The day after tomorrow was Monday, Matt realized, the day he'd have to decide what to do. Would he take the easiest way out and accept the job—all the while knowing the only thing he did right to deserve it was that he fucked guys instead of girls? Or would he take the ethically heroic path and pass up on a chance he'd probably not get again in years—not if Goodman had anything to say about it—and let his career take a nosedive to the pavement, and all the time he'd have to stare at the gloating grin on Goodman's face?

This predicament was one of the reasons he wished Rain were there with him, lying next to him and sharing the warmth of his body and his sharp wit. Together they could sift through all of it and come up with the right answer on how best to proceed—and not lose a single ounce of good karma in the process.

Matt shook his head and sighed. Ever since Rain had gone away six days ago, Matt seemed to think he was the answer to everything wrong with his life. That if Rain just came back, everything would magically sort itself out and they'd be together, living in the land of plenty, or the promised land of milk and honey, and all that jazz.

And that was another thing. Matt missed Rain's music too.

Every time a radio played softly in the background wherever he was—stuck in a car in traffic, or at a diner around the corner from his apartment, or at the supermarket getting groceries—he felt the twinge of pain in his heart. It wouldn't ease up, no matter what—and the world had suddenly become very noisy.

A loud, irreverent knock came from the door. "Matt, I know it's late, but you have a visitor."

Pulling aside the covers, Matt shivered at the cool air against his bed-warmed skin. He had on his dark-blue boxers and nothing else. Mitchell didn't wait for a reply because by now, from experience, he undoubtedly knew to expect a harsh shout back or a mere growl from Matt, so he just opened the door and stepped aside to let Rain in, then closed the door afterward.

All Matt could do was stare. He'd never seen Rain as he stood now before him, looking manlier than he'd ever been. He had on uncomplicated faded blue jeans, a bright-green button-down cotton shirt over a white T-shirt, and dark green sneakers. The really strange thing was he had no makeup on, and for the first time, Matt could see his face in its natural state out of bed. The man's pale-white skin shone a little under the banker's lamp light from the nightstand Matt had flicked on, his cheeks were flushed red, as if he'd been running during a winter frost even though it was summer, and his pale-green eyes were haunted and dark.

Stepping forward hesitantly but with a tender smile, Rain had his hands tucked in his jeans pockets, and he was swaying a bit on the soles of his feet. "Hi, Matt." He spoke softly, without all his usual flare, and his hushed voice lacked his typical melodious cadence, but there was a sweet loving smile on his lips—and Matt was baffled, and angered, by it.

As Matt stood up slowly from the bed, his tongue was glued to his palate, his mouth dry. Afraid a little, he asked, with a tremor in his voice that was part anger and part fear, "What do you want, Rain?"

Rain tugged on the hem of his shirt nervously and bit his full lower lip. After taking a couple of deep breaths, he began to speak—and it all came out like a flood, washing over Matt so fast he could barely keep up. "Matt, I love you." The momentary pause was not enough time for the stunned Matt to react as Rain pressed on, his voice gaining strength as it progressed. "I thought I'd been in love before, but I must not have been, because what I feel for you and with you is so much more. So strong, so powerful, so undeniable. It drowns out everything else—"

"But your music—" Matt interjected, puzzled, when Rain drew a breath to continue.

Rain stepped toward him, his gaze intense and burning. "Matt, *you* are my music. In fact, you are the center of my universe. With you I hear it, the Harmony of the Spheres, and I want for nothing but to be with you." Another step, right into Matt's personal space. "I thought I'd lost it, my music within, but I hadn't. It was just replaced by your music—and your love. You showed me that. I was so stupid I didn't realize at first that your music and my music became one. *Our music*."

Shaking his head, confused, Matt was at a loss for words but struggled on nonetheless. "But… you left me. You just took off without an explanation."

"Matt," Rain started, taking another step, placing his palms on Matt's bare chest—and Matt's heart rate began to race as if it knew that its love was near. "I was falling in love with you. You're wrong, Matt, if you believe I don't care for you. Yes, in hindsight I should not have left so suddenly, but I can explain. I had such a good plan in the works, you see, but clearly it backfired. I miscalculated the likelihood that you would not worry about me leaving for a bit—"

"Rain," Matt whispered, unsure. "You left, and you've been gone a week."

"I heard you talking with your brother," Rain said, sniffling a little, "and you were so sure that I didn't love you as much as my music, so I knew I had to do something to convince you. Take action. But I also knew I couldn't do that while I was still injured, so I went with Momsy. Oh, she's here too, by the way. Mitch gave her the other guest room again. Is that okay?"

Without its usual Southern drawl, Rain's mouth ran a mile a minute, and Matt had a hard time keeping up with the rapid pace. "Uh, yeah, I guess...." Shaking his baffled head, he said, "I—I'm having a hard time following your train of thought, Rain, and exactly what plans are you—"

"Oh, right, of course." Rain chuckled breathlessly. "I'm feeling much better now. My leg is almost completely healed, see? I got the gash checked at the hospital in Mobile yesterday—it's healed up nicely—and I can stand well enough and hold my own weight. And I got my voice back too."

The simply happy expression on Rain's beautiful face made Matt nod and smile faintly. "That's great, Rain. Really."

"That's when I knew I could come back." Matt had no idea what was going on, and he said so out loud. "Right, right, um... look, lovey, I didn't go back home just to recuperate, and certainly not to run from you or what we have. I had to see Daisy because she knows me, and she's family, and she had it, you see, darling, and I needed to get it so I could—"

"Jesus, Rain, slow down," Matt urged, his headache returning with a drumming bang.

"Oh, yes, right." Rain clearly tried to hold on to his control, but his hands were shaking fiercely, and his eyes were wide and unnaturally bright. "The real reason, my most fundamental reason, for leaving was to see Daisy. To get this," he added and dug out a small square box from his jeans pocket. "It belonged to Daisy, and to her mother before her, Violet. She used to dance Vaudeville way back in the day, did I ever tell you about her? She was quite an amazing burlesque starlet, and—"

"Rain, you're babbling," Matt said, unable to tear his eyes away from the little red velvet-covered box that could only be one thing, and it caused Matt's breath to hitch in his throat.

"Oh, sorry, darling." Rain chuckled again, anxiously. "I'm just so terribly nervous that you'll say no, and I really don't know what I'd do then, I really don't, because I love you, Matt, so very much that I can't—"

"Baby, you're doing it again." Matt stopped his lover, touching his cheek softly, and he could do that because now, at long last, he finally understood. And using the familiar endearment came out like second nature.

"Oh." Rain kept repeating the one-syllable word several times, nodding like a jack-in-the-box. "Um, here," he muttered and offered the ring box to Matt. "It's a family heirloom, you see, and I knew from the start I wanted you to have it. I mean I wanted you to have me first, obviously, but this ring right after that. I had to get the ring so I could do this right, to do this good and proper, since I only plan on doing this once in my life. And I want to do this with you, Matt, because I love you, and—"

Amidst the endless prattle, Matt managed to pop open the lid of the ring box and took a good long look at the magnificent ring. It was a spiral solitaire engagement ring forged of silver that held a single deep-green emerald in its setting between the ends of the spiraling curves. Matt had never beheld anything so beautiful—except Rain.

"It's a symbol of everlasting love, for our happily ever after," Rain whispered, his tone having lowered so deep Matt had to strain to hear it. Matt looked up to see Rain watching him, his lower lip trembling and his pale-green eyes moist with a glistening veil of tears. Then, without another word, Rain kneeled awkwardly in front of Matt, breathing rapidly and shaking all over, and asked, "Matthew Wetherton, I love you more than anything else in this world. I don't ever wish to be parted from you again. W-w-will you… m-m-marry me…?"

Dumbfounded, as seemed to be his habit with Rain, Matt stood in place, opening and closing his mouth like a fish caught on dry land. When he'd seen Rain in his bedroom tonight, there were so many possibilities running through his feverish mind of how it would play out—but not one of those scenarios had involved a marriage proposal. He could barely breathe, and his heart beat so fast he wondered if it might burst out of his chest.

"Say yes already, you dumbass, or I'll come over there and kick your ass," Mitchell's snarling voice shouted from the hallway, followed immediately by Charlotte's suppressed giggle.

At that Matt could only laugh, with the full knowledge that his cackling was about two steps away from turning into hysterics. So, mustering all of his remaining self-control, he managed to gasp, "Yes, love. I will marry you. And I love you too."

Letting out a sob but stopping any more from coming out by placing a hand over his mouth, Rain hustled up onto his feet and jumped into Matt's lap, and Matt took the lean man in his arms, holding him tight with every intention of keeping him there for the rest of their lives together. Granted, it might be difficult to go to work with Rain in his lap, but he'd manage.

"Oh, Matt," Rain murmured, still sobbing. "You're my music. I love you."

From outside in the hallway, Matt could discern Mitchell's loud whoops of joy and Charlotte's cries of happiness. He surmised they were probably hugging each other to death by now too.

But he didn't care when Rain's long, agile legs wrapped around his hips and his plump warm lips pressed against his jugular, nuzzling and suckling. Holding his lover's weight up by cupping his firm round globes, Matt lowered Rain to his back in the middle of his bed, reminding himself to get some background music so that the other occupants of the apartment wouldn't be disturbed by his and Rain's lovemaking.

But then Rain was kissing him on the lips, and the outside world melted away.

Chapter Twelve

"YOU did the right thing, darling," Rain assured Matt, lying beside him in Matt's king-size bed two days later and snuggling closer with a low contended purr, absentmindedly twirling his fingers over Matt's chest in tiny circles.

Earlier that day, on Monday morning, right on cue, Matt had gone straight to Mr. Griffin's office and politely declined the offer of the coveted managerial position in Griffin and Lyons Law Firm. It was one of the hardest things he'd ever done, but he couldn't accept a job that he only got because he was gay. Maybe if he had been more unscrupulous and ambitious. In the real world, one didn't earn any brownie points for doing the right thing, but more than likely, one got stuck with the bill while others partied away on your dime. Unfortunately.

But as it was, Matt had other priorities—one lying next to him— and these priorities kept him on the straight and narrow. And that's the way he preferred it too.

"Yeah, right as rain," Matt said softly with a smile, earning him a pleasurable nuzzle from his lover. "It didn't go all bad, at least," he reminded his lover of their earlier talk.

Yes, Matt had declined the job, fully expecting Goodman to get it. But apparently the man had read a lot into the private session between Matt and Griffin after the monthly department meeting and decided to do something drastic to get the attention of the senior partners. Unfortunately his desire to prove himself had caused him to cook the books for an important client, thus breaking the law—and exposing the entire firm to both civil and criminal litigation in the process. Griffin had yelled at Goodman behind closed doors for over an hour, and the rumor was that Lyons was going to attend the bawl-out from his villa in France, too, in a day or so. In order to avoid any undue attention or bad publicity, Goodman had not been fired but instead demoted.

Matt was not going to be Goodman's superior, and he was happy about that, and unsure whether it was to refrain from the temptation to gloat or to pity the poor man. Both of them were bad for a man's character and karma, so Matt took the whole thing as an opportunity to get his own bearings straight—and forget all about Goodman, who'd finally have to clean up his own mess.

The foremost good thing that had resulted from it all, however, had been Griffin's attitude toward Matt's refusal of the job offer. The man had seemed impressed by Matt's integrity and resolve. In the afternoon Matt had been recalled into Griffin's office and told that he'd be first chair in the upcoming Wyndham trial pertaining to charges of tax evasion. Wyndham was an important account for the firm, and Matt had taken the case eagerly, having worked on it for over a year but only as a part of the team—with Goodman in charge of the project then. Now the position had been left vacant, and Matt had jumped at the chance to prove himself in a court of law. Yes, being project leader meant longer hours, but the rewards were too good to pass up since there would be an influx of new billable clients—and thus also a substantial increase in pay.

"No, not bad at all," Rain agreed, kissing him on the cheek. "Sure, the project is only temporary, but it will lead to great things for you. You'll see. Trust me."

"I do trust you, love," Matt said, turning his head to reach Rain and kiss his lips. With a whimper Rain parted his lips and let Matt's delving tongue in, swirling and tangling his own tongue against and around Matt's. Matt tasted the remnants of chicory coffee in Rain's mouth under the fresh fruity toothpaste and his own natural flavor, and deepened the kiss to explore the sensual delight to his full satisfaction.

When Rain groaned louder, Matt broke the kiss with a hiss. "Shh... are you crazy? We have to be quiet. Absolutely no noise. Your mother and my brother are sleeping right down the hall. Don't you think we've given them enough shows already? Soon we should start charging them."

Rain chuckled with a wicked glint in his pale-green eyes, brushing his red-golden curls away from his eyes. "We'll be as quiet as mice, darling," he replied with a dare, sticking his tongue out between his teeth playfully. "Hush hush, lovey dovey."

Matt seriously doubted Rain could be silent during sex, but when his lover pursed those plump lips in a challenging manner and batted those long red-gold lashes, he knew he couldn't resist long enough to make a rational argument. Rain had him from head to toe, without contest. He could only give in—either now or later.

Sighing, he nodded, resigned. "All right, baby. But we do this my way, got it?"

"Oh, sweetheart," Rain murmured appreciatively. "I'll do anything you want me to any way you want it—and I'll even throw in a few things you've never thought of or imagined."

Matt thought he might not be able to catch his breath, let alone steady it, for the rest of his life as the pornographic images began to flow past his mind's eye.

Without adding more, Rain chucked his pajamas and underwear off so fast it was as if he'd crafted a veritable magic trick. The amazing vanishing clothes trick performed to perfection with a suave sleight of hand. Then Rain threw himself theatrically back against the headboard, giving Matt a languid glance from under his lashes, and propped himself upright in a sitting position, waiting and licking his lips like a serpent waiting for his prey to edge closer—only to be devoured whole.

Enchanted by his lover's melodramatic show, Matt laughed, and he'd make damn sure that Rain would deliver on his promises of sexual favors. But not tonight. Right now, Matt wanted to be in charge—and dominate less like a debonair gentleman and far more like a lecherous lover.

Standing up on the bed lazily, Matt undressed, sliding his pajamas past his hips in a show of his own—although he wasn't quite as elegant as Rain could be, but he was motivated and enthusiastic, thus giving it his all. After shimmying his pajama bottoms down to his ankles, he kicked them off into the distance, accompanied by Rain's delighted giggles as he snuggled to a more comfortable position on the bed to watch the private strip show.

"Oh, *darling*," Rain whispered, enamored. "We should have music for this."

Matt stilled with a warning glare. "Absolutely not. Don't even think about it."

"Killjoy," Rain murmured disapprovingly, pursing his lips. Huffing in righteous indignation, Rain waved his hand, twirling it around. "Go on, sweet cheeks. Dance for me. Shake that booty. Show me some skin."

Smirking at the ridiculous requests, Matt complied—but at his own pace. After unbuttoning his pajama shirt, he let it fall on the bed, and only then did he turn around to display his bare backside to his lover, who immediately began to giggle heartily at the sight—and then clap his hands loudly.

"Shh," Matt whispered, miffed, shaking his hands in a shushing motion, but Rain only pouted and crossed his arms over his bare chest, narrowing his eyes dangerously. "Oh, no you don't, babe," Matt said low. "No sulking, or I'll give you a spanking."

Shrugging in feigned impassiveness, Rain lifted his chin defiantly and turned his head away. "You couldn't possibly do *that*, darling. That would be far too noisy for the likes of—"

Matt fell to his knees on the bed in front of Rain, grabbed his arms, yanked him forward onto his lap, and gave his lover's bare butt a fierce slap. Rain yelped in a very feminine manner—though the sound was muffled by the fact that his face was buried in the sheet—and began to squirm as if his life depended on it. Chuckling, Matt gave his lover's butt another strong slap, and Rain shrieked—again the undignified sound was cushioned by and dispersed into the sheets— wiggling even harder to break free.

"Shh," Matt ordered coolly, keeping his tone threatening yet seductive. "Careful, baby. You don't want me to go rougher, do you?"

Rain stopped moving, his body heaving with deep breaths and quivering in anticipation, giving Matt a pretty damn good idea about what Rain expected—and wanted deep down inside. Caressing and fondling his naked prize, Matt admired the unobstructed view of his lover's exposed rear end, the firm apple cheeks glowing pale white under the light from the nightstand lamp.

After lifting Rain from his lap, Matt rested Rain on his back before him, intently watching the familiar signs of arousal displayed on his lover. The rapid breathing, the half-lidded eyes, the full parted lips, the dull red rising on his cheeks and chest. Matt cupped Rain's ass cheeks, one in each hand, and in a flash pulled Rain to his lap again, his lover's legs around his waist and Matt's rock-hard cock lodged in Rain's crease.

"Oh, Matt...." Rain moaned, closing his eyes and arching his back in the throes of passion.

"Shh...." Matt smiled mischievously when Rain looked up at him, dazed. "Not a single sound, babe," he whispered. "You still owe me my prize, remember? So be still and silent. Shh," he added, lifting his index finger against his pursed lips. Rain's eyes flashed, and Matt knew how outraged his lover felt at that moment. But Matt also knew how much Rain would enjoy acquiescing to him. They were both well aware of that fact.

Taking a determined hold of Rain's flanks, Matt bowed his head to kiss Rain's chest, then licked his way to a dark red nipple, suckling sweetly on the hardening nub before moving on to the other and latching on to it with single-minded intent. Rain groaned, and Matt felt him shiver all over in his arms. Wrapping his arms around his lover's back, Matt slid his tongue up to Rain's throat and neck and sucked several hickeys there just because he could.

After finding his way to Rain's lips, Matt claimed his lover's mouth in a deep, searing kiss. "You're hot as hell and sexy as sin," he muttered appreciatively before capturing his lover's lower lip between his teeth, nibbling little love bites, and Rain wound around him like a vine, like he often did.

"Oh, darling," Rain whispered, pleased, "I do love these sugar lips of yours."

Matt's probing fingers brushed briefly over Rain's leg and felt the raw scar there, and he pulled back to see it again even though hc'd studied it at length the day before. The scar was red, and he could see the faint remnants of the jagged edge around the long scar marring the otherwise unblemished alabaster-white skin. Though the scar was still fresh enough to protrude outward, it was smooth to the touch and silkier than the surrounding skin. Matt traced the line with his fingertips gently, being careful not to place too much pressure on the flesh.

Rain rose up on his elbows to watch Matt scanning his scar. "It's ugly, isn't it?" he mumbled, and Matt heard the self-conscious sadness in his trembling tone.

His gaze unwavering, Matt leaned down and kissed the scar, making sure to touch every inch with his lips. Shaking his head amidst the kisses, he said, "Nothing about you is ugly, my love. One day this will be nothing but a distant memory, the whiteness of it disappearing into your creaminess. And even then, if ever you feel self-deprecating about it, I will kiss it to mend it and make you feel like a princess."

Rain chuckled, the sadness giving way to joy. "Don't you mean *queen*, precious?"

Matt raised his head, quirking an eyebrow in a mocking fashion, grinning. "Touché." Caressing the wound gently, as if Rain's leg were fine porcelain and could shatter at the slightest petting, Matt sobered. "I don't want to sound morbid, but I can't help thinking something like this could happen to you again at any time because you are...."

As Matt's voice trailed off, Rain stiffened under his lover's touch. "I am—what, darling? A flaming queer? A flashy queen? A flagrantly obvious tranny?"

Yes, Rain was all those things, and it was redundant for Matt to say them out loud. Especially since his lover used the terms in a derogatory context, and it wasn't how he felt. But unless Matt wanted their relationship to take a huge step backward, he'd have to be honest. "Yes, baby. You're all that, and yet more than the sum of your parts. I love each and every part of you, and I don't want to change anything about you. But after you getting bashed, I can't help worrying. You can't ask me not to do that, because I love you so much that sometimes it hurts."

Rain's face mirrored every emotion rampaging through his head and heart, from the dark to the light. "Darling," he said, his voice cracking as his pale-green eyes changed color to a deeper green as tears veiled them. "Oh, Matt. I'm sorry… I guess I overreacted. Listen, I know you are concerned about my welfare, but I assure you, you don't need to be. It's not like Tiny is ever going to let me go anywhere outside The Sultry Sound on my own again, let alone my other hangouts, especially V-Sin-ity. He's going to shadow me from the club stage to the inside of my car. And by my car I mean your car, of course, honey. Tiny talked the owner of The Sultry Sound, Ms. Francesca—well, coerced, really—into bringing more security both into the club and to watch the outside like hawks. There are now three more beefcakes around, all of them hunky, hung, and delicious."

Matt raised an eyebrow, and Rain giggled.

"No, nothing's going to happen, darling." He smiled sweetly, the love shining from him as bright as the sun. "I will always love you, Matt. No one compares to you."

Nodding, fully cognizant of the truth of Rain's statement, Matt leaned forward to give his lover, companion, partner, and betrothed a kiss. "I love you too, babe." Serious again, he caressed the scar, as if distracted. "I just don't want you to get hurt again—by hooks or crooks. I don't know how I could survive…." He swallowed hard and licked his dry lips, feeling silly after all the reassurances from Rain that he'd be just fine and still not being able to alleviate his own fears.

Rain kissed him on one cheek and then the other. "No one can predict the future, my sweet baby love," he murmured, causing Matt to grimace at the gaudy, cheesy endearment. "All we can really do is deal with each and every personal crisis that may occur the best we can, because they cannot become crises of faith as long as we have faith in ourselves. And I know I will always have faith in myself, in you, and that things will turn out just fine and dandy as long as you remain by my side, loving me to death—oh, a poor choice of words, honey, I'm sure," he added with his Southern drawl, emphasizing it with a theatrical wave of his hand, which he then placed over his heart, batting his long red-gold lashes.

Never in a million years would Matt be strong enough to resist those eyes. Chuckling, he sighed, capitulating. "All right, love. One day at a time, then, I guess."

"Excellent," Rain exclaimed enthusiastically, clapping his hands before Matt grabbed them to silence him. "Oh, don't be such a *drag*, my dear," he huffed indignantly, shaking his hands free. "Pardon the pun, darling." Pursing his lips to give Matt "the look," he winked. "So, now that we've covered your concerns… can we please fuck now?"

At times Rain had the ability and inclination to be incredibly crass, Matt thought dryly. "Yes," he said, scooping Rain up close to him again until the man sat in his lap, their chests touching and their lips tasting. "I'm going to stick my naked cock into your bare ass, baby. Are you ready?" This was no empty threat since they'd discarded condoms the day before, when Rain had shown Matt his clean bill of health from the hospital in Mobile—Matt guessed a wealthy Southern ancestry and a well-connected socialite mother had their perks—and Matt had produced his own proof of his disease-free self, which he'd gotten at the same time he'd bought Rain's ring.

That same engagement ring he'd kept hidden in his pocket for what seemed like ages now adorned Rain's left ring finger. It was a simple flat-surfaced silver ring with an almost translucent milky-white moonstone in an oval setting. Everything about Rain was flashy, so Matt had chosen something innocuous.

Laying his lover down on the bed, Matt began Rain's seduction. A couple of kisses and a little nuzzling later, and Rain was ready, indicating his aroused state with a lingering hushed moan. Matt reached for the lube—watermelon-flavored—under his pillow, where he'd stashed it from their lovemaking before, and coated his naked cock with a rich dollop, now that it was stone hard and fiery hot, jumping at the prospect of entering his lover again. Matt doubted if he'd ever get enough of Rain to diminish the rabid foaming-at-the-mouth effect his lover had on him.

After giving his fingers a sheen of lube too, Matt prepared Rain's willing body for Matt's entry. "You feel so good, babe," Matt purred in appreciation, with his roaming fingers delving deep into his lover's tight passage, coating the inner walls with the creamy substance and curving his fingers around inside, searching for that sweet, sensuous spot within Rain that had him writhing. "So hot, so tight, so wet. Yes, I think you're ready to be flown into the stratosphere, love."

Lifting Rain's hips into his lap, Matt aimed the flaring head of his cock toward his lover's puckered opening and shoved in past the snug ring of muscle in a single forceful motion.

"Oh, Matt...." Rain groaned in a passionate uproar.

"Shh," Matt whispered, breathless, gliding into his lover's narrow passage balls deep and holding Rain tightly in his arms, scooping him closer to his heart.

"Oh, darling," Rain huffed, stirring from his arousal to showcase his reproach. Sounding remarkably lucid with a cock jammed up his ass, Rain snorted derisively. "What you're forcing me to do borderlines on cruel and unusual punishment. You can't just—"

Matt kissed Rain silent, allowing the man to tangle around him like a constrictor about to devour him. As Matt changed his angle and direction, various parts of his mouth alternated on Rain's skin. Lips, teeth, tongue, all offered in separate, intense doses until they assaulted and ravished Rain all at once, leaving Rain gasping in ardor that Matt felt practically pouring out of Rain through his shivering skin.

Heat built up fast inside Matt, filling his belly and groin with liquid fire. As his cock remained enveloped in the silky smooth viselike scorching blaze of his lover's ass, Matt bore down with zealous frenzy, desire burning him to ashes. Keeping his lips tightly fastened against Rain's lips, Matt began to pound into his lover like a piston firing. At first his rhythm was steady, fast and hard, but soon he began to falter as his passion overrode his strength and control.

His orgasm boiling in his balls, aching in the flared head of his cock, and tingling all over his skin, Matt could no longer keep up the kiss with Rain. Their hot breaths fanned over each other as they inhaled each other's breaths. Loving the feeling of moving in unison with Rain and being united into one being through the act of sex, Matt could no longer hold back the infinite pool of need he kept under wraps every day when he was unable to touch Rain, and liberated, it washed over him with the force of a tidal wave. Ramming into his lover with a pent-up yearning beyond his rational mind, Matt was barely aware of the savage moans and hushed whimpers coming out of Rain with each exhale.

"Oh, baby," Matt murmured incoherently, trapped in a red haze. "Gonna come."

Twisting his hand over Rain's thigh, Matt fisted his lover's cock and began to pump vigorously, smearing precum all over the hot hard shaft that burned angry red and twitched as if in agony in his hand. Stroking and grabbing, Matt made sure to cover every inch of his lover's cock to bring him to swift climax as his hips bucked upward hard.

"Matt," Rain cried out, his back arching, and he shot his load between them, warm liquid landing all over Matt's hand and their bellies and chests.

The sight and feel of his lover's orgasm pushed Matt over the edge. With an animalistic groan, he snapped his hips and came deep inside Rain, filling him to the brim with steaming-hot cum that Matt apparently was producing by the bucketload, since the spasms just wouldn't die down. He kept his cock buried as deep in Rain as he could, his whole body jolting with the fierceness of his release. White lights flashed in front of his closed eyes, his hips jerked of their own volition, and he was unable to catch his breath or control his orgasm as his balls emptied dry.

After what seemed like an eternity, Matt's body had no more to give, and he slumped over Rain, weak and boneless but sated and buzzing.

"Matt." Rain huffed and whispered, "Oh, you're heavy, you big oaf."

Faintly Matt became aware of Rain trying to push him off, and, using what little energy he had in his worn-out muscles, he shifted over and landed on his back next to Rain. He tried to recover a semblance of his regular breathing pattern and slow his heart, which had apparently jumped so enthusiastically during the awesome sex that it had lodged itself in his throat, beating away like a jackhammer still.

"Sorry, baby," he managed to mutter fuzzily as sleep was dragging him under with its dark-blue velvety covers.

Murmuring something unintelligible himself, Rain just patted Matt's sweaty, hot, quivering belly in a congratulatory manner, chuckling drowsily.

"Would you boys give it a rest already? A lady needs her beauty sleep." Charlotte's amused voice drifted to their sex-tired brains from across the hall, and Matt froze in place, suddenly completely conscious and utterly awake again. Yes, he'd known in advance the walls of his loft apartment were paper-thin on the mezzanine level, but sex with Rain had incinerated his caution to smithereens.

"Yeah, I second that. Are you two quite finished for the night, or what? I'm an athlete, for fuck's sake. I need my power naps." Mitchell's taunting voice reached them immediately after, also from across the hall, dripping with humor. Matt also noted that neither of them sounded sleepy, so he had every reason to assume he and Rain had been anything but silent in their affair.

Jesus, both of their guests—family members, no less—*had* heard them. "See? That's why I told you *shh!*" he scolded Rain, mumbling the comeback more to himself than his lover, since after the mind-boggling sex they'd just engaged in, he couldn't for the life of him chide Rain for anything.

Matt's cheeks grew beet red with embarrassment, but he was soon cured of that reaction when Rain yelled out crisply, "There's more than enough room outside in Momsy's SUV, you eavesdropping mongrels." As Matt burst into laughter, Rain murmured disapprovingly, "Next time we're getting a place with sturdier walls—or zero guest rooms. Got it, darling?" Then Rain just snuggled to lie at Matt's side, getting comfortable under his arm. Resting his head over Matt's heart, Rain sighed contentedly before nodding off.

To that statement Matt had nothing to add, so, grinning broadly like the lovesick puppy he was, he wrapped his arms around Rain— knowing they'd be stuck together tomorrow, smeared with dried cum— nuzzled Rain gently, and fell asleep too.

ℰpilogue

MATT and Rain's engagement party, and coincidentally their four-month anniversary, was in full swing at their loft apartment where they now lived together. It was well past 1:00 a.m., but the guests remaining showed no signs of imminent departure.

Matt's parents had stayed throughout the evening but had called it a night at around ten and settled in for a stay at a hotel instead of cramping into the already crowded guest bedrooms. One had been conquered by Charlotte and the other claimed by Mitchell and his wife Marian, and even though they offered to share, no one took them up on their generous offer. Matt surmised it was because everyone knew how Charlotte fussed and how Mitchell snored.

At some point—and no one could pinpoint the exact timing—Norma and her friends had started a horridly cliché and tacky conga line, accompanied by loads of equally cheesy lounge music and a gush of party people neither Rain nor Matt knew personally. Norma's friends, however, despite being flashy and flamboyant to the extreme, were nice and were there just to have a good time. They delved into the entertainment without resorting to the open bar.

Matt stood leaning against the doorway to the balcony, which opened from the living room, tugged off his bow tie, and chucked it on the couch. He popped open a few buttons of his snow-white dress shirt, getting more comfortable in the remnants of his tuxedo ensemble now that the formal part of the party had ended on a good note.

He kept watching in amusement as Rain danced the night away in his bright-pink latex pants and T-shirt, his hips doing the shimmy and twirl like no other could. His leg had improved in the month since he'd come back to Matt—although technically he'd never really left him to begin with.

Rain was all right, and because he was fine, Matt was all right too.

Norma shuffled past Matt to get to the balcony without saying a word. Following him with his gaze, Matt observed Norma finding his way to Tiny, who stood at the far end of the balcony in the shadows, nursing a stiff vodka on the rocks in a rather humiliating plastic cup—his first and last of the evening, since he wasn't much of a drinker.

"What now?" Tiny said, gruff.

Norma was looking particularly pretty tonight, dressed in an over-the-top pink sequin corset and low-riding, sequin-ornamented light-blue jeans. His electric-blue wig and equally sharp blue makeup gave him a sexy appearance, and he took full advantage of it.

In a flash he'd snagged Tiny's drink from his outstretched hand and taken a small sip before the man could react at all. "Oh, vodka," Norma murmured disapprovingly, grimacing. "How disgusting—not to mention predictable."

When Tiny snatched the cup back, his face went dark, and Matt changed his stance in an instant in fear that the two of them might actually come to blows. For an interminable moment, they stood in place and just stared at each other, Tiny's eyes piercing and furious and Norma's defiant and fiery.

It was hard to say who moved on who first—but then they were kissing.

And it wasn't small-time smooching, either. This was full-on mouth-to-mouth intimacy, exploration, and conquest. Lips latched on, tongues dueled, hands took hold, and groins ground in fabric-covered friction.

And perfectly good vodka drained from the dropped plastic cup on the balcony.

Matt's cheeks grew red at the private sight he was getting a sneak preview of. Looking away as quickly and inconspicuously as he could, he silently sauntered further away from the embarrassing witness position he'd been in, only daring to breathe when he reached the relative safety of the kitchen—and the comfort of the bar. He could never, ever say anything to anyone about what he'd seen. Consigned to a vow of eternal secrecy, Matt made a G and T and gulped half of it down in one sitting.

"There you are, darling." Rain's voice wrapped around him like a warm woolly blanket. "Come on, big boy, and dance with your betrothed." After taking Matt's drink and putting it aside, Rain tugged gently at Matt's hands and drew him into his embrace. They'd moved the couches back to the walls in the living room to make more room for people to dance, and now Matt was glad they had, because he was holding his lover in his arms with the certain knowledge he would never have to let go.

Smiling, he asked softly, "Are you happy, love?"

Rain kissed him and murmured against his lips, "Yes, happier than I've ever been, darling." Slowly, as he wrapped himself around his fiancé, Rain grew serious, locking his gaze with Matt's and swallowing nervously. "There was a time I feared we would never get here. But I always hoped and prayed."

Matt kissed Rain, pouring into the gentle gesture all the love he felt for him. "Sing for me, love."

With a wicked grin, Rain rolled his green eyes, going over the possibilities. When he finally settled on a beautiful piece, his melodious voice set out to conquer the stage. And as the room fell silent to hear Rain singing and to watch the two of them dance, Matt fell even more in love.

"*'Bout twenty years ago way down in New Orleans, a group of fellers found a new kind of music. And they decided to call it… jazz.*"

As the lyrics and the tempo began to pick up the pace, Matt whirled Rain around on his heels, twirling him around in pirouettes before pulling him elegantly back into his arms. Their friends and family clapped around them and began to add to the beat. A few guys—musicians from the club—divided their musical talent, one playing the piano and the others giving off a beat with their humming mouths and snapping fingers.

The song entered full swing, and Matt shook his legs intently to keep up with his light-footed Rain, who seemed to float on air as he spun around himself and swiveled around Matt, though ever remaining in his arms. The rhythm took hold of them both as they whirled in unison, and Matt kept Rain pressed tightly against his chest.

Yes, they might've been missing clarinets, saxophones, and bass and drums from the background, but Rain's music brought the lyrics and the cadence to life. With all the sweet sounds emanating from his golden throat, Rain breathed vitality and potency into the song and gave Matt an added cause to celebrate his love and union with Rain. As Rain continued to hum in his arms, Matt felt the suspended bliss hanging above him and surrounding him in warm tenderness, and he wanted for nothing more.

THE party had been like a wind-up toy. When the string had stopped, the jig was up. Literally and figuratively. People crashed and keeled over where they'd stood and slept where they had landed, be it on the couch, on the floor, or on the coffee table. After the fever pitch of the party had been reached, it had died down so fast it was as if someone had pushed a button to make everyone fall down unconscious. Not even the open bar had prevented the simultaneous slipping of people into dreamland.

Only two people were still left awake.

Matt held Rain in his arms, his face buried in his betrothed's red-golden curls as they danced in place in slow movements. Rain caressed the nape of Matt's neck lazily, unwilling to let go. Throughout the night they had kept slow dancing, no matter what took place around them, until finally their apartment fell silent and not even music remained—until they were the only ones left standing. It was as if the apartment were a warzone comprised of party balloons, silly string, colorful paper cups, and tossed-around pieces of clothing—and Rain and Matt were the lone survivors in the dead of night, where only the light of the glowing blue moon emerged through the shutters.

"I love you, Matt," Rain whispered in his lover's ear and kissed him on the temple softly, curling his fingers in his lover's sandy-colored hair.

In his whole rather eventful life, Rain had never felt like this before. Despite the strings of lovers and series of affairs, Rain had felt like the odd man out every time. But with Matt Rain felt comfortable to be himself—the flaming gay guy, the sultry lounge singer, the boy who loved women's clothes and played dress-up whenever he could. Matt didn't ask him to change or force him to be someone he wasn't. Yes, Matt would always have a trace of fear for what might happen to Rain when he wasn't looking, but it was something they could talk about and Rain could understand and relate to.

"I love you too, baby," Matt murmured into his neck, kissing the sensitive spot under his ear with passion, beginning to stir up Rain's sex until his cock began to jut out against his zipper and he had to shift his position abruptly. Matt chuckled teasingly, "Something up, babe?"

"Oh, you miscreant...." Pursing his lips, Rain pushed the man away roughly, huffing with feigned outrage, and stalked off toward the stairs.

"Thanks for the view, love," Matt murmured appreciatively, right behind him, ascending the stairs too, his gaze obviously fixed on Rain's rear end. At the top of the stairs, he caught Rain back into his embrace.

"Oh, you silver-tongued little imp," Rain whispered admonishingly but started to relent when Matt gently swayed him in his arms, cooing little incoherent compliments and sweet, dirty endearments in his enjoying ears.

As Matt began to guide him toward the bedroom, Rain knew that his dreams had not only come true but had been fulfilled to a tee. Those childhood dream castles in the sky, all pink and fluffy and seemingly unattainable, had become their permanent residence and love-filled home after all. Smiling happily, Rain fell into Matt's embrace as Matt led the way to their shared bedroom and joint life.

Along the way Rain began to hum a jazzy little ditty from back home—and he didn't care if the music vibrated from him or echoed from his lover, because now and forever, the two of them were as one.

Just when he thought there could be no more pleasant surprises in store for him now that he felt so disgustingly happy, Rain heard Matt murmur in his ear, chuckling, "You wanna top?"

SUSAN LAINE was born and raised in Finland to the best mother in the world, and she told her daughter time and again that she could be and do whatever she wanted in her life. However, it took her until her thirties to find the spark for serious writing by discovering the gay erotic romance genre which is what she mainly writes today.

Her formal education revolves around anthropology, but wishing in time to become a full-time writer, Susan does office work at her unfortunately necessary evil day job. When not working or writing (yes, it's her second job), Susan enjoys hanging out with her sister and friends in movie theaters and book stores. Her other pastimes include walking, swimming, and fantasizing about sizzling hot manlove. Some of her likes are Lady Gaga, chocolate, and doing the dishes (it's relaxing), and a few dislikes are sweating hot summer days, tobacco smoke and purposeful prejudice. She hopes to one day write a historical romance novel and a murder mystery, too, but all in good time—and there will undoubtedly be a gay romantic twist.

Visit Susan's website at http://www.susan-laine-author.fi/ or write her an e-mail at susan.laine@hotmail.com.

Also from SUSAN LAINE

http://www.dreamspinnerpress.com

Also from SUSAN LAINE

A SENSES AND SENSATIONS MYSTERY: 2

Love in
Plain Sight

Susan Laine

http://www.dreamspinnerpress.com

Also from SUSAN LAINE

http://www.dreamspinnerpress.com